ALCHEMY

AMONG THE SEVEN HOLY TOMBS

AF507940

ALCHEMY
AMONG THE SEVEN HOLY TOMBS

This book is a work of fiction. Names, characters, places, and incidents are the product of the author's imagination or are used fictitiously. Any resemblance to actual events, locales, or persons, living or dead, is coincidental.

Copyright © 2023 by Michael Joseph Dammit Sullivan

All rights reserved.

The scanning, uploading, and distribution of this book without permission is a theft of the author's intellectual property. If you would like permission to use material from the book (other than for review purposes), please contact theextraordinarymuldoon@gmail.com.

Cover Illustration: "Still Life with Chainsaw, Opium Pipe, and Teddybear"- Artist Unknown, early 19th century, rendered in smashed bug-parts and badger saliva on vellum.
Editing | Book Design and Typesetting
Enchanted Ink Publishing

ISBN: 979-8-9874583-1-0 (E-book)
ISBN: 979-8-9874583-0-3 (Paperback)

Thank you for your support of the author's rights.

This book is dedicated to YOU.

(pretty smart, eh? I certainly thought so.)

ALCHEMY
AMONG THE SEVEN HOLY TOMBS

SHORT STORIES BY

MICHAEL JOSEPH DAMMIT SULLIVAN

CONTENTS

FOREWORD

AND A *REAL* GHOST STORY

On the far southwest corner of Chicago, there is a neighborhood called Mount Greenwood. It has no mountains and isn't particularly wooded, green or otherwise. It's hemmed in by suburbs on three sides and several sets of freight train tracks on the remaining one, a bastion of sometimes ugly Plastic Paddyism and intemperance. More grit than glamour, this is where I grew up. The Mt. Greenwood of my youth was a slightly shabby blue-collar neighborhood inhabited largely by cops, firefighters, and Streets and Sanitation workers who were required to live inside the city, plus assorted tradesmen and laborers, all raising their families among the several Catholic parishes located there. The neighborhood's big claim to fame, geographically, was that the last working farm in Chicago was within its borders. Take that, Magnificent Mile.

Mt. Greenwood did boast a literary celebrity though, in the person of the late John R. Powers, author of, among other things, the Eddie Ryan trilogy: *The Last Catholic in America, Do Black Patent Leather Shoes Really Reflect Up?*, and *The Unoriginal Sinner and the Ice Cream God*. In the Eddie Ryan books, he called Mt. Greenwood "The Seven Holy Tombs," a nickname that referenced the many cemeteries in the area. I'd heard the term outside of Powers's books, and when I first started fumbling on a (yet unpublished) manuscript for

i

a novel, I felt the moniker was too poetic not to use. My efforts in researching the origin of the name turned up nothing, but the magic of the internet allowed me to send Dr. Powers an email inquiring as to where he had gotten it.

Of course, he had made the name up himself, and besides his talent for language, he turned out to be remarkably generous with his time and advice, discussing the Chicago of our respective youths, along with matters literary. During our handful of late evening phone conversations, he was also generous enough to give me not only his full blessing as to the use of the wonderful nickname for the neighborhood that he coined, but his brutally honest insight into the realities about achieving success in the world of writing fiction. It saddens me that if I ever *do* achieve success as an author now, I won't be able to phone him up and tell him how it went and thank him for his words of guidance. There is a chance that if I do make it, he wouldn't have been surprised in the slightest. There's also the chance that he thought the few passages I sent him were plain god-awful and he didn't have the heart to tell me to hang it up. In either case, I'm stealing the name *The Seven Holy Tombs*.

You were promised a real ghost story, and here's a good one:

The year was 2005, and the White Sox were in their climb to World Series victory. I'm not much of a sports guy or an athlete, but as a Southsider, it was awesome to see them field such a juggernaut of a team. I had been generously offered a short-term job as a night watchman at a construction site that stood on unused land reclaimed from one of the neighborhood cemeteries of lore. The construction office where I spent those nights was a trailer that sat between the townhouses being built and the sidewalk, inside the fence that marked the cemetery perimeter. Being naturally nocturnal, the job suited me quite well, my time divided between working out story ideas in a notebook and doing the odd rounds to check the property and chase the partying hooligans out from among the headstones. That autumn, Mars was also very close and even from the city appeared bright and pink in a clear sky. The cemetery in fall, late at night, was the perfect setting for a ghost story.

It was sometime between 2:00 a.m. and 3:00 a.m., and I stepped outside the trailer to stretch my legs in the cool night air. I found that if I stood very close to the trailer in the shadow it cast from the light thrown by the streetlamps, I could get a better view of the red planet, so I stood out there for some time looking at Mars and the stars. I heard him long before I saw him: some young and very drunk kid weaving his way up the sidewalk, shouting nonsense to nobody and angrily kicking the tall fence as he came along the cemetery. I kept an eye on him as he was both incoherent and acting violently, babbling loudly like a maniac. I was hoping he'd go away without incident, but just after he passed where I stood on the other side of the fence, he hooked an empty over the razor wire-topped fence and into the construction site, the beer bottle arcing high in the air and landing maybe a dozen feet from me. Maniac or not, I did not appreciate having to pick up after him. In my anger, I picked up the bottle, and what I had *intended* on doing, on my honor, was to toss it back in his direction, whizzing it past his nose, and call him Jackass. As soon as I let go of the underhand toss though, I felt pretty stupid since once the bottle inevitably shattered on the street, I'd have to go sweep it up dozens of bottle pieces instead of the one solid one I'd already picked up but decided to throw to make a dumb point.

Except, it didn't go as I had intended. As I said, I'm not much of an athlete, so my throw was off by about six inches. Instead of whistling past his nose like I'd hoped, the bottom of the bottle hit him square on the crown of his melon with a resoundingly loud *kunk!* It didn't break on his head, and miraculously, it didn't break when it clattered to the street either, which relieved me from having to sweep up broken glass. And my opportunity to call him Jackass didn't happen either, because when that bottle sailed out of the dark to clunk him on the ol' coconut, he took off down the sidewalk like a bipedal cheetah. For someone who couldn't walk without staggering just moments before, he sure could sprint in a straight line. He would have left the Road Runner in the dust. It wasn't until he took off that I realized he probably couldn't even see me standing in the shadows on the other side of the cemetery fence, and from his perspective, his discarded beer bottle had boomeranged out of the darkness and hit him right in the skull like God's own act of retribution.

The laugh hit me so hard, not only could I not say *Jackass*, but anything else for that matter. All of my breath leaked out of me in a convulsing wheeze. He was a block and a half away, over the railroad tracks, before I stopped hissing and started snorting audibly. There was no way he could have heard me by then.

So while I don't personally have a ghost story from that night, *he* does. Sure, my story has more of the facts and is little heavier on the true details, but mine doesn't hold a graveyard candle to his. His story is way better than mine. His has a bottle-slinging Phantom of the Burial Ground. Sometimes, I think about him in his old age, being asked by his grandchildren if he believes in the supernatural, and he can tell them the story, his hand to God, about the autumn night when the ghosts in the cemetery almost got him for good. Who knows what kind of effect his brush with the paranormal has had on him since then? Maybe he's a crusader for temperance, clean living, and reverence for the departed to this very day. And good on him for turning his life around.

On the other hand, he may also be some highly successful but unscrupulous publisher now . . . and if he is and he ever sees this: I'm the guy who conked you with the bottle, and I have more stories from the Seven Holy Tombs I'd like to sell. Drop me a line!

As for the rest of you, thanks for reading!

EARTH

A FILTHY SHORT:
THE HISTORY LESSON

The Storyteller shifted his weight to his hip beneath the shady tree, the wood and cord of his weather-beaten chair creaking. He eyed the question-asker from beneath his unkempt brows with a twinkle and continued to fill his briar pipe as he began . . .

"Oh aye, I know the place! I'm more than a teacher; I'm like a two-century-old oak, standing witness through time. I know the place well. I knew it when it was prairie swamp, back when the city was just the burnt timbers left of the fort smoldering near the lake! Yessir, not far from the Vincennes Trace, the old buffalo trail that ran from Tennessee all the way to the Great Lakes. Lots of tribes used the trail—Ojibwe, Miami, Fox, Sauk, and the like—but it was the Potawatomi that burned the first fort on the shore. Traders and trappers used the Vincennes Trace too. Even had a trading post not far from here," the old man said, jerking his thumb in a vague direction.

"Back in the mid-1800s the Germans and Dutch came to farm the firmer ground. Some of those little truck-farms held on for a century or so. A lot of the area was drained when the Irish came after the famine, building the canals. When the city burned down and the cow got the blame, lots of the sooty rubble filled in the remaining marshes.

"The city grew, and the population boomed, and the cemeteries appeared to receive Chicago's departed. The taverns and saloons appeared too, to receive the mourners and prevent their going home thirsty. As the Emerald Isle continued to export her sons and daughters to the City of Big Shoulders, plenty of them ended up here, a rowdy patch of the living among the quiet parks of the dead. Some of the more delicate lace-curtain gentry living farther east tried to make the area 'dry' in the years before the dreaded Prohibition to keep the locals from raising too much hell. That's when they declared themselves a village unto themselves."

The wizened old man tamped the tobacco down in the bowl of his pipe without pausing his story. "Yessir, that did not protect them from the Eighteenth Amendment! So with the whole country officially on the wagon, the locals voted to be annexed by the City by the Lake, the very same year Lindbergh landed in Paris with an empty lunch pail and a full bladder. The Twenty-first Amendment opened the beer taps again in '33, but the WPA didn't put in sewers until '36. But the locals were tough people.

"These same tough people went and fought the war, and when the cannons stopped barking, the babies started booming, and the local population density soared again. Oh, yes, I know this area. I know the cops and the firemen, the Streets and San workers, the ironworkers, the electricians, and the plumbers. I know their rotten kids and the parishes where they pray. I've seen their St. Patrick's Day parades, their softball games, their skeetching from cars in the snow, and all of the Plastic Paddy nonsense. I've seen them stop their cars in the middle of the street to have conversations that begin with 'Howzyerma!' and traffic be damned. I've seen their lawn chairs bloom next to the curbs in the winter and the cordite haze hanging in the air in the wee early hours of July 5th. The puking in the street, the pissing in the alley, and the fornicating in the park! I've seen the houses get bigger and the families get smaller and the McMansions grow where the clapboard shanties got pulled down.

"So yes, my old son, I know the area well!"

The Storyteller lit his pipe, drawing the flame from the struck match.

The question-asker looked down at the old coot from the cab of his idling truck. "Look, Pops, I just meant do you know if this is the way back to the Dan Ryan Expressway!" *That does it*, he thought, *I'm getting one of those GPS thingies.*

GOODBYE DEZZY

THE TESTIMONY OF THE GREAT MULDOON
FOR PUBLICATION ONLY AFTER THE
STATUTE OF LIMITATIONS HAS EXPIRED.

If it hadn't been so cold that night, Leon would have bled to death, so that's good. But who knows how many lives we endangered by forcing them to forgo natural gas heating on that frigid January night? I'd always known that saying goodbye to Dezzy would be hard, but I never would have thought it would almost cost me my life.

What could I tell you about Desdemona? She was dark and beautiful, with long wavy hair that was so black as to sometimes appear blue, like Superman's. She was loyal and loved me unconditionally, that anyone could tell. She also had the manners of an eight-year-old schoolboy. She could not only belch loudly, but also produce flatulence seemingly at will. She was the best dog ever. As well as being rude and crude, she was afflicted with a puppy sort of Tourette's syndrome, which prevented her from keeping her opinions about other people to herself. As she got older and lost her girlish figure, she took on the countenance of a large black sheep with a collie's head grafted onto it by some freak of mad science. If I went without grooming her for, oh say, a year, she looked more like a Vietnamese pot-bellied bison. Man, in high summer, with her thundering across the un-mowed grass just as the sun was setting over the alley and across the railroad tracks, it was like being a witness to this great nation in its infancy. A tear would damn near come to my eye, and right then, I would have given my left nut to be able to graft a pair of horns on her. You know, little curved ones like a buffalo's.

But my poor Desdemona was getting old and feeble. She'd had a long and good life for a dog with no marketable social skills, but I wasn't looking forward to doing the responsible thing I knew would have to be done soon. I'd hate to have to take her to a vet's office . . . she'd just know something was up. I'd rather she just pass quietly in a comfortable spot, like she'd want. Actually, she'd really want three pounds of shaved roast beef au jus, but that wasn't going to happen. Excepting the prime cuts, how can you give your best pal death with dignity?

Unfortunately, it was during one of those mid-January cold snaps that hits you right in the solar plexus as soon as you step from the comfort of the indoors. No matter how many layers you sport, nothing can prepare you for the soul-chilling experience of inhaling that sub-zero air. That thin air that's so dry it can make your nose bleed, though you wouldn't notice it as the snot froze uncomfortably right in your nostrils.

The funny thing is, when it got that cold, people stopped complaining about it. They'd just contemplate the temperature and say, "Fuck." It was the kind of cold where, when you had to step inside to answer nature's call, you'd be standing at the urinal and the frigidness of your fingers would make Little Adolph retract into your body like a frightened woodchuck retreating into his burrow. And worse was knowing that it would be some time before you could coax him out again, and you'd pray that in the meantime, your bladder wouldn't burst and give you peritonitis.

It made me doubly sad that the cold would prevent me from putting her down and burying her in the yard—her yard, her domain, the only home she'd ever known.

Goddammit, it was Dezzy's yard, and that's where she should stay. The burial was the real problem. Back once upon a time, they would stack the departed in question out in the snow until first thaw, but I didn't think they did that in cities nowadays. What did they do when a person died during a cold front? I mean, sure they have all that hydraulic digging equipment and the like, but this frozen ground was like iron. What the hell did they do, blast?

Just to show you how out of my mind I was at this time, I was stuck by a slow freight train out in front of St. Mary's Cemetery, right in front of the answer to the $64,000 question for twenty-five minutes, and I didn't even glance over until the train had passed and traffic began to lurch forward. There in the new section of the cemetery, smoking away like a chimney, was a large casket vault-shaped heater. It was heating up a large casket-shaped piece of cemetery ground soft enough to install a casket-shaped hole, rather quickly too, if you were sporting some of that fancy archdiocese hydraulic equipment.

Then the brilliant idea struck me . . .

I mean, hell, the big steel washtub that we filled with ice and beer for barbecues in the yard could easily fit two and a half Dezzys, so it could theoretically heat up enough ground to bury 150 percent more deceased dog than I'd have when the awful time of obligation came. All I would have to do was dump the bag of leftover summer charcoal into the tub and drag it into the prairie over the tracks and get a nice fire going for a few hours. That would hopefully soften the frozen ground enough to dig a proper grave for my little princess. Then it would be a simple matter of putting one humanely between the eyes to end her suffering and a few tasteful words about dust to dust and the land of endless T-bones and postal carriers ripe for the mauling and all of that religious crap. I knew she'd approve.

Friday. Right after dark so as not to arouse suspicion if any of the neighbors just happened to be bored and looking out their back windows into the prairie on the other side of the tracks, which was goddamn unlikely. Hell's bells, even in darkness, the freight yard was a sight so depressing it would have given Steinbeck the blues. Plus, on a Friday night in this neighborhood, a single gunshot could go quite unnoticed.

Yes, Friday would be the night. That way, I'd have two days to mourn and keen, and I'd be over the initial shock by Monday night when I had to go back to work. I wasn't worried about the guys at work seeing my teary-eyed. Hell, they'd all see me cry openly when I told them about paying nine bucks to see that piece of crap movie about the liner and the iceberg. It's just that I was afraid of crying at work and the tears freezing my eyes shut. If that happened, I could easily wander into a whirling propeller, and then they'd be using the washtub to heat up a hole in the yard for *me*.

My brother had given me some codeine pills from when he broke his leg that I was saving for a special occasion, but I could part with two to make sure she wasn't in pain when the awful but necessary deed went down. And I could put her on her favorite blanket with her squeaky toy and favorite ball so she would spend her last time on this plane surrounded by her favorite things, minus the roast beef. I could bury her with all that stuff. It would be like the burial of some kind of dog pharaoh. I even had fleeting visions of putting a marker on her grave inscribed with something like *Chasing Cars Down the Streets of Glory* or something similarly dignified. As terrible as this task would be, I was starting to feel better about the whole thing.

———

WHEN FRIDAY NIGHT ROLLED AROUND and the time for preparations arrived, Leon came by to help. It is said that a good friend will help you move, but a true friend will help you move bodies. Leon was a true friend, the kind that would reliably have your back in any bar fight he started. Like a true friend, he brought with him a bottle of Bushmills Black Bush and a case of Dew. A perfect choice, that combination—one for courage and fortitude and the other for energy and sharpened wits. I would need both badly that night. Thank the gods that I had a couple bottles of Black Bush in the cabinet myself already. I gave Dezzy the codeine wrapped in a piece of salami so that this night would be a peaceful one for her. I'm sure she appreciated it.

That little bitch better have appreciated it. As it turned out, we wound up needing them more than she did. We took the washtub and bag of charcoals over to a perfect area in the prairie, and I cleared a spot in the crusty snow. I dumped the whole bag of coal into the tub and used the bag as tinder. Leon poured a dram of the good whiskey onto the coals as a ritual accelerant, which really made it a proper wake. Jesus, did that stuff burn then.

We went in to drink for a couple of hours while the roaring flames died down and the coals started to glow brightly. Then the labor began. We went out with a shovel to dig the hole, but when we tried to move the washtub, the handles seared our hands right through the leather of our gloves. So we went back inside to get a crowbar and a hammer to hook onto the handles so we could move the tub to the side for the digging. And as long as we had to go back inside, we both drained another glass before we returned to work. When we moved the tub, there was nice soft mud underneath, but only for about a half a foot deep. Under that, it was like trying to dig a hole in a marble floor using a plastic spork, so we had to drag the blistering tub back into the mud to heat up some more of the ground. Again, thank the gods for the whiskey. It was going to be a long labor-intensive night. But far from a dry one, that's for sure.

We must have repeated the process seven or eight times, moving the tub, digging in the muck full of big rocks until the frozen ground threatened to break the shovel blade, replacing the tub in the hole, and returning to the house to check on Dezzy and drink away the cold and aches from the job. Eventually though, the perseverance paid off and we had a suitable hole. I looked back at the house where I knew she was sleeping, and I realized that I would have rather kept digging.

When we went in to get her, she was sleeping pretty soundly, but when I leaned down to pet her and she awoke for a moment and her tail twitched a bit, I felt as if she approved of what was being done—was maybe even grateful for the effort—and that helped calm my nerves a lot. That and the whiskey. Lots and lots of whiskey. My nerves were doing all right on that frigid eve, considering.

I guess it was around three when Leon drained the night's second bottle into our glasses and the final preparations had to be made. "You're doing the right thing," he said reassuringly as I dropped the first bullet into the cylinder of the .38 that had belonged to my grandfather.

I wiped the tear from my eye and absentmindedly reached for another bullet to load into the pistol.

"What the fuck is that for?" he demanded, motioning with his glass toward the second round. "Does your dog need putting down or did she steal your woman, for chrissakes?"

I shrugged.

"This is a solemn occasion. You're sending your pal on her final journey. This isn't Dodge City, Johnny Ringo."

I could see his point. Just a single bullet gave it more of a sense of holy ceremony. I clicked the revolver shut. We put on our parkas, and I stuffed the gun in my pocket. We drained the glasses and carried the sleeping dog out to the prairie beyond the tracks wrapped in her blanket with her toys.

We laid the bundle into the hole, and I started to cry pretty hard, I'm not ashamed to say. I patted her head to say my goodbye, and she replied by snoring loudly. That made me feel better, knowing that she wasn't distressed. I was distressed enough for both of us. I took the gun from my pocket and prepared to conclude the final act, but every time I tried to aim into the hole, a flood of tears would obliterate my vision and prevent me from seeing where I was aiming, even though Leon was shining a flashlight into the grave.

"I can't do it, man," I said hoarsely. I felt Leon's hand on my shoulder. At the time, it felt like brotherly empathy, but in hindsight, I realize he may have just been trying to keep his balance. "I hate to ask you this, buddy, but . . . do you think you can?"

"No problem," he slurred heroically. We traded places, and I handed him the pistol. "Just have to get to that zen state of mind." He closed his eyes with his arms at his sides, revolver pointed to the ground. He teetered to and fro right on the edge of the hole in his zen-like stupor. I was waiting for him to open his eyes and take aim so I'd know when to shine the light at Dezzy. The night was cold and absolutely silent for a moment.

BANG!

"What the hell was that?" he actually said, the dope, his eyes snapping open wildly as our ears rang.

The deafening staccato crack had sent us into momentary sobriety. As the answer dawned horribly on my hired assassin, the silence of the frigid night was only broken by Dezzy's feeble delayed bark, barely audible as she was barking in her sleep. When I realized that Leon had squeezed off the round prematurely and only in the general vicinity of Desdemona, I shined the light into the hole to make sure the moron hadn't winged her. I'd have never forgiven him for that, and neither would my dog. She'd have no doubt jumped out of the hole, pistol-whipped Leon, and put herself down. I wouldn't have blamed her. Now we had to go back inside for another fucking bullet. And another whiskey.

What we didn't know at the time was that Leon had just shot himself in the foot. I'm not kidding. Clean through his boot, two socks, and the meat of his foot just between the bones. And that's just the second funniest thing the bullet had accomplished, but I'll get back to that after we have a stiff drink. The only way we found the hole in Leon's foot was that we noticed Leon tracking something other than mud into the house, which turned out to be the pool of blood in his boot thawing out. *Serves him right for botching the job*, I thought. Leon, however, ranted like a spoiled debutante after her credit card's been declined.

"Son of a bitch!" he slurred, unlacing his boot and peeling off his perforated and bloody socks. "Goddamn, this is going to hurt in the morning, you prick!" Which was no doubt true as any of his pain was currently being drowned in County Antrim's finest export. On the other hand, I wasn't the one who'd shot the bastard.

"Ah, fuck you, Sergeant York," I retorted. I could see he had no problem wiggling his toes, so I didn't think he'd even nicked any bones. Shot himself in the foot, that just figured. He was pretty angry, but I really didn't care, so I just let him rant like a jackass. I did go get him a roll of gauze and the remaining codeine just in case the pain did set in. "Here, I'm all out of Kevlar socks. I'm so very sorry." I was kind of pissed at this wannabe Doc Holliday yelling and whining like it was my fault. Shoots himself right through his own fucking flipper, no shit. Few Catholic funerals can boast of miraculous happenings, and it's even rarer for canine funerals, I'm sure, and while it wasn't an appearance from Our Lady of 127th and the Expressway or an even more apropos a sighting of St. Francis of Assisi, it was a quarter of a stigmata. I'm actually not sure if Dezzy was really even Catholic, but this struck me funny at the time. I laughed as I poured us both another stiff one.

"What the hell is so funny? I did this because you couldn't even take care of your own stinking dog!" he ranted, cramming his bandaged foot back into his ventilated boot with a wince. Now he was just getting personal. My expression must have changed at this, because he started backpedaling immediately.

"No wait, man, no offense. I just mean your dog reeks bad, that's all. Really bad. Can't you smell it?" I do have to admit that seven years of inhaling jet fuel hadn't done the best for my olfactory senses, and Dezzy's hygiene was never top on my list of priorities, but that was no way to speak of the soon-to-be-departed. "I can't believe you can't smell that," he continued. "She must be decaying from the inside or something. Here, even my coat's got the aroma. Check it out." He proffered his sleeve, and I inhaled. It did smell a bit ripe, but it didn't smell like old dog.

"I don't know," I said. "That's more of a chemical smell than an animal one, like metal cleaner or natural gas or something."

"Natural gas! Yeah, that's it, like the stuff they mix with natural gas so you can tell a faulty stove or a broken gas main . . ."

It was right then that it dawned on us. We looked out the window to the hole where Dezzy lay, the coals in the washtub beside it sending the occasional spark up to the clear winter sky. Remember when I said the bullet did more than one funny thing?

"Aw shit," someone said. It could have been either of us. Or both. The silence that immediately followed only lasted for a moment. We saw a blinding flash.

BOOM!

The kitchen window that faced the prairie shattered into powder, and our breath was stuffed back into our chests. A sheet of flame fountained eighty feet in the air. It seemed all the more blinding because the power in the house was knocked out instantly. The scene across the tracks, not fifty yards from us, was a conflagration of Homeric proportions. We scrambled out of the house and ran for Leon's car at least as fast as Desdemona's little doggie soul soared, doggie heaven bound, even figuring in the rocket assist we had provided.

No Viking chieftain had ever received a more majestic pyre than the one we gave my Dezzy on that cold night. JFK may have gotten an eternal flame, but my darling girl got a whole mushroom cloud to herself just about.

We were knocked sober by the explosion, and the panic had taken hold. Leon drove us away from the crime scene at breakneck speed, which wasn't a problem since every police car in my district was at that time heading *toward* my house and was in too much of a hurry to notice us. Neither of us spoke a word until we were locked in his apartment, still breathing hard. I made a beeline for the liquor cabinet as Leon turned on the TV. It didn't take long before the results of the night's solemn occasion were being speculated upon by the local early news programs.

We sat on the couch barely speaking as we drank for almost an hour waiting for the 6:00 a.m. news, contemplating our options. There was absolutely no way anyone would believe that we had accidentally dug a canine grave right over a gas main and then accidentally punctured it with a bullet. And all of this on the coldest night of the year. There would just be no explaining this one.

The announcer on TV was reporting that the deputy fire chief at the scene was quoted as saying that vagrants frequented the rail yard often, and there was some speculation that a fire in an oil drum may have sparked the explosion due to a faulty main, but investigators would have trouble knowing for certain as the resulting crater was at least twenty feet across.

Shit, I thought, *you could put a whole kennel of dogs in a hole that size.*

I kept running to the window to check outside. I was that paranoid.

"Stop worrying," Leon poured us two tall whiskeys. "With all the firefighters running all around, they'll never find our footprints. We cremated your dog and every shred of evidence," he concluded confidently. He was correct on that point. That took some of the edge off, at least. "Hey, man, come quick! You can see your house from the news chopper!"

I'll have to admit, it was kinda cool seeing my own place from the air on the news, illuminated by the column of fire that still easily rose twenty feet above the roof height. But then it dawned on me that I was looking at an empty house. I no longer had my four-legged pal. The grief caught up with me as the sun rose.

"Here," Leon said, handing me my full glass. "Mission accomplished."

"To Dezzy!" I said, raising the glass as tears ran down my face.

"To Smithereens!" replied Leon, a little teary-eyed himself.

FITZY'S SECRET

ere's to Ginny, the one that took my virginity!" said the loud man, hoisting his beer glass. His lusty expression fell when he caught Charles's expressionless gaze in the mirror behind the bar. "Sorry, didn't mean to offend . . ."

"No apology needed, friend," Charles assured the man. He raised his whiskey glass, joining the toast, drained it, then finished the inch or so of his remaining beer chaser. It was time for him to leave. The evening was just beginning, and the bar would start filling with younger fellows stopping after work. He neatly folded the sports section of his newspaper after ensuring that he wasn't leaving the horse-racing section behind with the rest of the paper. He pushed the few dollars left in front of his stool toward the rear edge of the bar, put on his hat, and made for the door. "Liam, until next time," he waved at the bartender, receiving a respectful nod in return.

The evening was cool and dry, the light fading in the clear sky as Charles made his way home. The loud man's toast made him think of *his* first. All throughout his life, he'd thought back to her often, expecting to do so less and less as age and wisdom took hold of him but lately finding the opposite. Now with an older man's clarity, the more important points of his life, many only made salient in hindsight, came to his private musings more often.

She'd be in her late sixties now, maybe even seventy. *Tempus fugit…*

CHARLES HAD JUST TURNED SEVENTEEN. He had one year left of high school and absolutely no idea how he should proceed after that. His gram insisted he go to college—that was the only intelligent thing to do, in her opinion—but Charles knew that he could follow her wishes to the letter and still feel that the old woman was deeply disappointed in him. It was if nothing he did could adequately express his love and respect for the woman who'd raised him, and he felt every sigh of resignation she brought to their interactions. Most of his behavior was dictated around avoiding the guilt of having let the old woman down yet again.

His uncle Jimmy was the other side of the coin: he was sympathetic to the kid's plight, knowing full well what kind of psychological warfare expert his mother was. Charles idolized Jimmy. He was the epitome of cool: a tough but friendly man who'd earned respect from everyone in the neighborhood and was known for his rowdy past exploits. Jimmy was the only one left alive who didn't hesitate to call the matriarch out on her passive-aggressive tactics. More than once, Jimmy had cut off her melodramatic reactions by picking up the phone and demanding that the operator patch him through to the Vatican for fast-tracking the suffering woman's canonization.

The week before the junior prom, Charles had taken the terror-inducing leap of asking Rachel to go with him. Uncle Jimmy was the driving force behind that, prodding the lad to be bold. He hadn't even discussed it with his two best friends, as they would have been in total agreement that Rachel was far out of his league. One of the most smart and popular girls in the school who'd broken up with the captain of the senior hockey team weeks before, Rachel was a young person with a future. Against all odds, his shocking display of initiative took the pretty brown-eyed girl by surprise, and she accepted, maybe so Charles could be surprised too. Charles and his crowd weren't exactly pros when it came to dealing with girls.

For someone who didn't approve of Charles's hanging around with the neighborhood guys, or not hanging around with the neighborhood guys, or his showing interest in the opposite sex, or of the opposite sex showing any interest in him, Gram seemed unusually pleased to hear his good news that he'd asked Rachel to the dance. That was a shocking bonus for a young man who was already walking on air. Not even a flicker of disappointment or a brief lecture on how much his late grandfather had treasured and cared for the family car when he asked to borrow it, even after explaining that the plan was for the couples to spend the next day at the dunes on the lakefront.

The day before the prom, as Charles got home with the tuxedo he'd picked up from the rental place on the way home from school, Uncle Jimmy's midnight-blue Mustang Boss 302 was parked in front of their building. What a magnificent automobile. Uncle Jimmy had bought it when he got home from the Navy, and he treasured it with every fiber of his being. He even let Jimmy drive it once or twice, including one night a few weeks ago when he let Jimmy take it up to 110MPH on Doty Avenue, with a word of warning that it would be the last time he got to drive it if Gram ever found out.

He was embarrassed to parade in front of his uncle in his tux, but Gram insisted on seeing the fit, fussing over the details. Before he could take it off and hang it back up neatly, a car horn out in front prompted Uncle Jimmy to look out the window and wave at the driver, a pretty blonde in sunglasses.

"G'bye, Ma," his uncle said as he led Charles to the front door. Once out of the old woman's earshot, Jimmy theatrically placed a set of car keys and twenty-five dollars into Charles's hand. He stared at the keys in disbelief, his shock interrupted by a light slap on the cheek. "Hey, Ace . . . it's got four corners and a full tank. I expect it to be like that on Sunday night when I come back, understand? Oh, and one grain of sand left in the interior *or* in the trunk and you do your senior year from a hospital . . . understand?" He gave his nephew a final tap on the face and headed out the door. Wicked!

Rachel called after dinner. Right at the crest of his triumphant wave, the disappointment brought his good fortune to a frozen stop. As bad as it made her feel—*really*—she wouldn't be going with Charles tomorrow night. Her ex had broken up with his current girlfriend and wanted to take Rachel instead, and since they'd been together for so long and they'd only broken up just recently, Rachel couldn't let him go alone, and anyway, Rachel would see Charles there, and she promised to save a dance for him . . .

———

EVEN SO MANY YEARS LATER, he could still feel the scar tissue on his ego left from that moment. To say he had been stunned would be an understatement. It was the confusing silence that followed a good shot to the head in the boxing ring. And the feeling of shame that followed, worse still, was not being able muster up the courage to tell Gram what had just happened. It would've only reinforced her feeling of disappointment; he had convinced himself of that. He wasn't strong enough to face that with her. His lack of maturity had caused him to lie to Gram. It hurt him even now, all these years later.

———

WHEN HE TOLD HIS TWO best pals that Saturday morning, they were sympathetic, urging him to go anyway. They tried to think of other girls he could ask, but they all knew that was a lost cause.

"Look, Fitzy, you were just going to make a jackass of yourself with her tonight by dancing too close and getting her pregnant. You're much better off just coming for the party!" his friend Danny had said, full of camaraderie.

"You already bought the ticket, and you got your uncle's wheels. Come on," another made the case. "Your gram let you off the leash. Don't blow that opportunity! Or at least let *us* take the Mustang!" he teased, not making Charles feel any better, even though those were all good points.

———

CHARLES BARELY TOOK NOTICE OF any details on his walk home from the tavern, his head filled with the dredged-up memories. His focus snapped from replaying the drama of so many years ago, and he found himself stopped on a curb waiting for an approaching car to pass before crossing the street, a pile of dry maple leaves the color of saddle leather clattering on the sidewalk behind him. The minivan squeaked to a hasty stop when the driver, a smiling middle-aged woman, noticed Charles and bade him to cross despite there not being a stop sign or crosswalk on that street for a couple of blocks in either direction. Charles politely waved his thanks as he sighed under his breath for having to cross swiftly instead of at the pace of his old reminiscences. The evening air started to chill his ears and the tip of his nose, but his mature bones still felt the warmth of the early summer so long ago . . .

———

FEELING RIDICULOUS NOW IN THE tuxedo, Charles waited while Gram fussed over him before he left, insisting on taking his picture despite his protestations and the fact that the flash cube on the Kodak didn't work anymore. He almost stalled the car working the heavy clutch on the Mustang as he pulled away, taking the corner a little too fast, according to the squeal of the tires. He drove past the alley and made a much more cautious turn up the next block, parking about halfway down. He took a shopping bag from behind the Mustang's seat and slipped quickly through the gangway between two bungalows and into the alley. He opened the overhead door of the garage behind their building, closing it behind him as his eyes adjusted to the fresh darkness. Next to Gram's car, Charles changed into jeans among the smell of gasoline and cut grass, packaging his tuxedo back on the hanger inside of its plastic shroud to hang like a flag of defeat. He checked the window that faced the yard to make sure Gram wasn't looking out before slipping back out to the alley. He was back on the next block, confident that he'd gotten away unnoticed, but hadn't even gotten the Mustang's door open when he heard someone call his name, freezing him in place.

"Hey, Fitzy! Uncle Jimmy know you've got his car?" Maggie called from the porch of her apartment building, where she sat smoking a cigarette. Not one of Gram's favorite people, Maggie wasn't really much older than Charles, but she'd dropped out of high school to have her daughter, who was now about six.

"Hello, Maggie. Yeah, there's no need to get the police involved," Charles joked, getting a half smile back.

"Hey, I saw you in the tux like a maître d'. What's the story?"

Charles quickly laid the incriminating suit on the back seat of the muscle car. "Ah, nothing. I'll see you, Maggie," he said, about to make his exit.

"Wait, isn't it prom or something tonight? Why'd you leave all dressed up to change now?" she said, her prying seeming a little condescending.

"It turns out I'm not going. Got other things to do."

"Like what?" she teased, none of her business notwithstanding.

Charles shut the door and walked over to the porch, feeling no need to share his woes with every open window on the street. "Nah, my date canceled," he said when he was close enough for a more conversational volume. "No big deal. We're not dating or anything."

"Well, damn. She sick or something?"

Charles considered going with this explanation but must have paused too long.

"She standing you up? What a bitch." Maggie was well known for having a mouth like a truck driver to go with her lack of other graces, as any of Gram's friends from the parish would be glad to tell you.

"I don't think it's like that."

"Ah, to hell with her, Fitzy. You should go and have a good time without her," Maggie said, leaning back with her elbows on the next stair up. "Don't be a mope. Go dance with the other girls!"

"I might, Maggie. That's a good idea. See you around!" Charles walked back to the car.

"Hey, Fitzy!" she yelled just before he got the door open again.

"Yeah?" he called back, anxious to make his escape.

"So why did you leave wearing the monkey suit? Does your grandma think you're going?" she shouted for all to hear. "Why you sneaking off?"

Charles could feel his ears reddening. God, that's all he needed— having to explain everything to Gram *after* she'd heard about it from whatever neighbor heard it from this human bullhorn. "Look Maggie, I'd rather not have to tell Gram the whole story. That's all."

"You should still go, then."

"I'd rather just do my own thing," he said, turning to leave.

"Let me drive the Mustang!" she said enthusiastically. The idea was so ridiculous it made Charles snort out a chuckle. "Let me drive the Mustang, and I won't say anything to your grandma . . ."

Charles didn't even have to think that deal over. "Fat chance!" He laughed, much preferring yet another uncomfortable string of questions from Gram than one from Uncle Jimmy. "See you around!" He waved and made for the car.

"Take me for a ride, then," came the counteroffer.

"See you around!" he repeated, smiling.

"Hey, Fitzy, if I do you a big favor, take me for a ride?"

"What's the favor?"

"Not telling you unless you agree. That's the deal. Trust me, you'll want to hear what I have to say."

"Let's hear it," Charles said cautiously.

"Did you get a corsage for this little pair of tits?" Maggie asked. In truth, Rachel was far better endowed than the young mother—and with better manners.

"Yeah, of course."

"But you don't have it with you, so maybe you don't want to forget to pick it up?"

"Don't need it now," Charles said. He'd paid for it when he ordered it. Who cared whose garbage bin it wound up in?

"Yeah, but you wouldn't want the florist phoning up your grandmother with a reminder, would you?"

"Ah, damn. No, I don't," he admitted in defeat. In fact, Maggie had done him a huge favor. "Okay, hop in."

"Let's go!" Maggie squealed, bouncing to her feet toward the car.

"What about your daughter?"

"Nope, at my ma's house for a sleepover. I just got off of a twelve-hour shift."

"Want to grab some shoes?"

"I'm riding, not walking, dumb-dumb!" She laughed, almost skipping across the sidewalk. The tips of the pockets of her cutoff shorts poked just beyond the baby blue fringe, and what little she had, braless under her pale yellow tank top, oscillated with every hop. By the time Charles started the rumbling motor, she had already fondled the upholstery and was starting to go through the glove box, *ooohing* and *ahhhing* over Uncle Jimmy's fine auto. As he pulled away from the curb, working the clutch gingerly, Maggie was manipulating the rearview mirror to check how she looked in the sunglasses she'd dug out.

"Make yourself at home," Charles said sarcastically.

"May as well, you drive like a sissy!"

At the end of the block, Charles whipped a left-hand turn that slid them in their seats like an amusement park ride, the motor snorting to a roar. Maggie let out a shrieking laugh, clutching the door for dear life.

———————

Darkness was dropping quickly as Charles trudged away down the sidewalk to his home in nostalgic revelry, almost impervious to the cold aside from his numbing ears and running nose. He smiled at the memory as he brushed his upper lip with a handkerchief from his pocket, eyes down, watching his own shadow slither as he moved from the glow of one streetlight to the next. What a car that had been!

———————

When Charles had returned to the car, corsage box in hand, Maggie nagged him to put his tux on and go, date or no date. She said he'd be a chump to let Rachel keep him from going out and kicking up his heels. She seemed full of nags and criticisms; maybe all women were stuck in a state of constant dissatisfaction. Just to prove his own stubbornness, he abandoned the route back to Maggie's street and made a beeline for the expressway, driving as fast as he dared, hoping not to incur the wrath of traffic enforcement. They were well out of the neighborhood when Maggie asked slyly, "Um, Fitzy, where are we going?"

"For a ride!" He laughed.

He headed toward downtown, driving to the lakefront. The wind whipped through the open windows, completely drowning out the blasting radio when it cut out under every overpass. They sailed under the neon lips that meant quality carpet cleaning and the ballpark that passed by them on the left. Just south of the Loop, he made his way to the side drive through the park among the museums, the sun occasionally hiding behind the skyscrapers. As he drove slowly, lake to his right and city to his left, they cruised past a swarthy man with a silver mustache manning a pushcart.

"Pull over! Get me a hot dog!" she demanded.

He bought three, and they sat on a bench facing the Mustang and the twilight in the southeast. Maggie asked him what he was going to do once he graduated. Charles told her that *everyone* insisted that he go to college, despite having no money for it. Sure, he'd probably get some minor scholarships, but deep down, he really had had enough of school. Lately, he'd been kicking around the idea of the Navy.

"Don't be a chump!" she dismissed. She told him to try to get into a union or something. She told him that she'd never put herself in a position to have someone else making decisions for her. She could take care of herself, she kept insisting. "Look at me. I was never smart enough for college, and I did my own thing even with everyone in the neighborhood judging me. I don't care. I'll be fine."

He wasn't going to argue. Why argue with the advice from someone whom Gram would refer to as *the unwed mother*?

Maggie broke the silence by throwing the wadded-up foil used to contain a hot dog at him. "C'mon, get me home. You got a prom to go to." Had Charles not picked up the foil ball off the grass, it would have stayed there.

Charles cruised a few downtown streets in the rumbling Mustang before heading back to the neighborhood, the sun setting and the air cooling as he did. The sky above them was indigo blue when he pulled up just across from Maggie's building to drop her off.

"Go and meet up with your buddies," she counseled firmly as she opened the door, the dome light seeming harsh.

"We'll see . . . I might go drive some more."

Maggie sighed theatrically and rolled her eyes. "Don't be a dope. Go have fun with your friends. Someday, you won't be able to." There was something wistful in the way she said that before closing the door behind her. She walked around the front of the car, and it occurred to Charles that he should turn on the headlights before pulling away.

Just before she crossed the street, he called, "Thanks, Maggie."

Instead of crossing, she walked to the driver's window and leaned in. "Look, Fitzy, I know what will help. Come on up and you can have *one* beer. That'll make it easier to show up late. One and you're out with your friends, deal?"

Up the four sets of stairs, she led them into her apartment, a small close stuffy place that faintly smelled of cigarettes and drying paint, sparse with the exception of the little girl's toys and clothes scattered about. Maggie opened the back door from the kitchen and invited Charles to sit out on the screen porch on a small gliding couch, the light from the kitchen illuminating the overflowing ashtray on the small iron table in the corner that also held a battered transistor radio. He noticed his own bedroom window plainly visible from where he sat.

Maggie soon joined him with two cans of Pabst, a pack of Dorals, and a lighter, the screen door slapping closed behind her, spring creaking. They cracked the cans open, and he followed her lead of throwing the ring tab into the ashtray. It was nice and cold, and Maggie's features briefly flared in vivid orange as she lit a cigarette, the chorus of crickets coming up from the yards below.

He was mere yards from home yet thousands of miles away, sitting silently in the dark with his thoughts when it all became a blur, tasting of sour beer and acrid tobacco smoke, fumbling and awkward and soft and foreign.

And there on the back porch in the panting darkness, incredibly but all too briefly, Maggie was his first.

CHARLES COUGHED AN AUDIBLE LAUGH as he walked, feeling the genuine warmth of gratitude all these decades later. One might blame his watering eyes on the chilling breeze or car exhaust from the street, but in truth, it was from the memory of that perplexing confusing joy. He laughed to himself again. Maggie was his first. As clumsy and clueless as his efforts were, she was his first.

TWENTY MINUTES LATER, MERCIFULLY, SHE was technically also his second. The encounter was not so brief this time, thank God, and felt more natural, even with a few words and manipulations of guidance from someone way more experienced. They sat next to each other in silence for some time before she pushed his still-curious hands away gently and slipped back into her clothes.

Charles caught her features in the flicker of the lighter again, and he croaked, "Thank you, Maggie."

He got a teasing chuckle in response. She lay back in the corner of the glider as he dressed absentmindedly, and by the time he was tying his shoes, she was stubbing out the cigarette.

"Okay, kiddo. I've got to get to sleep, and you have a dance to crash. Get out." She propelled him steadily back through her apartment, saying, "Go, have a good time. I'll be fine . . ." Her words had a condescending edge, but she kissed him gently before shoving him out the door with a laugh. How could he express his profound gratitude for her act of kindness?

"Hey, Maggie," he said, looking back from the hallway outside her door.

"Goodnight, Fitzy," she insisted.

"I hope it was okay," he said, a little too meekly.

She laughed. Pushing the door closed, she said, "It was fine. You were fine. I'll be fine . . . Now scram!" and gave the door a final shove, shutting it completely.

Charles stood for a few seconds, then lazily made his way down the stairs. Before rounding the landing, he looked back and noticed two shadows in the light from the crack under her front door where her feet stood. *Did that really happen?* he wondered as he made his way down the flights of steps. He had an idea and left the front door propped open with an unclaimed newspaper from the front porch. When he got the driver's door open on the Mustang, he looked back up, maybe to wave goodbye. All the lights in her apartment were out now, and the slight rustle of curtains he detected could have been real or he could just have imagined it. He drove away, with the car rumbling mightily.

He cruised the streets of the neighborhood with his thoughts for a bit before returning to her street and parking far from her house.

Returning swiftly on foot and letting himself back in as quietly as possible, Charles climbed the stairs gently at the side edges to minimize the creaking. He laid the corsage box in front of her door and made a quick stealthy exit, kicking the rolled-up paper back to where he'd found it.

It was still early enough to change into his tux and keep his promise, but once he got out on the main streets with the grumbling engine and his racing thoughts, the only thing to do was head back downtown and cruise around the tall buildings, feeling like the king of the city.

The next morning, he woke up to the sound of someone knocking on the window in the parking lot of the beach at the dunes. Panicking at the thought of it being a cop, he jolted awake with a jump. It was his friend Danny. Most of the group was unloading coolers and lawn chairs from the three or four cars they'd taken. They all took turns giving him a ration of grief for not going to the dance.

"There he is, the last virgin in the school!" one mocked. "Should have come, Fitzy. It turned into a regular Roman orgy, and you missed it!" he said, getting several laughs and crude agreements before others chimed in with graphically embellished tall tales of their romantic exploits of night.

Danny and Charles carried a large cooler across the rippled sand toward the water. "You should have come, Chuck. It wasn't much, but we had a decent time," Danny told him.

"*You* would have had a good time, wallflower!" Paul called from right behind him. "Tell him what happened, Danny!"

"Oh yeah!" Danny laughed. "You *did* miss it! Rachel and her boyfriend showed up. He was completely sloppy drunk. Dumb bastard puked right before they walk in. He wouldn't have gotten in anyway; he smelled like a brewery on a hot day. I mean, he puked *all* over. Rachel was as mad as a wet cat. Hockey coach had to drive the kid home. He's probably in trouble over it. Rachel sat crying for almost an hour until her dad came and got her."

"Thank God he showed up. All the girls had to go sit with Rachel and listen to her blubber. You should have been there to be Prince

Galahad!" Paul added. "Too bad you were at home crying about Rachel!" He laughed derisively.

"As a matter of fact, I had an adventure of my own!" Charles said, the secret burning inside of him.

"So what did you do with your night?" Danny asked.

Charles closed his eyes to put his thoughts in order before sharing his story.

"Me?" he began, jerking his thumb back toward the Mustang. "I cruised around all night in that wicked machine!"

They wouldn't have believed him anyway.

———

THE PORCH LIGHT ABOVE THE door caught wisps of Charles's breath as he let himself inside, finally home. It was warm inside the foyer as he hung up his coat and hat on a hook, the cold leaving his bones in fits as he rubbed his hands together.

Young Father DeCicco, two years out of the seminary, recently transferred from Africa, and a little too eager to please must have been listening for the door, so quickly did he glide into the front room of the rectory.

"Enjoy your walk, Father Fitzpatrick?" the young priest said obsequiously.

"Yes, fine, Robert," Charles replied, much preferring the quiet of his thoughts to his colleague's company at the moment. "Messages?"

Father DeCicco consulted the note in his hand. "Nothing major. A reminder about the archdiocese meeting on Thursday and two estimates on the boiler upgrades for the school. Details are on your desk."

"Very good, Robert," Charles said, easing himself into a chair.

"Pardon me, but you seem deep in contemplation, Father Fitzpatrick," the young dark-haired man pushed. "Would you like me to handle Mass tomorrow morning?"

Charles waved his hand dismissively. "Oh no. Thank you very much for the offer, Robert!" he replied, putting effort into not sounding too harsh with the well-meaning younger man. "I'm saying a Mass for someone tomorrow."

"Oh! And who would that be, Father?"

"Maggie Fielder," Charles replied.

The younger priest didn't recall the name from those of the parishioners he knew but was nervous that perhaps he should. "I see, Father. Is she unwell?" Father DeCicco asked, hoping that was the right question to ask.

"I really don't know, Robert," Charles replied. There was a slight pause before he added with a chuckle, "But wherever she is and however she's doing, I'm sure she'll be fine!" He laughed.

Father Robert DeCicco laughed too, although he had no idea why.

THE VANISHING HITCHHIKER

hanks, mister. You're very kind on this windy night!" Ernie Kawolczak said in a thin falsetto, hair from his cheap blond wig whipping in the wind as he slid into the passenger's seat.

"Where you going?" the father said, his eyes darting to the folded bills on the bench seat between them, which Ernie quickly palmed in his white opera gloved hand before tucking it away in a fold in his flapper dress. It looked to be about three bucks—not a fortune, but good for a couple of beers and a few songs on the jukebox. Anyway, the shoes were killing his arches.

"I'm just going home from a dance. I don't live far . . ." As the car pulled away onto Archer Avenue, Ernie stole a glance at the three bored kids in the back seat of the sedan, who were watching the iron gates of the huge cemetery reflect a strobing pattern of streetlights as their dad picked up speed and maneuvered into the left-hand lane. "Just turn left up here at Seventy-Ninth if you please, mister. It's not far."

"Whatever you say, young *lady*," the father said, emphasizing the last word for the sake of the children and giving Ernie a conspiratorial wink that he made sure the youngsters wouldn't catch.

"Hey, mister, are you going to a Halloween party or something?" the little girl asked from the shadows in the back seat.

"Oh no, honey!" Ernie replied, trying to giggle femininely. "I'm going home from a dance. I just broke up with my boyfriend . . . Anyway, isn't Halloween tomorrow?"

"Yeah, that's right! Halloween isn't till tomorrow, so you wouldn't be going to a Halloween party," the dad chimed in, impressed with the young man's quick thinking.

"I'm not far from here, sir. You can drop me off on this corner." Ernie gestured, eager to get back to the saloon. Swinging the car door open, he said to the family, "Thanks for the ride. You've been very kind."

"Our pleasure, young lady, and good luck with your boyfriend!" The father winked again theatrically with his left eye as Ernie shut the door, and then the car pulled away. Ernie walked up the side street a few dozen yards to be sure he was out of sight of any children that may still be watching him. He fished a Lucky from his clutch and lit it on the fourth try because of the wind. When he was sure the coast was clear, he turned around and headed back to make his way to the gin mill on his aching and wobbling feet.

"Mary!" the baritone chorus of a half dozen ersatz blond flappers greeted him as his stepped into the warm close air of the tavern. He finished his smoke in one drag as he made his way to a barstool and stubbed it out in an ashtray before putting his three dollars up on the bar. Chet was already drawing a draft from the taps and set it down in front of Ernie.

"Better than a poke in the eye with a sharp stick," Chet said to Ernie, trying to make the young man feel better. "Not like it was when I was a boy though. That's for sure. Man, back in the late forties, early fifties, a group of decked-out fellows could keep quite a party going on a night like tonight . . . especially with the baby boom."

Ernie took a long sip of his beer. Al, three stools to his left, chimed in: "Of course, we all knew the hustle at the time too. These new kids, a lot of 'em don't have the patter." He gestured toward the men's room, obviously referring to someone in particular. "Three bucks ain't bad for a few minutes of acting, kid. Be proud," he said. Al had no room to talk. He was almost twenty years too old to play this game, his thick dark brows and five o'clock shadow in stark contrast with his long blond wig and looking quite matronly in his tight sequined dress. It made Ernie wonder what was fueling Al's perennial enthusiasm for the tradition.

"So who ain't 'got the patter'?" Ernie asked Chet, jerking his head toward the lavatory.

"Ah, some young college kid in here tonight. No idea what he was doing. Chased away some nice families coming on too strong, they tell me. Looked a fright too . . . Anyway, Stosh has him back in the can doing his makeup and giving him some pointers. If you're going to play, you gotta respect tradition!"

"That's so true," Ernie said. He didn't necessarily agree but thought better of arguing with his bartender while his hard-earned three dollars disappeared quickly down his throat.

"It was a kick back then, helping families make some memories . . . You looked the part, you acted the part, made a few coins enough for a good rowdy time after with the gang. Boy, I wish I would've been able to see the faces on those kids on Halloween when someone mentioned the legend. Even if you didn't catch it on the radio or in the newspaper, someone would bring up Resurrection Mary. I had a pal that was such a dedicated Mary that he used to go to St. Vincent's and buy a few extra white sweaters. If someone tipped large, he'd have the dad drop him off at this very bar"—Chet tapped the wood counter three times to emphasize— "and 'accidentally' leave a sweater behind. When Pops brought the kids back to return it on Halloween, everyone in the bar would play along. What a hoot! For a few years, they had a picture of some blond dame in white taken from behind up on the bar, and they'd tell the kids it was a shrine to Mary since the tragedy back in the twenties! You should've seen the chins of those kids hit the floor! What a riot!" The old bartender roared with laughter and happy memories.

The wind assisted the door flying open as another bedraggled flapper stepped in out of the chill.

"MARY!" the crowd cheered as Ricky scuttled in, his eyes adjusting to the light.

"How's the game, Rick?" Chet called as the thin man slid onto a stool, counting out six singles.

Al whistled. "That's pretty good for this late, kid!" Al said, genuinely impressed.

Ricky waved his hand dismissively. "This is for three hitchhikes, maybe a dozen kids total. Not even a dollar a munchkin! He took a pull from the beer Chet put in front of him while picking the cost out of his earnings and wiping the foam and lipstick from his mouth. "Still, it beats working!"

"That's the spirit!" Al said, draining his mug. "Doesn't look like business is going to pick up. Maybe I'll make my way home, leave it to the younger fellows . . ." Al stood up and started arranging his white feather boa around his shoulders when Stosh and a now-stunning newcomer exited the men's room. Stosh presented the younger man to the crowd like a proud stage mother.

"Jean Harlow or what?" Stosh queried those assembled. "Get out there and make us proud!" Stosh said to the first-timer, the other Marys giving the newbie a round of applause and wolf whistles as he made his way to the door.

"Hold up, kid," said Al. "I'm going home. I'll shoot you up Robert's Road and drop you off at Archer, save you a walk." The two far-from-feminine flappers made their way out into the night.

Ernie pushed his empty mug toward the bartender and went through the change in front of him.

"Never mind, this one's on me!" said Ricky, holding up two fingers to Chet.

"Why, thank you, Ricky!" Ernie said, toasting him when his beer arrived.

"Going out again?" Ricky asked as Ernie scratched is scalp beneath the cheap wig.

"Not sure. Probably not. Wind's picking up, and business isn't. Might be time to head home."

"Thinking that myself."

The door opened again.

"MARY . . . and MARY!" Ernie and the crowd greeted two grizzled blond hitchhikers in white party dresses that shambled into the bar.

"How's luck?" asked Chet, drawing two more mugs.

"Lousy," one said. "This game is played out!"

"Look at youse," a powerfully built but well-turned-out flapper said from the end of the bar. "Youse are probably scaring them away, and you can't be out there in groups either. This grift don't work unless you're out there alone! Sheesh!"

"He's got a point," agreed the bartender. "Guys just don't put in the effort anymore."

"Sez you! Walt's got a plan to put a new spin on this game. It's a humdinger!"

"Oh really? Spill it!" Chet demanded, but the crowd had to wait for Walt to return from emptying his bladder. The conversation turned to next season's baseball, and they had forgotten about this new plan when Walt finally emerged from the bathroom, adjusting his package as well as he could beneath his dress before sitting down. A good forty minutes and two beers had passed before Chet decided to interrogate him: "Okay, Walt. How are you going to save Halloween?"

"I don't know if it's going to save Halloween exactly," Walt warned the crowd, "but I was telling Bob that I had an idea: what if some late night, we took a blowtorch from my job at the plumber's and charred some handprints into the cemetery gates? Looking like we were trying to get in? Huh? People would come to see that, and it would be there all year-round to remind people."

A quiet fell over the crowd as the wheels turned in their heads, imagining the possibilities.

The deep thought was shattered by the door opening once again to a hitchhiking blond flapper.

"MARY!" everyone shouted as Stosh's protege returned, looking both triumphant and embarrassed.

"How'd you do kid?" Chet asked.

"Make us proud?" added Stosh.

"I did okay, I guess," said the newcomer, sitting down and ordering a round for all the Marys.

"A round, you say? Musta done pretty good!" Chet beamed, filling the glasses as the newcomer placed his money on the bar, the amount of which amazed everybody.

"Thirty-five bucks! Holy cats!" Walt exclaimed. "You hit it out of the park on your first time. We have a winner!" The assembled crowd agreed in a jumble of calls of admiration and congratulations, which the embarrassed the young man a little further.

The young man raised his glass in a toast to his well-wishers and took a long sip.

"So how many kids were in the car? Give us the details," Stosh prodded.

The newcomer set down his glass and looked puzzled. "Kids? There weren't any kids in the car . . ."

MARY KATE MACMANUS WILL NOT SELL

Hey, I hear that crazy old bird that spit at you finally croaked!" Phil said, hanging an economy acoustic six-string up on the wall, perfect for beginners. "Happened a couple of weeks back, they say," he added.

Jerry looked out the window of the music store at the dilapidated house across the street. Surely they'd pull it down now and build something commercial. He wondered if the crabby old lady had left the house to anyone. He assumed that at least the empty lot between the house and the corner was still going to the church. Maybe she left them the house too, as a thank-you. Most of all, he wondered if the car was still in the battered garage.

It had to be a 1960 or 1961 Ford Fairlane. Doubtful if it had more than a few thousand miles on it. Last time he had seen it was maybe thirty years ago when Jerry's dad still ran the place, and Jerry had looked through the garage window, past the clutter, to see the dusty white car sitting there. Apart from flattened tires and probably rodent-eaten wiring loom, it looked like it was one car wash away from being in a dealer's showroom.

Mary MacManus was an angry crazy old broad. The neighborhood had a few crazies that were area fixtures sometimes referred to as the "walkers," spotted all around the area walking angrily and almost always locked in an animated one-sided argument. Mary would harangue and scold the sidewalk, children, other pedestrians, traffic, parked cars, and all manner of deities, all without breaking a strong determined stride as she gestured violently. Everybody gave Mary MacManus a wide berth.

In the summer, she wore a wide straw hat, like something that would be worn by rubber planters in Central America, and in the winter, anywhere between one and three woolen beanies and a long puffy down parka, but always sported men's sneakers that had to be several sizes too large. There was no way, even with all of her walking and sidewalk-pounding, that her hooves were that big. She couldn't have weighed more than ninety pounds with a pocket full of change and carrying her lucky brick, and her face and scraggly gray hair spoke of a harsh life.

Phil hadn't even worked at the music store when the spitting incident happened, but when her name was mentioned in conversation, someone would eventually bring up the incident. Mary MacManus sightings had been declining steadily over the last few years and now were quite infrequent, even for Jerry, who worked just four lanes of traffic away from the front porch of the elderly and mentally touched woman. Her demise would certainly account for his not seeing her much lately, and with luck, that would remain so. The thought of a spitting Mary MacManus poltergeist was not a pleasant thought. Still, Jerry had no animus against the old woman and hoped she was finally resting in peace. She deserved a peaceful afterlife, he felt, after having been trapped in that body for ninety plus years with that troubled mind as a roommate.

Mary had become a minor reluctant celebrity about twenty years ago or so, right after the owner of the tavern four doors down retired. Mary's house had once been the farmhouse for one of the small Dutch truck farms in the area. By the time Mary and her husband bought the place in the forties, the neighborhood was thriving, and her house and the two flanking empty lots were among some of the last residential houses on 111th Street. One lot stood between her and the side street, across which stood the church, and the other lot was a buffer between her and the storefronts. When the tavern owner retired and decided to sell, a developer snatched it up and along with it, most of the other property on that side of the street, with an eye to putting in a multi-business park that stretched the length of the block. His plans required him to have access to both side streets, and within a few purchases, only Mary's house and two lots stood in his way. With such a minor obstacle, he put his plans into action and started knocking down the old buildings farther down the block.

Except, Mary Kate MacManus would not sell.

She ignored the offers that came through her mail slot, and within a few weeks, the developer was sending people to the house to knock on the door and set the dog to barking. Mary would look through the window at who was knocking and just walk away. Agents of the developer would try to approach her on her stomps around the area, but this never ended well, sometimes with law enforcement having to warn the harassers to stop antagonizing the old loon.

The offers increased, and so did the abuse and vitriol heaped upon the representatives sent to reason with the old woman. While the chamber of commerce was sympathetic to the businessman's Scary Mary problem, she wasn't doing anything not well within her rights. She didn't seem to have any relatives that could be enlisted to help the nutty old woman see the benefits being offered, and that's when the little PR campaign started. First, the flyers to the local businesses and neighbors, apologizing for the holdup of the development designed to bring income and prosperity to the area. After that, people dropping by the stores and shops on the street, asking why nobody had started a petition to convince Mary Kate MacManus to sell her run-down house and ugly empty lots and actually help the neighborhood.

Word of the PR campaign spread quickly. Team Lunatic outnumbered Team Corporate Greed by a huge margin in the area, but most really didn't care until the PR campaign got too personal. He spread the word far and wide that not only was he offering Mary Kate much more than the property was worth, but he'd also taken it upon himself to find her a nice condominium in the area where she could keep her dog and never worry about upkeep again. He was really doing the crazy old lady a favor. But his largess didn't win over many more of the locals, who saw the tactic for what it was.

The developer decided to resort to what the locals felt was dirty pool: he started laying the foundation for having Mary Kate MacManus declared mentally incompetent, possibly even having her committed. That was a step too far for the locals. Sure, she frightened the children and yelled at lampposts, but she paid her bills and kept the part of her lawn that wasn't bare patches cut short and her sidewalk shoveled in the winter, even if Jerry made it a point to do it himself. The developer went so far as to have a man with a video camera keep watch on her, documenting her rantings and ravings as she made her rounds. When the cameraman started getting bold and approaching the tormented woman too closely, things got ugly. Before Mary Kate MacManus went over the edge and assaulted the fellow, some neighbors got involved instead, telling the man off and shouting at him to leave the old woman alone.

The cameraman was on his game the day of the spitting incident, right out in front of the music store. He was filming Mary yelling at the parked cars, and Jerry's mother looked out, and it broke her heart to see the crazy old woman harassed, so Jerry went outside to tell the man to knock it off, for the sake of his mother. Jerry yelled at the cameraman to get a life and stop bothering Mary, and when Jerry turned around, Mary stood there angrily, yelling at Jerry, "Kiss my ass, you filthy Jap commie!" before launching a gob of crazy old lady loogie that landed on Jerry's shirt with an audible *WHAP* and storming off. For the record, Jerry was German-Irish and held no particular political affiliations, so Mary's outburst at him forever remained a mystery.

Shortly thereafter, a reporter from the local newspaper—not one of those big newspapers, mind you, but the smaller area one that mostly handled high school sports, Boy and Girl Scout paper drives, and local parades—got wind of the story and took up Mary's crusade. The first article was headlined *David Vs. Goliath* and told the basic story of the old woman who wouldn't sell, the paper running a photo of the stalled construction project. The reporter was working on a follow-up telling the story from Mary's side and was looking to interview the old woman. He'd gone to her house three times looking to talk with Mary Kate MacManus, but the two times she did answer the door, he was met with a hail of profanity and empty Schlitz cans to accompany the sound of the barking dog.

It was after this last volley of attack that the reporter came into the music store to talk to some of her neighbors. This newspaper fellow was really doing his homework. Neighbors told him about Mary's crazy rantings around the neighborhood, and he shared some of the facts of Mary's life he'd dug up with Jerry's parents.

Mary Katherine had married Daniel MacManus in the late thirties, and they bought the house before the war. When Dan, a railroad engineer, was killed at work in the early fifties, Mary was entitled to a large insurance pay out, as well as Dan's railroad pension. It was shortly thereafter that Mary's cranial trolley started leaving the tracks it seemed, but nothing too major. Her mental issues were compounded by further bad luck. She remarried twice, once to a fellow named Fisher and eight years later to a man named Talbridge, neither of whom could stand Mary's mercurial personality for too long apparently, for they both left her without an explanation within a few years of matrimony. Mary spent the remainder of her time alone, save for the series of dogs she kept, growing crazier yet still keeping the house together. Money wasn't an issue with the railroad pension coming in every month and her frugal lifestyle, and she kept to her raging babbling self for the most part, until the developer made her a local celebrity against her will. And the developer had the resources to make an issue of Mary Kate MacManus's fragile mental state and put it to the courts.

Except, as crazy as Mary Kate MacManus was, evidently she was no fool. No sooner had the wheels of justice started turning to force her into a home than some ace private attorney decided to take up Mary's case pro bono. Maybe this attorney's heart had been softened by the article in the paper, or maybe it was perhaps that Mary had spoken with the pastor of the church across the street from her lot and told him that it was always her intention to leave that corner lot to the church for extra parking when she passed. It was probably just a coincidence that the attorney in question had done most of the parish's real estate paperwork over the previous two decades.

After four more years of legal deadlock, the developer gave up, selling the strip along that block of 111th Street to make up his losses and turning it over to a general contractor, who put in a modest row of commercial shop fronts and some new houses on the side street. The reporter no longer worked at the small paper but wrote the follow-up story titled *MARY KATE MACMANUS WOULDN'T SELL* and sold the story to his former employer—a tale of triumph of the little guy over the forces of greed.

That story ran about fourteen years ago or so now, the whole commotion long blown over, Jerry thought. And now the crazy old woman was dead. He told Phil to keep an eye on the music store so he could go across the street, maybe see if that Ford Fairlane was still in the garage.

When he got a break in traffic long enough to cross, two squad cars pulled up in front. The officers pulled spools of yellow tape from their trunk.

"Can we help you?" one cop called to Jerry.

"No, I own the music store," he said, pointing. "I heard that old Mrs. MacManus had passed."

"Well, we're securing the scene. You best get back to your record store!" the mustachioed cop suggested firmly.

Evidently, Mary Kate MacManus's body had been found as a result of a wellness check some weeks ago. Since then, the crew sent by the bank to clean up and appraise the cluttered house had found an old potato chip can buried in the basement containing over $97,000, all in pre-1973 currency. Twenty feet from that, they also found the buried skeletons of George Fisher and Malcolm Talbridge.

RITUAL

He walked up the wooden steps to the back door of the apartment, wrapped up in his own thoughts as normal. He moved through the kitchen and dropped the day's mail on the small desk against the wall. As usual, he stripped off his work clothes while heading for the bathroom to shower. He stood in the doorway between the bedroom and bathroom, holding his undershirt in his hand, and stole a glance at the single bed pushed up against the wall before throwing his shirt into the laundry basket.

MY DEAREST THERESA . . . IT HAS been 3,067 days since you left me. It isn't getting any easier. I am so tired, my darling. Even on the odd occasion when I sleep through the night, I feel as if the cosmos was doing me the double injustice of both taking you and leaving me. I cannot understand this. If there is indeed a God as you so firmly believed, I can only tell you how much I hate Him for what He did to me.

SHOWERED AND DRESSED, HE SAT at the desk. Before he sorted the bills, he opened the top left-hand drawer. It contained a sealed letter to his sister with some instructions and final wishes. It also contained a pistol and a single bullet. With the drawer open, he went through the bills, tossed the junk mail, and wrote three checks that went into the reply envelopes. He didn't have much, so his sister wouldn't have too big a chore taking care of things. She was a good sister and had been a close friend to him always. He made it a point to try not to cause her too much burden, whatever the case.

————————

I HAVE NO IDEA WHY my sister's car wouldn't start the night we met. Remember the looks on our faces when it started right up the next day? I didn't mind going to pick her up from that party, but I had no intention of staying. I was even going to decline the first beer they offered me; I fully intended to bring Becky home and turn in early. I wasn't even going to walk through the house to see anyone; I wasn't even going to leave the kitchen where I sat down. I still don't know why you looked so surprised when you walked in looking for more sugar for your tea. You were at a party; didn't you expect to find more people in the kitchen too? I know you believe now what you couldn't have possibly believed then—that I am really a quiet person! I had never talked that much before that night; it was as if meeting you had burst the floodgates. We talked at the kitchen table for an hour until I drove Becky home, and you were sitting on the porch waiting for me to get back when I pulled up again. We sat talking on the porch for a few more hours until we walked across the street to the park and sat on the swings talking. By sunrise, I was holding your hand. I would have held it all day too if I didn't have to work that morning.

Was that night really our first date?

That soldier boy you sometimes dated stood you up and you called Becky to ask her if she thought I would be free. We bought sandwiches from the deli and parked by the airport, sitting on the hood of the car while the planes took off over us. This time, I was holding your hand before sunset and was holding you in my arms not long after.

———————

He stood by the window watching the daylight fade. He would stand for long periods of time, the apartment silent except for the ticking of the clock. He didn't even hear his own sighs anymore. When the hunger rumbled in his belly, he made his way to the refrigerator to see what it held. As he opened the door, the half-empty bourbon bottle on the counter caught his eye. He looked at the amber liquid behind the label marked with a date in marker. He turned his attention back to the contents of the fridge. It would be leftover chicken and maybe a potato baked in the microwave tonight. All washed down with iced tea.

———————

Theresa, my love, I never thought to tell you how lucky I felt being your husband, but I felt that constantly. It pains me now that I never tried harder to let you know my feelings. Somehow, you always knew without me having to express myself, and that was always a great comfort to me. I could never stand having to explain myself, and then you came along, and you always just knew. I hope you also knew how grateful I was to have you in my life. I should have told you often. It isn't a case of not noticing what you have until it's gone; I knew then how lucky I was and how happy you made me. Do you know some of the times when I was happiest? When I was working on some car in the yard, working on an engine, and I would pause and look up at the house. Sometimes I would see your silhouette in one of the windows; I'd catch you looking at me. I don't think any king in history ever felt as grand and important as I would just then, having such a wonderful woman gazing at me like that. I never said it, but I wondered how I had gotten so lucky. And without fail, you would eventually walk out to sit with me as I finished up. Sometimes you brought me iced tea, but if you knew I was having difficulty, you would bring me a beer. And on those beer days, you would ask me to explain the problem I was encountering and how the piece worked and how the engine worked together. Then you would laugh at me because the only time I really kept speaking without prodding was when I was talking about mechanical things. Oh, Theresa, so many other things I should have told you without you having to draw it out of me. I just hope that magically somehow you knew them all.

There were so many things that passed between us that we never discussed, things of such indescribable sweetness that it breaks my heart again and again to remember. It couldn't have been too long after the wedding that I first noticed that when I would get ready for work so early as you lay in bed that you would steal the shirt I had worn the evening before and hold it to your chest as you slept for a few more hours. From then on, when I got ready in the morning, I would put my shirt on the bed within reach instead of throwing it on the pile. Sometimes, when I would come in to kiss you goodbye before I left, I would find that you were wearing it instead of the nightgown you had worn to bed, clutching my pillow to you like a surrogate lover. I tried to tell you how beautiful you were often, but I never had the words to tell you how beautiful you made me feel.

Supper over, he washed the dishes and put them in the drying rack. Some dishes never seemed to get put away. His plate, his glass, the mug for his morning tea were all permanent residents in the rack beside the sink. Things were so different in the apartment than in the old house. Maybe the smartest thing he'd done was get rid of the queen-size bed in favor of the single against the wall of the bedroom. Too many nights while sleeping had he futilely chased her ghost across the mattress to drape his arm around her. He would wake with a start to find himself right at the edge of the bed, teetering. And for just a moment, he would be puzzled as to where she had gone.

———————

How could it have happened to us, Theresa? It was like a tragic accident on the highway, at the same time sudden and shocking but unfolding in painful terrible slow motion. At first, I wasn't even bothered that you were feeling so tired. You were always so active and vibrant, I just assumed your body needed some rest. But when we realized that you were getting weaker, a panic went through me that I can still feel today. And when the blood work came back and that damned doctor was so sure there was nothing to do about it, we sat in the office holding each other and crying.

I should have been able to be extra strong for you, my Theresa, but you know now you were my whole world. I am ashamed that you saw me being so selfish, especially after the news that had just hit you, but please forgive me. My world was crumbling, and there was nothing I could do about it. Then the second doctor. Then the third. Then the awful treatments that did no more than make you feel hollowed out and exhausted. And I could do nothing to save you. I hate me for that. Theresa, if I only knew, if I only could've gotten to that damaged and faulty part of you and fixed it or replaced it with something new. I would have done anything to make you whole again, to restore your spark, your vibrancy, that blinding light you always radiated.

How could you have asked that of me, Theresa? You couldn't have known what kind of torment you were sentencing me to . . . In those final days, that terrible waking nightmare, the needles and tubes, the over-polished hospital corridors, the harsh buzzing lights, sitting in that goddamned chair watching your frail body lose the fight. My Theresa, you know I couldn't deny you anything. Why would you make me promise you that I would go on? Couldn't you have asked anything else of me? I could not imagine the agonies of hell coming close to the hell of continuing without you.

THE EVENING NOW QUITE DARK, he sat at the desk again with the lamp on. His tool bag was open on the floor at his feet as worked on yet another broken toy. Kids in the neighborhood would leave them on his back porch occasionally. People at work would find them and give them to him. If the toy had an owner, they would find it in a milk crate on his porch when he was done. If it was a found or salvaged one, he would leave it at the church with the charity donations. Lately, when he dropped them off, he had gotten into the habit of lighting a candle while he was there.

———————

CAN YOU FORGIVE ME, THERESA? I couldn't keep my promise to you gracefully. More of me went down into the ground with the casket than was left above. Please understand that.

I am ashamed, my love. I fell apart. I know you would have me behave differently, but I could not endure so easily. I could not face living with half as much courage as you showed while facing death. My spirit was defeated as fatally as your body was. I sat in that empty house just staring into the shadows. The parts of me that weren't completely empty held only pain and bitterness. I wasn't able to sleep for more than a few hours without waking up in indescribable agony before I turned to the bottle. I am ashamed, and I know you wouldn't have approved, but in oblivion, I found the only peace I could achieve. And if I could make it through the night, the next day would come, and I would start the labor of surviving alone all over again. By this time, my tears had all dried up. I could do no more crying, no more weeping. I was powerless and had to endure the empty pain inside. One bottle an evening eventually was no longer enough. Oh, my sweet Theresa, without you, I am truly broken and will not be whole again unless by some miracle I am somehow rejoined with you. I can only go on if I hang on to that hope, and I want to deserve that. I want my pain that I have had to endure to buy me that salvation. I had something so perfect once, and I want it back. It was over three years ago that I put the bottles away. It wasn't easy, but it pales in comparison to the determination I have to keep my last promise to you. My love, I cannot promise you that I won't stumble, but I promise you all the effort I can muster. I hope that even now, you are as kind with your understanding as you were while we were together.

My Theresa, you were the best part of me. Even now, my love for you continues to grow. I will endure the pain and heartache tomorrow in hope that we will be reunited whole again. I will try to keep my promise tomorrow. Please come visit me in my dreams. Lend me some more strength and hope. Help me behave like a man worthy of your timeless love.

IT WAS TIME TO READ for a bit before turning in to bed. He walked through the apartment, turning off unneeded lights. He paused before the desk at the wall and gently pushed the upper left corner drawer closed. He was through another day, another promise kept. Tomorrow would be 3,068.

GOODNIGHT, MY LOVE.

LARGE BROGANS TO FILL

The expression on Banger Fogarty's face was peaceful, although his jaw was somewhat slacker than he'd carried it in life. His wispy hair had been carefully combed over his lightbulb head, and he'd been dressed in his best light brown suit. How were the mourners to know that it was really Banger's corpse after all? More than a few of them wouldn't have been shocked if the deceased sat up in his coffin and started telling people off. That would have proven the cadaver's bona fides as the miserable bastard he'd been in life. At least one visitor inquired of Banger's sister whether the box in which he had been laid out was sturdy enough to keep him in for good.

Timothy P. Fogarty, Parlor C was spelled out in white plastic letters on the black felt sign board, right next to some poor dead sap whose parents had named Julian Callendar, Muldoon noticed. If ol' Jules had murdered his parents for that alone, and Muldoon had been on the jury, the man would have walked. *That's a case of abuse, plain and simple,* he thought to himself. And speaking of abuse, he walked into the room where Banger Fogarty lay clutching a rosary in his waxy paws and thought of the endless abuse that had been hurled his way from the guest of honor. There were quite a few from the neighborhood sitting around. He ran into Russ Fraser on his way in, and they exchanged greetings.

"I didn't know Banger's name was Tim," Russ said. Then seeing a framed picture of the old curmudgeon as a young curmudgeon wearing a uniform, he added, "And I sure had no idea he was in the RAF! Come to think of it, I had him more pegged as the Luftwaffe type . . ."

Muldoon nodded, looking at the hand-colored studio portrait of a young Banger squinting defiantly at the camera, his forage cap at a rakish angle on his short wavy hair, looking ready to pound seven shades of shite out of anyone who looked at him crossways. He almost laughed at the frail angelic look he'd taken on in death.

"You're not fooling me, you ornery old cuss. Go ahead and say something!" he whispered to the corpse.

Getting no reply, he added, "Hope they seat you right next to Ian Paisley!" He waited a full five seconds for the shower of invective and, receiving none, fully embraced the idea that Banger Fogarty was indeed dead.

Leon stood alone at the moment, receiving condolences from the mourners. Muldoon waited for a lull. When it came, he approached his friend and shook his hand. "Sorry about your uncle Banger," he said sincerely.

"Muldoon! You have no idea how much this would have meant to him! I mean, he hated a lot of people—most all of them, it's true—but he really, really despised you," Leon said solemnly, patting Muldoon on the chest for emotional emphasis. "Out of all of the people who *really* got on his tits, you were easily in the top fifty."

"Thanks, man. Very kind of you . . . How's your ma holding up?"

"She's fine, went back for a highball. Want a snort? I have a good bottle in the back room."

———

SHOCK O'KELLY STOPPED BY twenty minutes later. The huge, bearded man wore a kilt as usual, a habit which drove Banger Fogarty up the wall when he was alive, and the pain-in-the-ass saltwater turkey gave the hairy giant an earful about it every chance he got. The big fellow paid his respects at the casket briefly, offering condolences to Leon and his mother before taking a seat in the last row, just behind Muldoon and to his left. "Look at him as youngster, Doonsie. Did you ever picture him as an angry *young* man?"

"How about it? How would you like to be some poor limey bastard that had to work under him?" Muldoon replied in quiet tone.

"Did you know he was in the RAF?" Shock asked.

"Yeah, we talked about it a couple of times. That's where he got the name Banger. He used to load bombs on Vulcan bombers," Muldoon said, remembering some of the sour old man's service stories.

"Wait," Shock said in surprise. "The Royal Air Force trusted someone with his accent, his political views, and his simmering rage with high explosives? And Buckingham Palace still stands?"

"Yeah, screwy, eh? Old Blighty must have been desperate for manpower back in the sixties."

Leon joined them, sitting in a more comfortable chair along the wall yet close enough for conversation.

"Muldoon says the British let that mad old bastard handle real bombs back in prehistoric times. Is that a fact?" Shock asked Leon.

"Yeah, imagine that," Leon confirmed.

"I bet when the Troubles started up, he was on a load of watch lists!" The huge man chuckled.

"My ma said that's how he wound up here. Banger was living in, like, Liverpool or Manchester after he got out of the air force. When the bombings started, he couldn't break wind without some cop asking him a litany of questions. My parents and my uncle Jim were already here, so he went where he had family," Leon explained.

"Where he hated it!" Shock added.

"Yeah, why wouldn't he go back to Tipperary?" Muldoon asked.

"Ma was just talking about that," said Leon. "Banger did go back for a year or so back in the seventies. Most of his friends had been gone for over a decade. He'd been living in Chicago for long enough that the neighbors thought of him more as a Yank than a local, and he hated Dublin."

"Of course he did!" Shock snorted.

"Naturally!" added Muldoon.

"So Banger didn't fit in anywhere anymore, no place that felt like home, so he came back here to fulfill his life goal of telling us all that we were idiots! Real, grade A, misinformed Yank gobshites!" Leon beamed at the memory of the old man.

"So lucky for us, MI5 thought Banger might have been in the IRA," Shock O'Kelly pondered.

Muldoon turned around and did a passable imitation of Banger's brogue: "What do you mean IRA, you Yank gobshite? You mean the IRA that came out of the Republican Brotherhood or the Anti-Treaty IRA? Eh? I think you mean the Provisional IRA, you thick lummox, unless you're talking about that shower of cunts, the Real IRA . . . we're not even talking about the Continuity IRA!"

"You mean the pinheads or the stickies, you daft tool?" Shock replied in a fairly decent imitation of the departed as well. "Ye feckin Americans, thick as shite in the neck of a bottle!"

"And what would you clueless wonders know about the Battle of the Boyne? Nothing! Uneducated wasters, the lot of you Plastic Paddies!" Leon added.

Oh yes, Banger Fogarty despised Plastic Paddies and all of their misguided ways. The slightest celebration of Irish Americanism brought the bile up from deep within him. It was an itchy scab that Banger couldn't help but pick. He'd watch local Gaelic football and hurling matches and disparage the playing styles of the local youngsters. He'd attend sessions at the local bars and clubs and criticize the musical interpretations. Nobody in the blighted New World could *possibly* get it right.

Banger was especially fun to be around during St. Patrick's Day celebrations. There were so many myths, misconceptions, and half-truths for the bitter old man to rail against. According to Leon, his uncle Banger waited for almost an hour on a frosty March morning to yell at the woman who'd hung a sign in her shop window wishing the neighborhood a "Happy St. Patty's Day!" demanding to know who St. Patricia was, when her feast day was celebrated, and if she'd meant to honor St. Paddy instead, informing her that she'd failed miserably. Offering old Fogarty a green beer was akin to riverdancing in a mine field.

In a facsimile of his uncle's voice, Leon growled, "St. Patrick's color was BLUE!"

"St. Patrick wasn't Irish, you damn fool. He was a Romanized Briton!" Shock joined in.

"When I was a wee lad back home, nobody'd ever *heard* of corned beef!" Muldoon did in his best imitation.

"Pipe bands playing Scottish pipes, wearing kilts—those are from Scotland, not Ireland, you cabbages!" Leon added.

Shock O'Kelly commented that Banger had never forgiven him for a particularly heated conversation regarding kilts one day years before, when he'd reminded the old man of the kilt-wearers in the early Gaelic League trying to adopt an Irish form of Highland dress to foster a sense of nationalism. The profanity-laced rebuttal lesson had been one for the books.

"You feckin Plastic Paddies, not a cop-on among you!" Banger had pronounced when he was done berating the big fellow.

"Muldoon used to wind him up about Chief O'Neill saving all of that traditional music," Leon told those assembled. By this time, a few more of those familiar with the deceased had joined the rough circle to share their stories of Hibernian abuse. "He starts asking Banger if he couldn't accept how much real culture was being preserved by the diaspora Micks when the real Micks back home were doing their damnedest to forget it. Where would uilleann piping be without Chief O'Neill?"

"How did Banger take that?" someone asked.

"Tell 'em what he said, Muldoon!" Leon prodded.

Muldoon twisted in his chair to face the majority of the interlocutors, and in his best Banger Fogarty impression, he squinted one eye and growled, "O'Neill was a flutist, not a piper, you dimwitted whelp!" which brought laughter from those assembled.

"Son of a bitch!" Shock O'Kelly said, closing his eyes and throwing his shaggy head back as if receiving divine instruction. "Oh my God, it just occurred to me! Know how if someone tried to use a Gaelic word or phrase, they were always saying it wrong?" There were groans and nods of assent all around. "You know, everywhere I've traveled, if you tried to learn a bit of the local culture or lingo, the locals found it to be a sign of respect and maybe even charming if you didn't get it quite right. Some places, they're so shocked at you trying to be polite, they mistake you for Canadian."

"Yeah, so?" Leon asked.

"Yeah, well, not so with the Gael in my experience—Ireland or the Scottish Highlands, for that matter. Trot out what you've learned, and someone will be more than glad to tell you how wrong you are!"

"Interesting, now that you say that," Muldoon mused.

"It just hit me! The only reason anyone studies Irish history or language is to correct other people!" Shock proclaimed.

"Oh my God! You're right!" Leon agreed.

"That's it, I'm writing a book dedicated to your uncle Banger," Muldoon said to Leon. "I'm calling it *The Easter Rising, 1916 . . . and Why You're Feckin Wrong About the Whole Business*!"

"Oh, that's beautiful!" Leon said.

"Absolutely fitting!" Shock agreed.

Banger Fogarty may not have approved of the laughter at his expense at his own wake, but if that were so, it was the first time in history he'd kept his opinion to himself.

―――――――――

JUST OVER AN HOUR LATER, the trio found three open stools at the bar, right under charcoal portraits of both Michael Collins and Chief

Francis O'Neill. Mariah, the bartender, poured out the shots. Leon raised his glass.

"Lads, here's to Uncle Banger. Hope he's giving an earful to that double-crossing Spaniard de Valera right now! *Ar dheis De go raibh a anam!*"

"To Banger!" the other two said before sinking the whiskey reverently, savoring the smoky burn.

"That's not how it's pronounced, you Yank gobshites. Just feckin say, 'May he be at God's right hand, for Christ's sake!' Your palsied tongue is making my ears bleed," came a mumbled disapproving Mayo voice from a weather-beaten old man two barstools away, his white-haired, crimson-faced head shaking sourly at his half-empty beer glass. Without even looking in their direction, he added, "And de Valera wasn't a Spaniard. His father was. De Valera was born in New York! Eejits!"

The three exchanged looks as sly smiles crept along their faces.

"Will you look at that?" Muldoon said. "The torch has been passed!"

AIR

A BREEZY SHORT:
KATIE'S FRIEND

Who were you talking to?" asked Katie's mother, who'd heard her laughing and chatting away from downstairs.

"My friend Maggie! I play with Maggie when there's no other kids around!"

"You have an imaginary friend?" her mom asked, amused.

"Yes, my imaginary friend!" Katie said, hearing that term for the first time and liking it.

"Is Maggie nice?" her mom asked.

"Yes, very nice!" answered Katie.

Katie had other friends, but when she was alone, she still had a good time with Maggie. She was a big help when Katie's parents split up. That was a difficult time for her. Her imaginary friend understood.

It was very good to have an imaginary friend, because sometimes you can be lonely when there's nobody to talk to or play with, and an imaginary friend can keep you from being too bored when the grown-ups are busy. And the best part is that an imaginary friend is one you never can lose. Katie loved that thought.

One day at school, their teacher had them write a paragraph about their best friend. Most kids wrote about other kids in her class, but a few kids wrote about their best friend who went to another school, or maybe a cousin or brother or sister. Katie was the only one to write about her imaginary friend. Katie got the best score in the class, but she left out the part about Maggie being an imaginary friend because it wasn't important.

Her mother was happy Katie got the best score but thought Katie was getting a bit old for an imaginary friend, especially since she had so many good friends at school, which was true. And sometimes those friends weren't around, and sometimes Katie didn't feel like being alone. Maybe her mom knew best. Katie wasn't sure. What Katie was sure of, was that Maggie understood. Maybe all imaginary friends were like that.

As Katie got older, she was busy enough to rarely be lonely and was starting to enjoy time by herself more and more, so she saw Maggie less frequently. But when she did, she enjoyed it as always. An imaginary friend is one you can never lose.

When Katie was in middle school, her grandmother passed away. It made her sad, especially since she didn't know her grandmother very well. Katie's grandmother lived in another city, and besides visits a couple of times a year and infrequent phone calls, their main line of communication was birthday cards and school pictures with a nice note written in felt tip on the back. Katie and her dad flew to Arizona for her grandmother's funeral. Katie's father introduced her to some of her relatives, whom Katie had either never met or met once a long time ago.

And even then, Katie had Maggie, her imaginary friend she'd never lose.

She didn't play with Maggie at the wake, but there Maggie was in an old photo album, smiling up at Katie as she and her father spent time looking at the pictures.

"Here's one of *my* grandmother," her father said. "Her name was Marguerite." But Katie already knew that nobody called her that. Katie also knew that her father was only six when his grandmother died in the car accident on that icy road shortly after the holidays.

"That's my uncle Bert!" said Katie's dad, pointing at a good-looking man in a smart suit.

"Oh, Herbert, look at you!" Katie said.

"You've never met him. Neither did I. He died in the war, in Italy, I think," her father said.

"His B-24 was shot down over Romania," Katie told him. "He was missing and presumed dead, and the family didn't get confirmation for several months. But your grandmother prayed the rosary for him every week, and the day he was killed, he visited her to let her know he was fine. That helped her a lot," Katie let him know.

"How do you know this, Katie?" her father asked.

"My imaginary friend told me."

FEBRUARY 1944, THE PACIFIC

Technician Fourth Grade Max Delatour scanned the radio's dials and instinctively looked at his watch. The B-25 was still about two and a half hours out of Torokina, where the crew would hand the Mitchell over to the armorers at the maintenance base to add more .50 guns to the plane, enabling the bomber to be more effective against Japanese shipping.

Max was alone in the rear of the Mitchell. If this hadn't been a ferry run, there would've been a dedicated gunner in the rear fuselage to give him company, but this flight, there was only a crew of four: himself and the three forward of the bomb bay, Major Bart Howell and Lieutenant Dan Smith, the pilots, and the other enlisted guy on board, First Sergeant Tim Mooney, the flight engineer.

The burden Howell carries must be massive, Max thought as he unfolded himself from his seat and wobbled his way to the waist windows of the plane. Below, the Pacific Ocean stretched to the horizon in all directions, causing a knot in his stomach. Without a navigator on this flight, it was up to Howell and Smith to find their destination. If Howell was more than a few degrees off on his flying, they could miss their destination and be swallowed up by the blue expanse that covered a quarter of the earth. The thought scared him more than the thought of aerial combat with the Japs, where at least you could fight back . . . not that Max had ever been in aerial combat. Sure, he'd seen the occasional Japanese plane, usually pointed out to him by another crew member— maybe a Betty bomber or one of the huge Mavis flying boats—but he really hadn't shot at anything since qualifying back in the states.

Major Howell had done this run from Port Moresby to Torokina several times before. Max was sure that Howell wouldn't get them lost. The weather was good, and the skies were clear except for some high cirrus. He looked at the featureless blue ocean again before going back to his seat and his radios.

———

NAVAL AIR PILOT FIRST CLASS Masajiro Kenda scanned the skies around him. Although his primary mission was scouting for Allied shipping, he kept close watch for enemy planes. Masajiro was proud to fly one of the first Rufes in his squadron, a float-version of the superb Zero fighter. The large float under the fuselage and the two pontoons under each wingtip robbed the Zero of precious speed and maneuver- ability, but it had a range of over a thousand miles and could operate from the hidden seaplane bases that the Imperial Japanese Navy had se- creted throughout the Solomon Islands. He only carried one hundred rounds each for the two fifty-caliber machine guns under the cowling for the sake of weight, but the devastating twenty-millimeter cannons that were in each wing had full magazines and were a match for almost any target, be it airplane or PT boat.

Kenda was almost at the edge of his patrol range and had yet to sight evidence of the enemy. He could curse his bad luck, but he remembered that despite having been robbed of an opportunity for glory, he was still serving his emperor and country. He turned the floatplane in a wide arc and began the long flight back to his forward base. Perhaps he would draw another patrol in the late afternoon. The thought of returning to base without having fired a shot would make the usual supper of tinned fish, rice, and pickles seem even more monotonous.

Kenda let out a sigh, but it caught in his throat when a speck in the haze to his right caught his attention. Miles away and several thousand feet below him, there was a plane heading east. There was no question of it being an Allied aircraft, and this far south, the enemy would probably not be expecting an attack. He opened the throttle and started a sweeping shallow dive to move into a position to attack the target. As the minutes went by, his adrenaline started to flow, the excitement of the hunt sharpening his senses. Gradually, the faint spot grew in his vision. It was a medium twin-engine bomber. Eventually, he could see the twin tails—a Mitchell bomber, the same kind that had struck Tokyo in the raid that had shocked his nation so terribly!

The opportunity to strike one of the same species as the hated raiders thrilled Kenda. He focused hard, making sure that some small mistake wouldn't rob him of his chance. The enemy plane so far took no evasive action. The crew was either stupid or complacent or both. Kenda kept close watch on the tail, waiting for the winking of the tail guns, but even as he flew closer, it seemed as if he were invisible to the Allied bomber.

Masajiro lowered his goggles over his eyes and tensed his body for the attack.

———

Captain James Taggart USMC pointed the nose of his F4F Wildcat back north toward his base at Vella Lavella. After three fighter sweeps in the previous five days, it was a relief to draw a duty that wouldn't take him up the "slot," the area of heavy fighting up toward Rabaul. The Wildcats of his squadron had been taking a pounding lately, and the primitive conditions were taking a heavy toll on the already outclassed fighter. Jimmy Taggart looked forward to the day when his squadron would get upgraded fighters and would be facing the Japanese on something approaching equal footing. This day, he was scheduled to test fly two F4Fs that had repairs done after the last sweep.

This Wildcat was almost ready for the glue factory in his opinion. Patched too many times, overstressed once too often, and abused far beyond its design, this bird was old and tired long before its time. Yet it still flew, and besides its anemic engine and sluggish controls, Jimmy would sign off that it was ready for duty once again. Just to be thorough, he took the Wildcat up to twenty-four thousand feet to ensure that the turbocharger was working properly and test the oxygen system.

The cold thin air was quite a change from the sweltering muggy jungle into which the forward base of Vella Lavella had been carved. On the ground, sweat-drenched clothing would never dry completely, and the boot leather rotted away right on your feet. Any minor cut or abrasion would refuse to heal and remain a weeping festering wound. But up here in the rarified air, it was cold and crystal clear, and despite his personal feelings toward this particular F4F, he had to admit the engine was humming along splendidly.

He was scanning the instruments for engine temperature, RPMs, and manifold pressure just to ensure the engine and turbocharger were performing up to scratch when a quick glance below at eleven o'clock revealed in the distance the Mitchell being caught unawares.

"Ah shit," he muttered out loud, instinctively pointing the Wildcat's nose toward the trouble while grasping his throat microphone. "Unknown Mitchell, you got an Injun behind you!"

THE CRACKLING OF THE EMERGENCY radio in his headset jolted Max out of his seat. He was already racing past the waist gun positions when he heard the co-pilot yell, "Delatour! Tail gun!"

KENDA WATCHED THE MITCHELL BOMBER grow in his windscreen. Without taking his eyes off his quarry, his hands automatically went through the ritual of feeling the switches to ensure that both machine guns and cannon were selected and armed. His stomach muscles tensed, anticipating the defensive fire from the enemy gunners. Were they asleep?

The bomber skidded violently to the left. So, he wasn't taking this prey unaware! His nimble scout-fighter easily kept the bomber in his gunsights with easy correction.

Almost there! At this range, Masajiro could see a figure in the rear fuselage scrambling to make the tail guns through the pilot's violent maneuvers. And in the top turret, just aft of the cockpit, a blond head appeared as the twin guns spun around to take bead. The gunner's first shots went wild, and those were the only shots fired from the American bomber.

Masajiro had chosen the moment to fire when all four streams of ordnance would just about converge on the fuselage of the twin-tailed plane. Bullets chewed the metal skin and the cannon shells slammed and exploded in the doomed aircraft as Kenda coolly stitched his shots right up the middle of the target.

———

JIMMY TAGGART CURSED LOUDLY. THE Japanese Rufe was just that much faster than his Wildcat to keep him from knocking the Jap off his attack. "Damn, damn, damn, damn!" He was mere seconds from bringing his guns to bear on Kenda's fighter but could only watch helplessly as bullets and cannon shells ripped the bomber apart like a buzz saw. He could see small fires burning and sparking inside the Mitchell and a fine mist of gray fuel vapor pouring from the starboard wing root. There was a blinding flash as a cannon shell burst right next to the top gun turret, leaving a huge gaping hole ripped from the turret down the skin just behind the pilot's seat

"Oh, you bastard," Taggart rasped under his shallow breaths. When he just about had the pipper of his gunsight on the Japanese plane, he snapped his attention from the mauling the bomber was taking. As he squeezed the trigger, he felt the stubby fighter shudder from the rumbling guns. The shredded Mitchell, smoking and listing lazily, flashed underneath Jimmy's Wildcat as he pressed his attack against the agile Rufe.

———

JUST AS MASAJIRO WAS PULLING up to bring his plane around for the coup de grâce, he heard the chatter of guns behind him. He pulled up steeply and craned his neck around to see the stout gray Wildcat making an attack run from behind. He pushed on his throttle to make sure his engine was wide open and pulled the control stick back to his stomach to bring the Rufe into an almost vertical climb. Even with the added drag of the large float under his fuselage and the smaller two under his wingtips, no Wildcat could climb with the modified Zero. He kept climbing until he was sure that any F4F trying to follow was stalling far down below him. Masajiro banked steeply to survey the scene; the Mitchell bomber was losing altitude in a lazy curving descent while oily vapor trailed from its right side. It hadn't burned or exploded, but the plane was definitely out of the war for good.

Between Kenda and the crippled bomber, the Wildcat circled close to the bomber in a futile gesture of protection. He checked his fuel gauges and stole a glance at his wristwatch, then scanned the skies for any more Allied fighters and pointed his nose for his home base, grateful for a successful patrol.

———

DUST AND TEARS FILLED MAX'S eyes. The wind roared in his ears, and as he became aware of his body, he realized he was lying uncomfortably in the rear fuselage of his plane. Scraps of paper and grit whipped around in the churning wind rushing through the B-25. The wind had been knocked out of him; it felt like he'd taken a bad football tackle. He struggled to get a full lungful of breath, but a pain in his left side and back stabbed him with any movement of his body.

Max heard himself groan. That seemed to shock some part of him to consciousness. He became aware of the sound of the two engines, one missing badly. The air stank of ozone and avgas, and the realization shocked him further into painful clarity. He had to get up. He had to see the situation. He may have to get out in a hurry.

The searing pain drew the moments out to an eternity as he forced himself to kneel and stand. As the adrenaline cleared his head, he took in the scene of destruction: huge jagged holes had been ripped through the plane from ceiling to floor; the smoking radio rack was a mass of twisted electronics and charred wires, small sparks still dying in the gaping tangled holes; there was blood on the floor.

For a second, dizziness and nausea swept over him. He had never seen so much of his own blood before, and he wondered if he had died, until the shocking pain reminded him otherwise. He had to check on the flight deck. He had to ignore the pain and make his way through the tunnel next to the smashed and sputtering radio rack, past the empty bomb bay, and up to the cockpit. There was no question of doing otherwise.

––––––––––

THAT JAPANESE SON OF A bitch had pulled up at the last moment and started climbing like the proverbial homesick angel. As Taggart pulled up sharply to try to draw bead on the Rufe before he pulled out of range, Jimmy cursed through gritted teeth and clenched muscles. Goddammit, there was no way this iron pig was ever going to catch the lighter faster Japanese plane in a climb. As his speed bled off in his near-vertical climb, he let out an audible sigh and eased off the stick and kicked his rudder, bringing the Wildcat into a chandelle turn to head back and check on the Mitchell. One and a half corkscrewing turns brought him up behind the savaged B-25, slightly above on the left side of the bomber. He grasped his throat mic and tried to hail the crew but got only static as an answer.

It was a miracle the plane stayed in the air at all. You could hardly call it a Mitchell anymore; it was more like a Mitchell tail and two Mitchell wings held together with a tangle of scrap aluminum. The Rufe's cannons had gone through the fuselage like a bread knife hacked through a cardboard wrapping paper tube. He kept trying to raise the flight crew as he passed slowly by the descending plane, surveying the damage. Just before he pulled abreast of the cockpit, Jimmy gasped out loud.

The hole punched through the side of the cockpit was almost double the size of a domestic doorway. Through the twisted metal, he could see bright daylight where he couldn't see warped structure smeared with gore. The co-pilot's side of the windscreen was translucent from the blood spattered around the cockpit. Taggart could see the pilot slumped limply over the control wheel, while the co-pilot's head wobbled drunkenly as his hands grasped and clutched for the control levers.

Jimmy held his fighter in formation next to the crippled B-25, the feeling of helplessness churning in his guts. He was desperate to see some sign of life in the bomber. He wished to see someone, any member of the crew fit enough to get out and hit the silk before the plane made its inevitable crash into the blue ocean.

And as if he had made it happen by his own will, Taggart saw movement in the fuselage of the Mitchell. Someone was making their way forward onto the flight deck.

———

THE PAIN FROM BENDING, STOOPING, and climbing to make his way forward froze the breath in Max's throat. He reached behind him to feel the area where he'd been struck, but he recoiled in horror when he brought his left hand back sticky and caked with his own blood. The pain shot through him, but he steeled himself against it and made it through the low passageway to the forward fuselage on determination alone. What he found there was surreal. The scream of the engines was joined by the shrill whistle of the two-hundred-knot wind howling through the gaping hole in the right skin of the plane. He ducked under the distorted mechanism of the top turret, keeping his eyes forward. Whatever had happened to Mooney, Max Delatour did not see. Or maybe he saw it and instantly denied it. The scene never made it to his awareness. He kept moving forward.

Out the captain's windscreen, he could see that they were in a shallow dive toward the ocean. Major Howell was slumped forward in his seat. A shell had burst just behind him, destroying the seat back and punching a fist-sized hole in the major's back. Lieutenant Smith had a vicious wound in his shoulder and neck and was grasping drunkenly as he bled out.

Max had to get to a parachute and out of the plane. He stooped to look through the crawlway into the nose. Every surface he saw looked damaged. When he turned to look at the left propeller whirling just inches from him through the gaping hole, he got another shock. There, not twenty yards away, a stubby Marine fighter flew in formation like a guardian angel. It was faded dull gray, worn, and patched, but from where Technician Fourth Grade Maximillian Delatour stood, it looked like the picture of invincibility itself.

Another stab of pain jerked him into sharp focus. If the Wildcat was keeping formation, the Mitchell had to be relatively stable for now. Max moved forward and, straddling the passageway to the nose, reached over and unlatched Major Howell's safety harness. The shoulder straps had been severed, and only the lap belt held the major in his seat. Max, gasping with the searing pain in his side, slid the major clumsily to the floorboard and climbed into the pilot's seat.

He was met with an undecipherable array of dials, switches, and levers that he had ignored so many times before. He could see forward and to his left well enough, but the gore on the inside of the windscreen obscured his view to the right. He looked at Lieutenant Smith. He had stopped moving, and his ashen face revealed that he had finally let go. Placing his boots on the pedals and his hands on the control wheel,

Max gingerly moved them around, expecting the ripped airplane to break into smaller pieces with the strain.

To his surprise and relief, the Mitchell reacted. It was sluggish and sloppy, but it was under a measure of control. Max put his hands on the throttles and gingerly pushed them open a hair, listening to the sound as the big engines reacted. Although the right engine occasionally missed, he seemed to still have two engines at his disposal. He glanced to his right to see if his guardian angel could see him at the controls.

———

TAGGART LOOKED AT THE PROFILE of whoever it was that slid into the pilot's seat. *This guy has some set of plums on him*, Jimmy thought. That was no airplane he'd just taken control of; it wasn't even a collection of parts. It was a flying charnel house and was only staying together by a miracle. This guy might've had the right idea though, because according to Jimmy's rough guess, they were only about twenty-two minutes out of Lavella, which would make ditching much safer and help a lot closer.

The youngster piloting the bomber was looking right at Jimmy. Jimmy nodded and gave him a grim smile, then made a chopping motion with his flat hand in the direction of the tiny atoll where safety waited. He wished to hell that he could raise this guy on the radio and get an idea what his plan was, but for the moment, he could only keep him company.

———

MAX SAW THE MARINE'S GESTURE and nodded. Wherever the jarhead wanted to take him was fine with him. It would have been a relief to be able to talk to him over the radio, but just the ability to see the friendly face of someone who knew where they were going made all the difference to Max up above the expanse of ocean in a bomber that's best days were now behind it.

Max was sweating profusely and keeping his eyes on the Wildcat to his left. He was in diabolical pain and feeling chilled, and any glancing around the interior of the plane brought waves of nausea, so he kept his attention on the fighter plane outside. His whole body ached, wracked with the tension of keeping the Mitchell under control. The thought flashed through Max's mind that perhaps it was better that he *didn't* know what all of those dials and gauges were for, since they were sure to contain more bad news at the present moment, and he had enough to worry about as it was.

The minutes crawled by. How much fuel did he have? The gauges he found gave contradictory readings. Some of the dials' needles bobbed furiously, while some lay on their pegs, dead and useless. Every so often, at moments like these, Max was gripped with a raw feral panic. He had no idea what he was doing, what was next, or what he was supposed to do when he got there . . .

When he saw it, it was big enough that it had to have been visible for some time: a group of emerald-green and blinding white islands emerging from the haze. He had made it past the Solomon Sea, almost to safety.

The Wildcat waggled its wings to get his attention. The little fighter was starting to descend, heading down for the larger island beyond the first. Max eased the stick forward to get his nose down and eased the throttles back a small amount to keep the same distance from the Wildcat.

What happens when we get to the island? He had no idea how one landed a training plane, let alone a battered Mitchell bomber. He would just have to trust the marine to lead him in. He would swing down to the runway and chop the power by hauling back on the throttles; that's all he could do.

Just then, he remembered the landing gear handle in front of Lieutenant Smith. When he saw that he was lined up for the runway, he would put the wheels down and just keep slowing it down, trusting the fighter to lead the way.

Up ahead, he could make out the blinding white line that cut through the coconut trees that hemmed in the runway. This was it.

He leaned over Smith's body to lower the gear when he heard a weak gravelly voice: "Don't do it, Delatour. You'll stall us right into the water . . ."

Max jumped at the voice. There, sitting upright in the lower hatchway, Major Howell had sat up. His eyes were distant and his face the color of pale lilacs. "You got to lower the flaps, Delatour. Here." The major rose slowly from the floor, steadying himself with his cold ashen hand on Max's shoulder.

———————

TAGGART ALERTED THE TOWER THAT he was leading a crippled B-25 in. The crash alarm had already rung on the ground, and Jimmy could see the emergency vehicles starting to move into position. He eased his throttle back to let the injured bomber move abreast of his Wildcat. The Mitchell was floating up and down and overcorrecting, trying to keep on course. Was he losing this guy? *Not now. Not when you've made it to fourth down and inches from the goal . . .*

Jimmy eased the throttle back a little more to look to see how the young pilot was doing. He felt the Wildcat start to buck and shudder as he drifted dangerously close to stalling. The cockpit slid into Jimmy's view. He could see the young pilot hunched over the control wheel and another crew member standing beside him—an officer, by the looks of him, injured but evidently conscious and mobile. Taggart was grateful they had two heads in the Mitchell working on their problem. That would increase their chances considerably. He caught the young man and the officer looking in his direction for an instant and gave them a confident thumbs-up as a gesture of good luck.

The officer looked at Taggart, returned the thumbs-up, and then saluted. Jimmy returned the salute and left the pair to land the bomber.

———————

"Here's the flap lever in front of the throttle," Major Howell yelled over the howling wind. "We're going to bring her right in." The whine of the electric motor was barely audible over the wind and the rough engines as the flaps were lowered to their first position. The blinding white coral airstrip grew in their windscreen, maybe five miles away. The air was bumpier down low and the plane noticeably mushier as the engines were throttled back. "Watch the throttles, Delatour. Don't let it settle too low. Keep the near end of the runway in the same spot in your windscreen. Let's give it one more notch of flaps . . ."

Max toggled the switch and felt the plane buffet as the flaps came down some more. He had to jockey the throttle to keep the nose aimed at the spot on the runway as the major had instructed. They were passing over a shallow lagoon, almost to the runway.

"Wheels," Max said absently, leaning over for the handle.

"Forget them! We have too much damage. We're going to belly her in. You'll be fine, Delatour. Fine job. Last notch of flaps . . ." Max wrestled with the bomber as the flaps lowered again. The pain in his side was stabbing him again. Sweat was pouring off of him, and he was having to work hard to focus his vision. "Keep the nose up, Delatour. Fly her all the way down, and keep the nose up. Let the plane settle. Soon as you hear a scrape or feel a jolt, you cut the engines, understand?"

"Yessir, Major. I understand," Max croaked back as the tops of the trees started flashing by the window. His whole body ached from battling the damaged airplane. He stole a quick glance down to see the major had slid to floor, half sitting, half lying down, his face quite gray.

He had the throttles almost completely retarded as the plane sank to the blazing coral runway. Max felt a sharp jolt as the propeller blade on the right engine struck the coral. As he chopped the power, he eased the control yoke farther back, mushing the aircraft right in on its belly. The jolt slammed Max forward, but later, he wouldn't even remember cutting the throttles.

———————

THE FLIGHT LINE JEEP HAD run him by the wreckage after he'd handed the Wildcat back over to the crew chief. They were preparing to bulldoze the carcass of the Mitchell off to the side of the runway, where the engines and other equipment could be cannibalized without interfering with air operations. The nose section was bent up at a bizarre angle from the force of the landing and the damage the weakened fuselage had sustained. Jimmy and the driver looked at the smoking hulk wordlessly in disbelief before the driver dropped him off at the operations shack.

Taggart filled out his flight report, as well as the check report for the F4F he had flown today. Droplets of sweat fell from his forehead and off his nose onto the thin paper, marring his handwritten notes. After handing them to the intelligence officer who sat sweating at his desk, Jimmy walked out into the blinding daylight again and toward the Quonset hut that served as the base hospital. He had almost made it to the door when Doc Heiser stepped out, blinking in the sunlight.

"You lead that Army bomber in, James?" Doc asked, cleaning his bifocals on his khaki shirttail. "Damned horror show."

Taggart dug a pack of cigarettes from his shirt pocket and offered one to the Navy doctor, who took one eagerly. He lit one for himself and passed the flaming Zippo to Heiser. "Did they make it?"

The doctor took a deep drag and tilted his head to one side. "One survived. Tech sergeant. The orderlies are still digging parts of the radio out of his back . . . The other three bought it in the attack. The kid will do all right—may not even lose the kidney—but he lost a lot of blood. Shock. The corpsmen were taking him out of the wreckage, and he came to and told them to attend to the pilot, who was dead on the floor next to some other fellow's legs. The co-pilot died right in his seat. Bled out from a throat wound."

"Ah, damn. So the pilot didn't make it . . . Damn shame. It took them both to bring it in." Jimmy shook his head.

Doc Heiser squinted at him. "The co-pilot was the last to go, James. The other two were killed instantly."

"I saw him move right before they set it down, Doc, and that's the smoking-hot gospel."

"You saw a corpse in a bucking airplane bounce around, Captain. I examined him. That cannon shell turned the contents of his chest cavity to pudding when it exploded. Trust me, he never knew what hit him."

Taggart opened his mouth to reply, but no words came out. He shrugged, turned, and walked away, leaving the doctor to finish his smoke.

LONG DAY OF A SHORT FELLOW

Out of the sun, he stalked his prey, a three-winged Fokker. Marty could tell by the color scheme that the unwitting pilot flew for the Baron's dreaded circus. It was dangerous to follow the Hun much farther into enemy territory, but he was almost close enough to attack the German pilot who'd not yet sensed that he was being followed. Marty put his trusty Sopwith into a dive, gaining speed, then when the timing was perfect, pulled up slightly, the underside of the triplane filling his Vickers's gunsights. Just two brief bursts of machine gun fire and the Fokker shuddered violently, black oily smoke billowing from its motor. The German plane did a violent flicking wing-over, starting to shed fabric and structure as it plummeted to the ground. Marty watched the hapless foe as it tumbled from the sky, mentally adding the enemy plane to his already impressive tally.

In his foolish revelry, Marty didn't realize that he was also being stalked from behind, and his split-second loss of attention cost him dearly. The motor of his Sopwith banged and sputtered and started belching smoke as well, while bullets hummed past his ears and shredded the fabric of his wings. He was done for.

The high pale sun made drunken circles in the sky above his head as his crate started to spin as it fell faster and faster toward the hard earth below. Marty struggled with the stick and rudder, using all of his skill to try to bring the doomed Camel down in one piece in hopes that he'd be in one piece as well. After what seemed to be an eternity, he finally got the damaged aircraft under enough control to make a crash landing mere feet from the ground. He choked on smoke as flames licked his boots from the fuel-soaked floorboards, sideslipping and careening toward a suitable piece of ground. He raised the nose at the last minute to stall the wrecked craft, and the Sopwith crashed hard enough to jar Marty's bones and throw him against the safety harness. Wasting no time, he freed himself from the upended fuselage now starting to burn furiously. He fell to the ground and ran for the cover of a small raised mound of dirt, waiting for the fuel to explode.

Marty sat panting, his mind racing. He had to make it back to Allied lines and avoid German patrols that would be drawn by the column of black smoke and orange flames emanating from his beloved airplane. As he sat and tried to regain his bearings, the red Fokker that downed him buzzed low overhead, the haughty Baron saluting Marty as he streaked past. Marty shook his fist.

"Martin! Martin!" came the familiar voice. Marty stood and slapped the dust from his clothes as he ran from the empty lot and down the alley, climbing the back fence instead of using the gate.

"Martin James Curley! Use the gate, will you? Come in and wash the dirt from your face quickly I need you to run to the store . . ."

———

THE COAST SEEMED CLEAR, THE street nearly devoid of pedestrians, but this was no time to let his guard down. Enemy agents were everywhere, and in foreign lands like this, there were hidden eyes behind every curtain.

It was too quiet; Marty sensed a trap. Walking down the sidewalk nonchalantly so as not to rouse any suspicion, he chose his moment to dart between two parked cars and out of sight. Watching for any enemy tails, he waited for a car to pass before darting across the street for the shady cover of some tall shrubs. His heart racing and his senses heightened, he ran as silently as possible through the gangway and into the next alley, keeping an eye out for any opposition. He only had a block and a half to go to the rendezvous, darting down the alleyway from cover to cover, only once spotting an enemy agent disguised as a mailman, who didn't see Marty. Amateurs.

Scoping the place where the exchange was to be made, Marty's heart sank to find the route blocked by not one, but three enemy agents. Thinking fast, he moved the nuclear plans from his pocket to his sock, just in case they jumped and searched him. Emerging from his hiding spot, standing tall, Marty walked right up to the building, feigning complete innocence. Unfortunately, Marty was recognized immediately by Hogan, the leader of this particular assassination squad. One slipup now could cost Marty everything. Marty's and Hogan's eyes locked as Marty approached the door. The game might've very well been up.

"Hey, Marty!" Hogan called as the other two heavies kept pitching pennies. "Buy me a pretzel when you go in!"

Thinking fast, Marty replied, "Can't. Ma counts my change," in the local lingo, which Marty spoke flawlessly since his training.

"Ah, you suck!" Hogan replied. "I was going to give you a ride on my minibike!"

That was a lie. Hogan didn't have a minibike. And Hogan knew that Marty knew that he didn't. Marty sensed a double cross.

Inside, it was quiet except for the hum of the overhead fan. Working quickly, Marty grabbed the needed components and presented them to his contact, an elderly man of Mediterranean extraction. Marty looked over his checklist before making the exchange. Then an idea hit him as he caught sight of Hogan and his cronies through the glass door. He pushed two pennies out of his change toward the old gentleman in exchange for five doses of powerful cyanide disguised as bubble gum.

"Tell your mom and dad I said hello," the old man said, giving the proper sign.

"I will. Thank you, mister." Marty gave the countersign.

Hogan and his henchmen never suspected Marty's trap, the fools. To put them at ease, Marty took one of the doses himself. The remaining one in his pocket contained the antidote.

———————

THE ONCE VAST HERDS OF buffalo were dwindling now. Sometimes Marty walked for days without encountering any. The West was changing, and even his beaver traps stayed empty for weeks at a time. He made his way lazily through a meadow. By his side was the grizzly bear he'd raised from an orphaned cub. A gentle breeze blew, and the bear's nose twitched.

"What is it, a war party?" Marty softly questioned. If they were Sioux, things might be all right, Marty having spent several seasons with one of their top medicine men. If they were of the Flatnose band, Marty might have cause to worry. He kept his wits about him.

There, up ahead on the trail, an old warrior approached.

"Martin, you should have Daisy on a leash if you're walking her in the park!" the old chief said in his broken English. Definitely Flatnose.

"I have her leash here," Marty replied, slowly fishing the nylon lead out of his pocket in the manner of Flatnose custom. "She always follows me though. I take it off when there are no other dogs around."

The man nodded. Both friend and foe on the prairies knew of the scout Marty, a man of iron words. "Well, make sure she doesn't do her business on the sidewalk, Martin. Other people have to use the park too." A usual Flatnose challenge. Marty respected the treaty, but would brook no disrespect.

After he bade the chief a good afternoon, he turned his back on the old chief and led his grizzly away, showing that he had no fear. He headed back to his cabin. The days on the prairie had parched his throat to dust.

As Daisy flopped down to nap on the tile floor, Marty opened the door under the sink so he could step up on the bottom of the cabinet to reach the metal measuring cup and faucet. Filling the cup several times with cold water and emptying just as many times in a short series of breathless gulps, he satisfied the thirst of both his gullet and the front of his shirt. He eventually found himself on the front walkway, but only after having jumped down from the first step, then from the second step, then from the third step, then from the fourth step twice. He skipped jumping from the top of the porch on account of what had happened last time. Maybe later in the summer he'd have perfected his technique.

At the end of the block, the mailbox was protected from errant traffic by a large rock painted lemon yellow. From this rock, Marty could just jump well enough to climb on top of the box without stepping on the grass, which was often heavily booby-trapped. From his perch, he could keep watch down two streets in four directions.

The air seemed to crackle with electricity as the silvery craft glided in from behind with a low mechanical buzz. It stopped abruptly, coming to a rock-solid hover around the corner from his house. It was flat and circular, as long as a football field. The buzzing got louder, and a hatchway opened from just under the edge, depositing an advance party for the invasion.

The extraterrestrial scouts had been altered by their alien technology to adapt to our atmosphere yet remained otherworldly in their ignorance. Their appearance was small but grotesque, and they ran about awkwardly, giving away the truth that they were really far from human. Their speech was shrill and loud and shrieking and harsh to Marty's earthman ears. One of them beckoned, even calling him by name, no doubt pulled from his thoughts telepathically. Ignoring the attempt to lure him closer to infect him with some weaponized extraterrestrial germ and spread a contagion worldwide, Marty slid down from the mailbox and made his way home to harden the defensive perimeter against the alien invasion.

Back at Headquarters, Marty's mom sat smoking a cigarette at the kitchen table, a sweating glass of iced tea half-finished in front of her. She was reading from the parish bulletin as the radio droned softly.

"Marty, I think we're going to put you in the arts and crafts day camp up at the library. That'll be fun. What do you think? Don't want you to waste your summer being bored!"

Arts and crafts camp? Who has time for that shit? Marty asked himself.

That's Headquarters for you.

THE GREATEST WEREWOLF
STORY EVER TOLD

Father Charles Fitzpatrick accepted the offer of a lift up to the tavern graciously, even though he found Shock O'Kelly's company trying at times. He'd only made it half a block from the rectory when the opportunity to be chauffeured presented itself. The old priest slid into the passenger's seat of the battered yellow pickup, the case for his regret mounting quickly when he saw that the big ginger fellow was wearing a kilt. As hard as he tried not to, he involuntarily rolled his eyes.

Shock O'Kelly often wore kilts. His sister made them. She was a good one—a loyal parishioner, a good neighbor, and a dedicated mother. Father Charles liked her. Her brother, a large and often obnoxious brute who wore a full red beard and his hair past his shoulders, was more difficult to like. Long past used to having his authority challenged, a benefit of his holy office, Father Charles tired quickly of having his opinions questioned by the cocky and unkempt agnostic.

His heart is in the right spot, and however wayward, he is still one of God's flock and your brother, the priest reminded himself. And sometimes, Thomas O'Kelly wasn't so confrontational.

"Kind of you to offer the ride," he told the enormous fellow, determined to ignore the ridiculous clothing choices. "How's your sister?" he asked, punctuating his question with a click of the seat belt.

"Well, Father, she'll be delighted to hear we're out bending the elbow together!" The grinning neanderthal laughed. "To the boozer! Tallyho!" he shouted, gunning the pickup away from the curb like it was an aircraft carrier launch.

"Thomas, have mercy!" The suddenly terrified clergyman groaned, the record being set for the amount of time it took to be tired of Shock's company. He clutched the shoulder belt and closed his eyes. The fool was wearing a kilt, for Pete's sake, on the South Side of Chicago, nowhere near Scotland and not a pipe band in sight. And now the man was trying to give a priest a heart attack. *Arrested development, that simple,* he thought. *Everything is a joke, and every day is Halloween. Disgraceful for a man of Shock's age, to be honest,* the parish pastor thought. Yet another near lunatic further cementing the reputation the neighborhood had for a dearth of mental hygiene.

"Aw, we're fine. Open your eyes, Padre Mio!" Shock chided loudly. The priest hadn't even noticed that they were only doing slightly above the speed limit after the reckless pull-away until he risked a peep with one eye. "Unless you're just shy . . ." The driver batted the eyelashes of his vivid blue eyes at the older man and pulled the hem of his kilt down to better cover his hairy knees modestly. *A kilt,* Father Charles thought. Jesus, Mary, and Joseph, the world was going insane. *Bad enough to be a borderline freak of nature, why compound your problems by dressing in a freakish manner?* He played the nagging question in his head. *No, the Lord asks us to love our brothers unconditionally.* Even those who chose to make asses of themselves, he was sure . . . He'd keep his opinions to himself. There was nothing to be gained by acknowledging O'Kelly's choice of hairstyle and fashion.

"Hey, Father, do you think Jesus ever got sore because his birthday was on Christmas?"

"You know, we're not in Scotland, Thomas," the older man said, unable to let it lie any longer.

"Damn straight, Chuck. Hence the locomoting on the right-hand side of the road." The driver gestured at the road ahead, his hand flat like a hatchet. "If I'm not mistaken, the result of the spat between Hank the Vee Eye Eye Eye of Old Blighty and your boss, isn't that a pistol, if not canon?"

"Is that a fact, Thomas?" asked Father Charles, making sure his tone conveyed the fact that he was merely humoring his driver.

"No real clue, Father, just something I heard. Can't be sure of anything but existence, right? *Cogito, ergo sum*, according to Descartes." Shocked worked the clutch and gearshift with grace. "Of course, if you think my kilt is silly, you wouldn't want to listen to a frog with a girl's name either . . ."

"Thomas, I'm more inclined to listen to a Frenchman of letters than a Chicagoan who insists on dressing like he thinks he's in Scotland, to be honest."

"Ah, but I *know* I'm in Chicago, and kilts are rarely worn by Scotsmen these days. I've been there!"

"So why do it here? Especially since you're not Scottish?" he asked, knowing full well he would regret it.

"Partly to air out the lads, mostly to put a smile on your saintly face!" Shock O'Kelly laughed, gunning it to make the light ahead.

"I fail to see the difference between a kilt and a skirt, Thomas," the clergyman pointed out.

"Absolutely. No more than the difference between a cassock and an evening gown. I'm right with you there, Father," Shock verbally pointed back. *Checkmate, Bishop,* he thought to himself.

A block and a half from the destination gin mill, they passed a disheveled man fishing a trio of aluminum cans out of a refuse can on the sidewalk to join others in his well-worn garbage bag.

"Son of a bitch, that looks like Dougie Gray!" Shock exclaimed.

"I believe it is, Thomas," Father Charles said a little sadly, adding, "Poor soul."

"You said it, Father Chuck. Nuttier than the rat shit in a pistachio warehouse!"

Dougie Gray and Shock O'Kelly had been in fourth grade together. Dougie had been in fourth grade the year before too, and wound up in the fourth grade for some of the next year as well before some bright spark in the education system put forth the wacky idea that maybe Dougie required some extra scholastic attention.

He was a nice kid, for the most part, but borderline feral. There may not have been more than two summers of Dougie's childhood that didn't see him wearing a cast on random limbs earned on his more clever adventures. At the age of sixteen, Dougie and the education system parted ways, and as he lived with his widowed mother, he was able to contribute to the household, mostly working part-time handyman or labor jobs, until he found his real niche in life: roadie for touring middling-act heavy metal bands. The lifestyle was a match made in bedlam for him, lasting for twenty years or more while he lived his dream life and the chemical indulgences rewired his already questionable neurology. Eventually getting too old for the harsh underpaid roadie life and with his mother getting frailer, he returned to the neighborhood and odd jobs. Things got far more interesting for him his second summer back at home, where after a week of consuming a particularly economical purchase, a series of spiritual visions revealed his true purpose: Dougie Gray had been chosen to be a Prophet of the Lord.

"I wonder when they let him out?" Shock pondered out loud.

"I believe he's been out for a couple of months, good behavior," Father Charles informed him. "I would have gladly gone to any parole hearing for him to speak on his behalf, but he no longer recognizes the Church."

"Is that a fact?" Shocked asked, parking right across from the tavern.

As the unlikely pair walked in, Shock called to the bartender: "Liam, how about two shots and two pints for this arrant knight of the Church and this humble sinner?" He hung up his denim jacket beside the priest's windbreaker, waving hellos to a few regulars toward the back who shouted their greetings.

"Father, Shock, how are ya?" the barman welcomed. Liam had been in the neighborhood for three years now, ever since blowing in from Galway. The priest took the end stool and started shuffling through the short stack of newspapers lying nearby, his position taking advantage of the daylight streaming in through the windows. Shock stood at the bar, looking at the silent afternoon television hanging near the ceiling as the bartender poured.

"Nice dress," came a quiet but snide voice from the party of three at the table in an alcove beside the entrance. The bar seemed to get extra quiet.

Smartly kicking his right boot behind the heel of his left, the big man in the kilt executed a very military 180-degree pirouette to face the direction of the comment. Three fellows in their younger twenties were feeling their beer, their youth, and their superior numbers but stopped in mid-snicker as Shock stepped forward and looked them over. They weren't known faces from the neighborhood as far as he could tell. Some suburban kids slumming it, he figured. He looked them each in the eye and smiled.

The big man smiling down at them was almost twice their age but at least four inches taller than the tallest of them—and broad. And although there were two more of them, the friendly smile and the pale eyes put a stiff January wind right up their alimentary canals.

"Well, son of a bitch! You fellas fashion consultants or something?" The big man grinned warmly. "Looking to lay some sartorial wisdom on me? Oh goody!" A slight giggle started to rise in his voice. Behind Shock's back, the barman shook his head slowly in a warning to the strangers.

"Oh, marvelous," the old priest muttered, not looking up from his paper.

"You said it!" the large man added. "You know, the monsignor and I probably passed a dozen taverns to get to this one, and here are just the guys I wanted to meet!"

The young men sat, not knowing how to proceed.

"No, just neat kilt, is all," one said meekly to stop the yawning quiet.

"Yo, Shock, your pint!" the wise barman said loudly, placing the glass next to the full shot glass on the bar.

"Thanks, Liam!" Shock said after a brief pause. Before he turned back to sit at the bar, he gave the trio an exaggerated wink and said, "Oh, we're all going to have some laughs, the four of us!" in an overly friendly tone. "Well, Father, we've arrived!" He raised the shot glass to the priest before draining it slowly. The priest raised his in reply and took a sip of the whiskey.

"Of course, if you didn't insist on dressing in a high school girl's uniform . . ." said the priest in a hoarse stage whisper, hoping he was making a point.

"Coming from a fellow wearing an outfit most associated with pedophilia these days," came the quiet gravelly reply from the man who didn't care if he was making *his* point too strongly. The barman snorted a chuckling cough at the exchange and shook his head where he stood washing glasses.

Shock watched the shapely weather girl gesture soundlessly in front of the wavy tie-dyed map of the US projected behind her for a while and drained half of his pint before contemplating joining his nervous new friends at their table. His attention was stolen by the sight of Dougie Gray checking the gutters for discarded cans and scanning the heavens for signs from the Almighty. He wore extremely faded baggy workout trousers that had once displayed a loud pattern, a yellow raincoat, oversized basketball sneakers, and a White Sox hat. His long sparse wavy hair was turning silver quicker than his full mustache, and his face was weather-beaten by the hard living on the road and the hard partying that came with it. His recent sojourn as a guest of the State of Illinois Department of Corrections seemed to have failed to dim any of his spark or spirit.

It had been an unfortunate matter that occurred during a particularly harrowing episode of Dougie being tested by agents of the Dark, when deep in a self-inflicted haze, he happened upon a double-parked delivery truck idling in front of a hardware store not more than a mile and a quarter from the tavern, the driver inside the store solving some logistical issue. Before the delivery man knew it, Dougie had driven away in the large cube truck and unloaded the entire cargo of backyard bug zappers into the garage of his mother's house. Two hours later, police located the stolen truck, now empty, double-parked in front the same hardware store, idling away.

Several weeks later, there was a major break in the Case of the Missing Bug Zappers when Dougie, having gotten good news from his dealer but low on cash, remembered seeing some surplus in the garage and proceeded to try to shift a few door-to-door down his block. Unfortunately for the Prophet Dougie, the sixth door he knocked on was answered by the wife of the very Chicago police sergeant who'd been working the desk on the afternoon the truck temporarily disappeared.

The story around the neighborhood, as told by witnesses who'd actually been at the court building the day of the trial, was that although Dougie had been well-behaved, lucid, and contrite when dealing with his public defender, he seemed to take a hard turn when up in front of the judge.

When asked how did he plead, Dougie reportedly replied, "Buh-zzzzzt!" for reasons known only to himself and to the Lord.

"Excuse me?" the judge was said to have asked, so Dougie put his mouth closer to the court microphone.

"Buh-zzzzzt!" he repeated, hoping to be much clearer this time, to no avail. Things weren't helped at all when Dougie answered every subsequent question put to him with "Buh-zzzzzt!" even as his court-appointed lawyer tried to get some control of his buzzing client.

Once the book had been thrown at Dougie for his lack of decorum while addressing the court and he was being led away in cuffs, his frazzled legal counsel lost his patience with Dougie and berated him, asking just what the hell kind bullshit that was in front of the judge when they'd worked out the best course of action beforehand.

Dougie had looked the lawyer in the eyes sincerely and said forcefully, "Well, *maybe* I didn't understand the question!" before being taken for processing.

"There he is, lads!" Shock said to the priest and the barman. "The Patron Saint of Paint Huffers himself!" They all looked out the window as Dougie meandered by. "We should buy him a drink!" He stood to go fetch the Prophet in.

"No, please, no, Shock!" the barman protested in his thick brogue. "You're as weird as I can stand it to get in here. Please no."

"Do you really think it's wise to give that unfortunate man alcohol, Thomas?" the priest added compassionately.

"With all the industrial MKUltra rocket fuel stuff he's done throughout the years? No worse than children's aspirin!" Shock insisted, now committed to his act of charity. "Don't worry, Liam, it will only be for a beer or two, and I'll watch over him. He won't bother either of you," came the promise, in exchange for which he received one sigh and one eye roll.

Shock strode outside to greet Dougie.

"Dougie Gray, you old ring-tailed lemur! You're out! C'mon in and let me get you a brew!"

The booming invitation startled Dougie a bit, but he warmed up considerably, recognizing the shaggy ox in the kilt. "Oh, Shock O'Kelly! Wow! God bless you, brother!" Dougie said, transferring his quarter-full bag of cans to his left hand to shake Shock's huge mitt vigorously.

Shock guided the grizzled Prophet into the bar, sitting him at the table in the alcove on the other side of the entrance from the nervous trio of strangers finishing up their final round in a hurry. Dougie stashed his bag of cans along the wall and took off his raincoat, revealing his faded concert tee. Before he sat down, he removed his ubiquitous well-worn dog-eared and hand-annotated copy of the Bible from his bulging fanny pack. They got some pleasantries out of the way while Shock fetched his guest the promised beer and another for himself. The trio of young men took that opportunity to make a quick departure, which made Shock a little sad.

To Shock O'Kelly's absolute delight though, Dougie the Prophet wasted no time in sharing insights from the fascinating spiritual wonderland in which he walked. He flipped through his Bible and announced, "Your soul is plugged-in, brother! God really likes you!" he said enthusiastically.

"You getting this, Father Chuck?" Shock called over his shoulder, barely hearing the priest's groan of dismissal.

"Sometimes when I study my Bible, the angel Gabriel will come and show me things."

"Like what?"

"Lots of things. Sometimes really bad things to come—disasters and that kind of thing," Dougie said, his mood suddenly heavy.

"Son of a bitch, that bites," Shock said sympathetically.

"Oh yeah, like he'll show me mudslides in Paraguay, but I can't warn anybody because I don't *know* it's Paraguay because I don't recognize it, so I feel really bad because I always sucked at geography, you know? Hey, didn't we go to school together for a while?" the burdened Prophet said, suddenly remembering, his mood lighter.

"Yeah, Dougie, we were in grammar school together."

"Thought so. You weren't so big back then."

"Not as I recall," Shock replied.

"Hey, your sister still play the bagpipes?" Dougie asked, pointing to Shock's kilt with a finger from the hand that held his glass. "I think I hear her practicing sometimes when I walk past the cemetery."

"Yeah, that could be her. She still plays. She's good!" Shock assured him.

"Oh yeah, brother. She's talented. You can tell that the spirits in the cemetery like it when she comes to play for them!" the Prophet assured him.

"Really, Dougie? How can you tell?" Shock asked.

"Oh, you can tell, dude. Once you let in the Light," Dougie said, closing his eyes briefly and pointing upward.

"Gabriel gave you this Light?" Shock said, scanning the ceiling just in case he needed to buy the archangel a beer as well. To make certain that he wasn't dreaming this surreal episode, Shock tried to conjure a blue apple in his hand—unsuccessfully. Nope, he was wide awake.

"You know, it may have been Gabriel, or it might have been the time I almost got electrocuted plugging in the stage monitors at an outdoor festival in Ohio. They told me my heart stopped! That was all part of His plan, Shock. I also got my sense of smell back!"

"Wow! Sorta like Saul on the road to Damascus!" the big man chimed in enthusiastically.

Dougie looked puzzled for a moment before replying, "No, man, I'm pretty sure it was near Cincinnati . . ."

Shock O'Kelly stifled a laugh at the accidental perfect delivery before calling to the priest: "Father Chuck, you should really join us."

"I'm fine reading the paper here, Thomas!" said Father Fitzpatrick firmly, never taking his eyes from the pages yet unable to filter the nonsense from the conversation behind him.

The conversation got far more secular for a bit, with Dougie telling Shock hair-raising stories from the road and jail, before telling the larger man the reason for the difference between man's higher spiritual nature and his baser coarser drives: "Yeah, Shock, check this out . . . Part of your consciousness isn't really yours! You got your spirit, right? That's what God gave you, but you also have this other spirit inside of you that isn't as holy."

"Demonic possession?" Shock asked, fascinated.

"No, no, brother," the Prophet said, shaking his head. "That's different. Although I expect possessions to be on the rise."

"Why's that?"

"Ah, the damn government scientists. They've been working on secret projects that have been awakening the evil spirits. Gabriel showed me. Underground labs. There's been a huge cover-up. You'll never see it in the news."

"Really?" Shock replied with genuine curiosity, then called, "Father Charles?"

"Leave me be, Thomas," the priest replied tiredly.

"But back to your consciousness," Dougie continued academically. "Some of it is actually a 'collective consciousness' made up of the colony of bacteria in your intestines. They work together like tribes of ants. They hijack your brain and give you some of your appetites. That's why people's personalities change a little over the years, as the colony changes as older bacteria die out and are replaced by new ones. So like, when you crave a candy bar, it's maybe not *you* that wants it; it's the consciousness of your gut bacteria that wants it!"

"They hijack your brain?" Shock asked for clarification.

"Oh yeah, brother, like that disease pregnant women can get from cat litter."

"Toxoplasmosis?"

"Her too, but any pregnant woman . . . they don't have to be Greek," Dougie explained gently while trying to remember if there were any Greek women in the neighborhood who'd just had a baby recently.

"And the archangel Gabriel showed all of this to you?"

"Well, him and nature shows. I love watching stuff about animals!" so sayeth the Prophet.

And to think, Shock O'Kelly thought to himself, *it was just going to be another boring afternoon.* He smiled in delight. "How about another beer, Dougie? I'm buying! Father Charles?"

"No, that's quite enough for me!" the priest said wearily. Obviously, he'd heard enough on what he'd hoped would be a quiet afternoon. "Time to stretch the legs for a bit. Thank you, Liam!" The older man put on his windbreaker. "Thomas, thank you for the lift." He added a heavy sigh before making his exit.

With fresh beers in front of them, the Prophet Dougie leaned in closer to Shock and half whispered, "I wouldn't have wanted to tell you this in front of Father Charles," his tone quite serious.

"Yeah, what's that, Dougie?" Shock asked, leaning in too, one eyebrow starting to raise.

"Something the angel Gabriel showed me recently. It's big, *really* big, and I don't think the parish priest is in on it. Might be too big for him to handle!"

"Sounds profound, Dougie!"

"Profound indeed, my brother!" the Prophet assured, taking a long sip that left a high-tide line of foam on his mustache that his tongue mostly wiped away.

Shock leaned in and rested his elbows on the table, readying every fiber of his being for the great revelation. "Okay, Dougie, I'm ready," Shock half lied.

"Okay, here it goes . . . I was studying my Bible, and I fell asleep while watching *Svengoolie*—you know, the monster movies?"

"I'm familiar," the kilted man assured the Prophet.

"Well, Gabriel gave me a vision, showed me things really clear." He took another sip as Shock's anticipation built. "Well, get this. You know how *Frankenstein* is clearly about resurrection? And *Dracula* ties into Holy Communion, with Dracula eating flesh and drinking blood and granting eternal life?"

Shock nodded, sincerely wishing that Father Charles hadn't tapped out so soon.

"Well, I was wondering how the Wolfman fitted in the picture," Dougie said, making it crystal clear to Shock as to why an archangel spent so much of his valuable time with the ex-roadie and possibly reformed bug-zapper thief.

"That night, Gabriel granted me a vision. It was like I was there . . . You know the Three Wise Guys from the Gospels?"

"Gaspar, Melchior, and Balthazar," the agnostic offered. Now he, too, was wondering how the Wolfman figured into this.

"Yeah, the very ones!" Dougie said, snapping his fingers, happily astounded for a willing and informed audience. "I knew you'd understand! I was worried, because what he showed me was really big!"

"Go on," Shock prodded.

The excited Prophet leaned in quite close and said, "Jesus sometimes wasn't really Jesus. They pulled a switcheroo!"

Okay, maybe Father Charles wasn't *ready for this kind of revelation,* Shock thought to himself, giving Dougie his rapt attention. "The Three Wise Men did this?" he queried.

"No, no, they were good guys," Dougie explained. "When they went to the Holy Land and saw that the Savior had really been born, they knew that the forces of evil would have a plan of their own, so from there, they went into the wilderness in Turkey to enlist the help of our greatest saint! Hey, Turkey is near the Holy Land, right? I'm no good at geography," Dougie asked.

"Near enough," Shock said, eager to get the rest of the story. "So who's our greatest saint?"

Dougie looked around the room and scanned the windows cautiously before whispering, "St. Judas!"

"Judas Iscariot?" Shock exclaimed, a little too loudly for the instrument of the Lord who sat opposite.

"Shhh . . . Yes, St. Judas Iscariot!" Dougie assured him.

"He was that much older than Jesus, huh?" Shock said, taking a large gulp of beer.

"Well, here's where it gets weird," Dougie warned, almost causing Shock to spray said gulp all over the tavern. *So* here's *where it gets weird?* Shock thought to himself as the Prophet continued. "Judas was hundreds of years old, a holy man and a demon hunter. He was known for saving villages from supernatural invaders. He could fight vampires and perform exorcisms and stuff like that. But he got bitten in combat with a werewolf and was cursed with being a werewolf. I think it's called lycanthropy by scientists."

Well, sure, if you were going to ask a reputable scientist about it, said Shock's inner commentary.

"Well, because he was now cursed, he lived like a hermit in the wilderness so when the moon got full, he wouldn't harm any people."

"Fair play to him for that," Shock mentioned.

"Very holy man, sure. When the Wise Men told him what was up in Bethlehem, Judas knew he had to protect the Son of God."

"Naturally."

"See, there's a lot of stuff about Jesus and John the Baptist stories that have been mixed up deliberately. The forces of darkness caused their own evil messiah figure to be born of a human woman. I won't disgust you with those details."

"But you know, Dougie, you could if you wanted," Shock prodded unsuccessfully.

"So at the same time, you had the Son of God and the spawn of evil alive in the same place, with the evil one always trying to steal the Son of God's thunder, kinda like what Stalin did to Trotsky," the burnout explained. Shock was floored at the out-of-left-field reference to Soviet history in a conversation that came almost entirely from two left fields over. Obviously, Dougie fell asleep to more than nature documentaries.

"So while the real Jesus was trying to bring salvation, this fake Jesus was laying the plans to use the power the church would eventually have. Still infects religions today."

Shock had no argument for that, to be honest.

Dougie continued, "So Judas was Jesus's right-hand man. They were inseparable, which is why Judas was wracked with guilt over not being able to save John the Baptist. Salome was the fake Jesus's girlfriend besides being a stripper. Her mom was deep in the cult of darkness. In fact, it was that old bitch who started the rumor that Mary Magdalene was on the game."

"Ah, I see, what a bitch!" Shock said to show support, any concerns he may have had with Dougie's tale being not well thought out quickly evaporating. Loony or not, Dougie was hitting all of the angles.

"Judas had his hands full protecting Jesus from all the people he was pissing off—the evil cult, the Pharisees, the Romans, the medical profession, all of them."

"But what about during a full moon?"

The roadie Prophet smiled and pointed at Shock with a glad-you-asked look on his face.

"That didn't bother Jesus, and when Judas was a wolf, he behaved himself around the Lord as you'd expect. I saw this in the visions! He'd sleep curled up at Jesus's place. Jesus would scratch him behind his ears, take him for walks. Sometimes they'd throw a stick around."

Unfortunately, this *did* catch Shock in mid-swallow, and beer foam rocketed upward to burn his sinuses from the inside. As he tried to stifle his coughing fit, he scrutinized Dougie's face through his own watering eyes. The weather-beaten character was clearly not joking. What a glorious day! Shock's heart sang even as his head throbbed from the foamy porter douche it had just received.

"Judas was so instrumental in getting the word of the Lord out, making sure the really important things like the Sermon on the Mount got recorded accurately, that he had to be taken out. That's why they framed him. All the other Gospels we have today are kinda based on what Judas left behind. He's really the original Gospel writer. Bet you didn't know that!"

"I certainly didn't!" Shock wheezed in agreement, thrilled to be breathing somewhat normally again.

"Oh yeah, you know how they did those early illustrations and stained glass that showed the Gospel writers? And they show Matthew as a man, but Mark has a lion's head, and Luke looks like a bull calf, and

John has an eagle's head? The Vatican has relics that show Judas as the fifth, and he has a wolf's head. Father Charles may even know about this, but he'd be sworn to secrecy if he does."

"One would imagine," Shock replied, hanging on every word. "So they hid away the Judas wolf images to keep the secret, huh?"

"That and marketing. There were still a lot of wolf attacks in small towns through the Middle Ages. Scared the kids," the crazed Prophet stated in full sincerity.

"Ah, wise," Shock said, letting it all sink in.

"Yeah, they framed St. Judas good, that's for certain. He was the most loyal of all of the Apostles, and today, he's looked at as the villain . . . The cult of evil, working with the Pharisees and Herod's men, they did him dirty!" Dougie looked off into the distance as if replaying the vision in his head. "Yeah, what they didn't leave out of the story was that he got paid with thirty pieces of silver. When they found out that he was really a werewolf, they cut up little silver Roman coins and braided them into one of their whips and flayed him with it. That's what killed him—the silver. Because, you know . . ." Dougie said sadly, his words trailing off.

"Yeah, werewolf," Shock said, nodding, trying to sound full of understanding. He drained his glass. "Well, Dougie, I think it's time for me to fly. Tell you what, I'll give you and your load of bauxite a ride home. I'm going to hit a drive-through. How about we get you a burger before I drop you off? On me!"

"That'd be really nice, brother!" Dougie Gray said gratefully, finishing his beer and starting to gather his battered belongings.

Shock paid the tab and put on his denim jacket, thanking the barman. He was in the process of steering the Prophet out the door out into the late afternoon when the barman heard Dougie say, "Hey, Shock, did you know silverfish are psychic? That's why as soon as you see one and you realize that it's a silverfish, they freeze!"

"No, Douglas, I did not know that," the huge man in the kilt said as the door closed behind them.

———————

FORTY MINUTES LATER, MARIAH CAME in for the start of her shift. Another blow-in from Ireland, Mariah was from Dublin and had a tough hard edge and a sharp tongue. The sexy but rough woman looked upon Liam as a backward culchie—a term from home meaning an uncouth country person. The condescending attitude kept Liam from thinking of her in anything other than angry carnal terms, and the friction between them was sometimes explosive.

Mariah put on her apron and poured herself a short beer, downing half before addressing her co-worker. "All right, Liam, I'm here now. What's the story? I see you've managed to keep from burning the place down," she said, her words barbed and slathered in acid as if goading him into confrontation.

"So a priest, a mental patient, and a guy in a kilt walk into a bar . . ." Liam said, fetching his hoodie from inside the office door and putting it on.

Mariah watched him say his few farewells as he waked toward the door.

"So, how does it end?" she asked harshly.

"It ends with me going home and having a bowl of soup, you slag!" he said as he exited.

ON THE ROAD TO JERICHO

One pilot and no passengers were on board. A single human, but plenty of spirits rode aloft on the two wings of the converted de Havilland bomber. Al's mother had always told him that the Holy Spirit would be with him, if you counted that, but more tangible spirits were on the plane in the form of sixty gallons of expensive Canadian hooch that was loaded in the bottom of the cargo bay in front of the cockpit that was intended for mail sacks.

Al Slattery didn't like the sound the engine was making. It was starting to get balky and for the fourth time, and he had to work the throttle to clear the roughness from her. Luckily, the Liberty motor had purred like a kitten while he was over the hundred mile or so leg across Lake Superior. Behind him to the north, tall angry clouds started to build, and that was another concern. He'd known quite a few pilots that had killed themselves by ignoring the weather and scud-running in front of a storm instead of taking it down and riding it out on the ground. Unfortunately, blowing his deadline would be almost as dangerous as having the wind shear drive the DH-4 into the earth.

It wasn't Al's plane. The last plane he had cracked up after the motor quit outside of Tulsa a few years back when you could still keep yourself fed barnstorming. He and his barnstorming partner, another grease monkey and spanner-spinner he'd known back at Kelly Field, had been able to make a bundle flying town to town selling rides and doing sloppy aerobatics over rural crowds who'd only recently started to get used to the sight of automobiles. Those were wild days, beating the hell out of the planes, keeping them patched and sleeping rough, building a bankroll and raising hell all the while. It was only five or six years or so ago somewhere in Nebraska that his partner's worn-out Standard J-1 literally fell apart after a wicked landing on a rough farm field, which delighted the crowd. They'd gotten enough of the farmers and oil roughnecks to put up sufficient funds for Al to deliberately crash his beat-up Jenny as well, flipping her over as it jarred to a stop. The local farmer wanted to charge them twenty dollars to haul the double wreckage off of his useless patch of dirt, and the local sheriff was going to hold the pair of aviators to it. Al and his partner struck a couple of matches and burned the broken crates down to the engines, wheel rims, and rigging wire and offered the farmer five dollars to haul the remaining scrap and the sheriff another five for a ride to the train station. The sheriff was jake with that arrangement.

The train conductor had a son who'd bought it in the trenches of France and let the two flying aces ride to San Antonio for free, where they purchased surplus Jennys in top condition for $300 each, cash, which still left plenty in their money belts. The medals on Al's flying jacket were what caught the conductor's eye. Both were real: the Great War Victory medal had been mailed to Al's mother's house for his time at Kelly Field, and the French Croix de Guerre had been purchased for two dollars at a pawnshop in St. Louis. The farmers who'd have to think about paying three bucks for an airplane ride would gladly pay five for a ride from someone who'd flown with Rickenbacker.

The gravy days of barnstorming were well over now, and Al's money belt remained empty for longer and longer periods. Running this whisky from just south of Thunder Bay down to Chicago would help build his bankroll a bit and keep his younger brother, Matty, in good stead with his underworld employers. Most Irish gangs were on the North Side, but on the far south, there were lesser-known organizations that kept the Italian outfit and its new boss from swallowing up the entire South Side. Matty was a powerful brawler and worked for Boss Taggart doing collections and security, despite Al's admonitions to steer clear of throwing in his lot with any players in the crime war. Matty had stubbornly said he could look after himself.

One of Taggart's associates, a well-connected businessman, could be convinced to look the other way if one of his company airplanes got borrowed for a day or three when needed, as long as it didn't interfere with legitimate business. The converted DH-4 mail plane suited some of the more clandestine needs of the bootleggers but was now sputtering and coughing as the black clouds started to catch up to the old girl.

Al knew it was the bad gasoline. Rudolph Heinz was an idiot. The father of a degenerate gambler, Heinz's even dumber kid owed Taggart thousands in juice on his bad bets. To keep Taggart's men from beating the younger Heinz to a greasy streak in the alley, the elder Heinz helped out on these secret high-speed booze runs. Behind Heinz's farm outside of Rhinelander, there was a large flat meadow that was perfect for a refueling stop. All Heinz had to do was to keep three barrels of gasoline on hand, bankrolled by Taggart, and help transfer fuel to the plane when needed. Then when the plane took off, he was to go into town and send a telegram to a small grocer's in the neighborhood that also sold bootleg under the counter for Taggart, who'd then phone Matty. If the telegram mentioned the dairy, it meant that Al and the plane should be at the place on the road just west of Joliet in about four hours. If the telegram mentioned the horses, it meant a delay.

Al had warned Heinz before about saving a few of Taggart's pennies on questionable gas and pocketing them, lest Al find himself with a dead windmill at four thousand feet with a load of illegal sauce and his pecker in his hand. As the Liberty engine sputtered more and more often, demanding Al's attention, he made a mental note to have a vigorous kinetic discussion with the dumb farmer if and when he ever found his way back. Unfortunately, keeping the cranky engine turning had badly distracted Al from his dead-reckoning. He was probably a little lost, but the bad motor and chasing storm made that less important.

The weather was closing in quickly, Al's ears aching slightly from the pressure drop. Being more than halfway home made the thought of pushing it a little farther tickle his brain, but there was the saying about there being no old bold pilots. And he didn't want to set down where he'd draw too much attention, as being caught by the law with Taggart's whisky meant a stretch in jail and losing Taggart's whisky meant a stretch in the hospital, at the very best. The winds were starting to rock the aircraft, and gusts were throwing him up and down violently. As the visibility closed in, Al rode the plane down to find a nice patch of flat field to save his hide. He couldn't even pinpoint the direction of the sun anymore, so gray was the sky. His watch told him it was nearly noon.

He was rather familiar with this route, but none of the terrain below was familiar. He was hoping to spot a set of railroad tracks or a big river or a town with a water tower, anything that would help him navigate, to no avail. To make things more urgent, the engine was sputtering more often and cutting out for longer moments as the fouled carburetor starved the engine of gas. Below, in the slightly hilly country, the only habitation he could make out was a small cluster of farms and what appeared to be a town hall or some such, with a large meadow just behind. Illicit booze or no, this was where fate had determined that Al Slattery had to land.

He flew a tight corkscrew down, watching the leaves on the trees. The prevailing wind had him land toward the whitewashed building, the land inclining slightly. He set up a good line into the wind, gently taking it to grass height, sudden gusts conspiring to raise him back into the air. His wheels touched the earth in brief jolts as he bounced along the meadow. He gently eased the rudder bar, taking care to not drag a wingtip skid on the undulating terrain and ground-looping as the pine trees ahead rapidly grew taller. Al felt the harness against his chest and shoulders as the tail skid dug into the grass, his engine now sputtering furiously. He felt relief, but only briefly.

As he taxied the wheezing plane closer to the tree line, he lay on the left rudder to cut a wide turn to bring the plane facing almost the opposite direction. He could tie her down here, the trees offering some protection from the gusting winds. Closing the throttle and cutting the magnetos to shut the aircraft down, Al heard the wind whistling past the wires and wings and looked up to an approaching storm, a wall of clouds almost black with hints of sickly green. He threw his helmet and goggles onto the seat as soon as he jumped down and laid his jacket on the silver-doped wing. From the cargo area forward of the cockpit, he quickly pulled out the pegs and rope to keep her from wandering.

As he worked quickly about a hundred yards or so from the white building, he laid out his priorities. He'd have to find a phone or nearest telegraph office and let Matty know he'd been delayed. Once that was done, he hoped the motor would be cool enough to reach in and remove the carburetors from between the cylinder banks so he could unclog the jets. By the time he could get them reinstalled, all of the filth from Heinz's cheap gasoline will have settled in the tank so Al could drain it out and run it through a makeshift filter before replacing it. Ideally, he'd do all of this quickly without having to answer any delicate questions that might interest law enforcement. If he were very lucky. If he called on the Holy Spirit, as his ma would say.

He stripped off the coveralls he wore over his clothes and put his jacket back on. There were two small canvas bags stashed with the cargo, one with a basic set of tools and the other containing spare pair of socks and the like. It also held his .45, purchased at the same hockshop when he picked up his French medal for gallantry, and Al debated whether he should grab that too. He decided against it for now.

The building was an assembly hall of sorts it. Clean and sparse, it had a lectern with a cross carved into the front and dozens of folding chairs laid out in neat rows. It was immaculately clean, the walls blinding white inside and out, and the only decorations on the walls were a wooden cross and the John 3:16 passage neatly painted below it. Opposite that, the Ten Commandments were listed within two tombstone shapes representing tablets. Next to a closet door stood a plain bookcase holding a few well-worn Bibles and hymnals, a couple of lanterns, and a few more odds and ends. Out a side door among a dense copse of trees stood two white outhouses with mossy roofs, and the front door opened to a porch that faced the gravel road. *Which way to go?* Al thought, trying to recall in which direction the closest farm was. He had no sooner stepped into the road than he saw a horse-drawn farm cart heading his way a couple hundred yards down the road to the right. He started walking to meet it.

"How are ya!" Al called, raising his hand. The man at the reins of the two draft horses nodded in reply, his lined and severe features giving him the look of the Indian on the nickel. His overalls were patched, his broad brimmed black hat well beaten, and his jet-black hair was cut home-style, straight across the bottom edge with scissors.

"Pastor will be along soon," the farmer said in a strong voice. "Trouble with your airplane?"

"Well, yes. That and the storm building. I'll have to make some repairs. Won't take me too long. Hey, I need to find a telephone or a telegraph office. I got to let my boss know that I'll be late. Where's the nearest one, could you tell me?"

"No phones nearby. Telegraph neither. Road into town washed out in the spring. Hasn't been fixed yet. Pastor will be along soon. We'll wait," the farmer said, prodding the horses toward the building. Al walked behind to where the farmer had stopped his cart at a place with a good view of the plane through the trees.

"Pretty, isn't she?" Al said. "You want me to show you a closer look?"

"No. It's a machine, that's all," the farmer answered, and that's where the conversation ended.

The sky was still dark, and lightning flashed in the distance, but the storm didn't seem to be creeping much closer, and Al walked back to the plane and opened up the cowl to cool the engine faster, as long as the wind wasn't rough enough to tear the flimsy panels loose. It would still be some time before the engine was cool enough for him to climb up and start working. He needed to get word to Matty within the next couple of hours at the very most. He pulled his tool bag out and took inventory of what he needed—wrenches, a screwdriver, he had some wire to clean out the jets. He looked up to see another wagon and a black buggy pulled up on the road in front of the white building. Al took the .45 and tucked it under his seat cushion in case he needed it in a hurry. Wiping his hands on a rag, he made his way through the trees to the group of men gawking at the stranger and his maroon-and-silver airplane. He tucked the rag in a back pocket. He was ready to go into his barnstormer barker mode to address and charm the crowd, hoping to win them over.

"God be with you, Brother!" the old man in the long black suit and black hat called to him from in front of the buggy before Al could even speak. "Brother Simon says that your airplane needs repairs before you can be on your way."

"Well, what I really need in a hurry is to find a telephone or get to a telegraph office, but yeah, Brother Simon is right. Just have to fix the carbs. Won't take too long," Al said, walking up to the gentleman and extending his hand. "Al Slattery, out of Chicago."

Two more wagons pulled up, and five more men piled out, all with dark features and tattered farm clothes, but clean, with white, white shirts in contrast to their tan skin and jet-black hair.

The pastor regarded Al's hand for a moment before shaking it, seeming a little reluctant. "I'm Pastor David, Brother. Your Christian name is Albert? Alfred?"

"Al is just fine, Pastor."

"What did your mother call you, Brother?"

"Aloysius, Pastor. My name is Aloysius, but everybody calls me Al."

"Brother Aloysius, I'm afraid you'll find no telephone nearby, nor telegraph office. Brother Simon should have told you."

"Oh, he did, Pastor. Even said the road to town was washed out, but there's got to be a way," Al reasoned with the minister.

"Can't be done, Brother," said the old man.

"Can't be done," muttered a few of the other farmers.

"I told him, Pastor," said Simon quietly.

All of the farmers were tall and lean, with a hard weather-pummeled look. They maybe ranged in age from their early thirties to their sixties, the pastor clearly being the oldest as evidenced by the quantity of silver in his hair. Their faces were all almost expressionless as they regarded the lost visitor.

Dammit, Al needed to get word to Matty. He'd wait with the two trucks from the scrapyard for maybe an hour or two at the most. After that, the plan could easily fall apart. Sure, there were plenty of places to land around Chicago, but most of them ran the danger of curious eyes and probing questions.

"What do you need for your repairs, Brother Aloysius?"

"Well, I don't want to impose, but if I could borrow a ladder and maybe a clean bucket or two, that would make things go even faster," Al said. He'd have to work at lightning speed to make his rendezvous on the road west of Joliet, even in perfect conditions, but the storm clouds sat like a fortress wall in the sky, periodically belching rustles of thunder.

"We'll do what we can to get you away from us as quickly as possible, Brother," the pastor said plainly. Al didn't know whether he should be taking offense or not, but he'd had frostier receptions a few times in the past. "Brother Boaz, would you have the charity to loan Brother Aloysius a ladder?"

"How big of a ladder does he need, Pastor?"

"Around eight feet would be best," Al said to Boaz.

"Brother Boaz, a five-cubit ladder would help our guest. Brother Asher, would you be kind enough to loan Brother Aloysius a couple of buckets from the dairy?" the pastor asked, always looking at Al.

"Now, I'm going to use the buckets for gasoline, gents, so just know that before you give me your best equipment . . ." Al warned.

"When you're done, we can rinse them at the pump beside the gathering house. Brother Asher will get them well clean after."

"You wouldn't happen to have a funnel too, would you, Asher— Brother Asher?" Al asked.

"Brother Asher, could you also locate a funnel for our visitor?" the pastor asked. Al got the hint; all strangers had to deal with the boss. Quite the opposite of Seamus Taggart, who only dealt with people outside of his inner circle in the most dire of circumstances. Al was wondering why Boaz and Asher hadn't yet moved.

"Brothers!" The preacher said, raising up both hands. All the farmers removed their hats and closed their eyes reverently. "Let us offer to the Lord our God a prayer that Brother Aloysius gets what he needs and can be back upon his way swiftly!"

There were a few echoes of "Back upon his way, Pastor" before they all said their amens.

"Amen!" the pastor said. The men replaced their hats, and Boaz and Asher left in their respective carts, in opposite directions. "Brother Aloysius, would you be so kind as to stay right here and give us time to discuss your predicament?" The question seemed to be less a question and more of a gentle instruction.

"Absolutely, Pastor David," Al said. "I really appreciate the help, and I swear I'll be on my way as soon as possible!" The slightest of winces from the pastor made Al wish he hadn't insulted them by making an oath so lightly. He didn't want to sour whatever welcome they were offering.

"Thank you, Brother Aloysius," the Pastor said, leading the remaining farmers into the gathering house.

Al turned back to look at the plane and the threatening clouds, glad to be on the ground until they passed. Perhaps he should pray to Ma's Holy Spirit. His time was getting short. He desperately needed the storm to pass and to get his repairs done quickly. Al checked his watch. Even if the thunderclouds tore through and left in the time it took to fix his crate, he'd still be pressed to make the meeting on the road to off-load Taggart's cargo.

Through the windows of the assembly hall, he could see the farmers and the pastor seated in a circle, the pastor talking while the men sat motionless, save for the odd nod or two.

Al paced a bit along the gravel road, considering his predicament. First, the carburetors, then the fuel. Then he would need some help to get the plane started. It wasn't impossible to hand-prop the Liberty engine, but it certainly wasn't as easy as a Jenny; one usually employed a Hucks starter, a mechanical monstrosity normally mounted on a pickup truck chassis and commonly found at the bigger airfields. Al thought he was pushing it with the request for a funnel; he wasn't going to bother the rubes by asking if they had a Hucks starter stashed someplace.

After several minutes had passed, Al glanced back into the hall. The heads were all bowed in prayer, save for the pastor's. His was tilted toward the rafters. Al fought the impatience glowing inside him, but a glance at the sky—gray and dense as granite—reminded him that he wasn't going anywhere soon. If the weather wasn't going to give him a break, maybe the holy revivalists could pray him some better luck. After several more minutes and no one emerging from the building, Al decided to cross the road into a neat copse of trees to relieve the strain on his kidneys.

There was slight thunder in the distance, the only sound save for the stream from his bladder slapping and bubbling the loamy soil beneath the trees. Through the pines, he spied what must've been the community burying ground. A good acre of meadow cut out of the trees, neat white wooden crosses laid out in rough rows. It was profoundly peaceful.

The sound of horse and wagon caught his attention, and he made his way back to the road to find the man called Boaz pulling up in his wagon. The pastor, standing on the porch of the hall, saw Al on the other side of the road and called out sternly, "Brother Aloysius! You agreed to stay put!" There was leashed anger in his tone.

"Sorry, Pastor, I didn't mean to wander far," Al said contritely, wondering what the fuss was about but in no position to ask. He put up his hands in a placating gesture. "Didn't wish to offend. I didn't understand how close you needed me to stay."

"Brother Aloysius, we expect you to be a man of your word!" the old man said sternly, bringing the blood to Al's ears.

"Again, my apologies, Pastor. I'll be out of your way soon." He thanked Boaz when he took the proffered homemade ladder from him and headed back toward the de Havilland. With the weather gods, the South Side gangsters, the Volstead Act, and the religious zealots all arrayed against him, Al was ready to start consuming his cargo himself—to hell with the money and Taggart.

The ladder was the perfect height. Fair play to Boaz. After redonning the coveralls and digging out the tools he needed, he got to work between the rows of still quite unpleasantly warm cylinders, unhooking the fuel line and dropping both carbs. Brother Asher showed up with the buckets before he was done freeing the second unit, which gave him a place to dump the gasoline out of the two components. Sure enough, the fuel was fouled with dark hard flecks.

"Thought so—rust. Look at that. Probably enough iron in here to make a coffin nail," Al said, showing Asher, who didn't seem interested. Asher only looked at Al and proffered a rough funnel, the seam hand-hammered. "Oh, that'll do fine, thanks!" the pilot said, getting no reaction whatsoever.

Rain started to fall, and Al closed the cowl and put the oilcloth cover over the cockpit, the heavy drops drumming on the fabric wings. The front porch of the gathering house gave protection from the rain, and Pastor David instructed some of the men to erect a small trestle table for Al's repairs. The old minister sat at one end of the porch watching Al work. The pilot started explaining what he was doing, but soon picked up that the community leader didn't harbor the least bit of curiosity for the mechanism's workings.

Al worked the throttle arm, letting the accelerator pump squirt a stream of fuel into a bucket before wiping the carburetors down and setting them on the brown butcher paper they had spread to protect the table. He cleaned the jets with a piece of safety wire and wiped the float bowls clean, making sure the needle valve was free of dirt and rust. He had both carbs back together and ready to be reinstalled when he checked his watch. It was dead.

"Aw, son of a—" he said to himself, suddenly mindful that Pastor David was watching. He'd blown the rendezvous, for certain. Matty would only wait with the trucks for so long, then maybe head back to Curley's grocery store to check for any word from Al. Dammit.

Winding his watch, he asked Pastor David if he knew the time.

"Will be evening soon, Brother Aloysius," came the reply.

Al worked through the falling drizzle, getting the carburetors back where they belonged. The stormy sky was still roiling and angry, and the light was failing. His belly felt full of lead with the realization that he wouldn't be heading back tonight. He laid out his plans as he crouched next to the DH-4, draining a bucketload of tainted fuel out of the sump, making sure the gas falling into the bucket was clean before shutting the valve.

Pastor David was still sitting on the porch when Al returned with the bucket of gas.

"What will you need to get going tomorrow, Brother?" the pastor asked.

"Well, I'll need some help starting my bird," Al replied. "Maybe we could make a set of chocks to hold her back while I start her. Will just need some wood about yay big." He gestured with his hands. "If we got two pieces of wood to hold the wheels and drilled them for a length of rope, I could start the motor and hop up inside, give one of the fellows the signal, and they could pull the chocks away. Easy." Al took a pencil out of his pocket and drew rough chocks on the butcher paper to illustrate. Pastor David looked at the crude sketch and nodded his understanding.

Al gently poured all of the dirty gasoline from one bucket into the clean bucket, filtering it through a piece of chamois cloth from his tool bag. He used a piece of safety wire to join the two buckets and the chamois as a ground in case static built up and caused a spark—a trick an older mechanic had taught him down at Kelly Field. The trick had no doubt saved Al from turning himself and his plane into a bonfire on more than one occasion. He poured until the first bucket held nothing but water and orange iron-tainted fuel.

Back at the plane, pouring the clean gas back into the tank was a little awkward, holding the bucket and funnel to pour into the filler tube just aft of the firewall. As the bucket got lighter, the task got easier, and Al managed not to slop too much gas onto the fuselage, which he wiped down well once the filler cap was back in place. He threw the bucket and funnel onto the grass before jumping down from the lower wing. He'd be ready to go as soon as the weather broke.

Al gathered the borrowed items and walked back through the light rain to the gathering house. He was no more than fifty yards away when an intensely bright bolt of lightning flashed in the sky behind him, followed by a roaring timpani of thunder. The pastor's buggy and another farm wagon were parked in front, mostly protected by the canopy of the trees. The table on the porch had already been cleared away.

"Brother Aloysius, it looks like you'll be our guest here overnight," Pastor David announced, his tone betraying his displeasure. Al wanted to assure the old preacher that he, too, wanted to part ways as soon as humanly possible, but before he could offer his apologies and gratitude, the pastor continued, "Brother Caleb will fashion what you need for the wheels of your machine. Brother Levi's wife, Sister Sarah, will send you supper and a few blankets. We've decided that you may stay here and shelter from the elements in the gathering house, provided you respect our community and our beliefs. We brook no sin here."

"Pastor David, I thank you and everyone for your kindness, and—"

"Brother Aloysius, we ask that you respect our community and refrain from wandering away from here. Our homes, our farms, our burying ground, we wish for nothing to be disturbed."

"I understand completely, Pastor David. I'm not looking to—"

"Have you been born again, Brother?" the preacher asked.

"Ah, no, Pastor David. But I was christened, made my communion, and was confirmed at Old St. Pat's," Al assured him.

"We shall respect you and your unfortunate adherence to the Vatican," the pastor said, his words dripping with pity. "We brook no sin here, Brother Aloysius. No smoking, no intoxicating spirits, no foul language. This is a holy place!"

The reference to alcohol brought a little blood to Al's ears. Did the old man suspect he was rum-running for the mob back home?

"I understand completely, Pastor David!" Al affirmed. At least he wouldn't have to bribe anyone with some of Taggart's hooch.

"There's a pump for the well around the side of the building and an outhouse beyond."

Two farmers exited the gathering house and drove the wagon away, acknowledging Pastor David respectfully without even regarding the stranger. In the gathering house, the table had been set back up with a lamp and box of matches. The rain let up, and the light was fading when a young man pulled up in a small wagon and entered carrying several woolen blankets folded neatly and a metal trencher covered with a kitchen towel. The young man greeted the pastor, placed the plate on the table, and tossed the blankets onto the polished wooden floor without even glancing in Al's direction. Al wanted to laugh as the kid quickly exited and was on his way in moments. *Must be Levi and Sarah's kid*, he thought, *the talkative one.*

There was tough smoked ham, boiled vegetables, and fried corn mush, along with fresh bread and butter. The pastor watched as Al sat down. Sensing the opportunity, Al said, "Pastor, will you say grace with me?"

"No, Brother Aloysius, I will leave you to your supper. Feel free to read a bit before you retire. We'll all pray for the weather you need to get back upon your way," the pastor said, gesturing to the Bibles on the bookcase.

"Thank you again, Pastor. Good night!" Al called to the departing preacher.

"God be with you, Brother Aloysius!" the pastor replied, sounding like a priest on a gallows.

The food was plain but hearty, and Al was grateful for it. There was almost nothing to rinse off the plate and cutlery in the creaking pump that dispensed clear cool water in the last of the dying daylight through the storm clouds. Al hung his gasoline-reeking coveralls on the railing of the porch, hoping the rain would rinse them a bit. It felt good to get out of his shoes and remove is tie and collar. Al's bed consisted of two layers of blanket for a mattress, one rolled up for a pillow and one to crawl under. His body was exhausted, but his mind wouldn't settle down.

As soon as the weather broke, he had to get back in the air to get Taggart's booze to the city. He had no idea how much of his cut the weather delay would cost him. He needed to build a bankroll soon. Coolidge had just signed the Air Commerce Act, and next year, both pilots and mechanics would require licenses. Pilot's licenses, if you could believe that—like there were going to be sky cops to pull you over at six thousand feet. Both of those licenses would cost money, and then he'd need to find an outfit to sign on to. He'd probably have to front some dough for part of an airplane to be successful at that. Al wanted to make a clean break from the mobsters, wanted Matty to be free of them too, but in the city, even legitimate jobs cost dirty money.

Al drifted off to fitful sleep, bothered by his thoughts before the noise woke him with a start. He sat bolt upright in the darkness in the unfamiliar surroundings, wondering if he'd dreamed the sound. He listened but could only hear the wind in the trees and light patter of raindrops on the roof and windows. He was about to lie back down when *there*! He heard something again, a muffled sound. He felt around in the darkness for the table that held the lamp and matches and fumbled around until he was seated at the table, lighting the lantern. The flare of the match blinded him briefly, and then his eyes adjusted to the soft glow of the wick throwing exaggerated shadows in the room and casting a bright reflection in all of the windows. He saw nothing out of place and was about to blow out the wick when he heard a skitter along the wall. That would explain it. A mouse, a rat, a stoat, a squirrel, or some manner of wildlife must've been running around and, out here in the country, no doubt several at once. Al regretted not grabbing his .45 from the plane. He hated rats.

Whatever it was, Al couldn't find it. He figured that it had retreated from the light. Turning the lamp low, he returned to the rough wool bedding.

When he heard the soft thump, he was up quickly and looking in the direction of the sound. One of the hymnals on the shelf had fallen over sideways. Al grabbed the lamp to look for the animal that was keeping him awake. He moved all of the books and found nothing. Whatever it was must have run off. He moved an old soda cracker tin on a middle shelf and checked behind it. Nothing. Al fumbled the cracker tin while replacing it, and it fell to the floor, clattering open loudly. The sound was such a jolt in the quiet night that it made Al jump, but the contents of the tin made Al's heart seize.

Inside were some assorted county deeds, a small ledger book, and a well-worn yellow envelope marked *Tithes* in lead pencil. Inside the bulging envelope was just over $7,100.

Al whistled. Wow, there was more than enough money in that envelope to buy a new house and a car! For all of their plain country ways and their tent-revival religious behavior, this community was loaded. A windfall like that could certainly turn a fellow's fortunes around, that was for certain. He held the stack of worn bills in his slightly trembling hand before returning it to the envelope and replacing the tin on the shelf. He whistled again to himself before blowing out the lamp and returning to his bedroll.

He lay in the darkness for almost another hour, immune to the occasional scurrying sounds, thinking about what it would be like to get back with that kind of dough in his pocket. Taggart could take whatever he wanted out of his cut for being late; it wouldn't matter. He could return the plane to the hanger at the Chicago Air Park and get himself a steak dinner across the street. He wouldn't have to worry about scraping together the stake for his pilot's and mechanic's licenses and could maybe buy into one of the lucrative airmail lines. He'd be set.

Too bad Al's ma had raised him to be more honest than that. On the other hand, who was to say just *how* the Lord provides?

———————

HE AWOKE TO A STORMING morning. Someone had been in during the wee early hours because the empty trencher had been replaced by one containing three hard boiled eggs and more bread and butter. On the porch was a pair of makeshift wheel chocks—two pieces of branch stripped of bark about five inches in diameter and a little more than a foot long, both drilled through to accept a long length of rough cord. That should do perfectly, as soon as the weather cleared. Once the storm broke, he'd be on his way. Al rinsed off the platter after he ate and sat on the porch waiting for the howling rain to pass.

He sat there all morning and most of the afternoon as well, and aside from answering nature's call in the dark outhouse and rinsing his shirt at the well pump out of boredom, that's how his day passed. He could explain a day's delay without word to Taggart's boys, but two days was another story. Someone had been promised that booze and was no doubt getting impatient. They'd probably be monitoring the police chatter to hear if Al had been caught somewhere and wondering if he'd absconded with it when no word came. Even if he showed up with the full load and a good explanation, Taggart would make an example out of Al just for the sake of his reputation. Al wouldn't put it past Taggart to give that job to Matty, just to make a point about loyalty. Al prayed to his ma's Holy Spirit for a break in the weather.

In his adult life, Al could only recall praying seven times before—once flying over the Dakotas when a thunderstorm blew up suddenly; once when being questioned by the cops about the cargo he was hauling; once when his dog got knocked down by a coal truck; once when it was rumored that Matty had been gunned down in a shoot-out; once when a doxie he knew down in San Antonio was two months late; once when Curley's daughter got scarlet fever; and once for his mother. The Holy Spirit must have been listening every time, except for Al's dog, the grocer's daughter, and his ma, and it apparently wasn't listening this afternoon either.

In the evening, the pastor arrived again with another plate of food, announcing, "Brother Aloysius, the weather tells me that the Lord has ordained that you stay with us for a bit longer," as he shook the rain from his hat and coat.

"With any luck, Pastor David, the storm will wring itself out tonight, and I'll be gone right after first light," Al said, trying to sound cheerful.

"On the Sabbath? Absolutely not, Brother Aloysius! It cannot be done!" the preacher bellowed sternly.

"Now, Pastor," Al reasoned, "I'd only need one of the lads to pull the chocks for me after I get started, and I'll be well out of your way!"

"Not upon the Sabbath! Absolutely not, Brother Aloysius!" the preacher repeated with something close to wrath rising in his tone.

Al fought his rising anger. How could he make these backwards people understand the reality of the situation? Even if the skies cleared right now, it was getting too late to head out tonight. Al walked to the door to scan the skies for any sign of letup. His coveralls and shirt were gone. He stepped out the door to see where they'd blown to. They were gone.

When he stepped back inside, the pastor told him, "Sister Sarah has taken your clothes for a good cleaning. You'll have them back before service tomorrow."

"Well, that's very nice of Sister Sarah, Pastor," Al said, attempting to hide his impatience. "But I'm telling you, the sooner I'm out of here, the better."

"We all agree there, Brother Aloysius, but tomorrow is the Sabbath. It cannot be done." The Pastor sat down in one of the folding chairs, paging through a Bible.

A few moments of reflection later, Al joined him, sitting at the table.

"Your mother was a godly woman, Brother Aloysius?" the pastor asked, breaking the silence.

"Well, sure, Pastor," Al answered, not wanting the conversation. "But still a Catholic," he reminded him—anything that might prevent him from extending his accidental stay any longer.

"And you were in the war, Brother?" the pastor continued.

"Well, not exactly. I was in the Army," Al said. He stood and fished the Victory medal from his jacket pocket, then laid it on the table. "Never went to France. I was down in Texas at a training field."

"And that's where you learned to pilot such an airplane."

"Yeah, well, I was a mechanic, and a pal of mine and I got an instructor to give us some lessons in exchange for, ah, things we could get for him," Al explained, skipping over some of the better parts of the story to protect the preacher's more delicate sensibilities. "After we were demobbed, my pal and I repaired some worn-out crates we picked up cheap and started barnstorming. Aw, we had a hell of a time!" Al laughed before he caught his transgression.

"Your mother approved of this lifestyle?"

"Sure she worried, but she raised us to take care of ourselves."

"Your mother still with us, Brother Aloysius?" the pastor asked gently.

"No, Pastor David. Bad cough took her a few winters ago," Al said, feeling the sadness creep up his guts. He couldn't wait to have this place getting smaller behind his rudder.

"Would she approve of what you're doing these days?"

Al chuckled despite his rising annoyance. While his mother would have much preferred her sons make their livings within the law, she also was no fan of Prohibition either, and that was gospel truth. And odd hospitality or not, he didn't owe the preacher any explanations.

"Are you an honest man, Brother Aloysius?" the pastor asked.

"As much as the next man, Pastor David. Sometimes I think even more so. But I'll bend the rules if I have to!"

"What does that mean, Brother?" the pastor asked quietly.

"It's complicated," Al replied before making the sign of the cross over the plate and removing the towel. That was the last conversation they had.

———

AL WAS UP EARLY THE next morning, the skies still gloomy but no longer raining. He walked out to check the plane, placing the chocks in front of the wheels and laying the rope, ready for someone to pull them away when needed. Before he re-covered the cockpit, he stashed the pistol back in the bag in the cargo compartment.

When he got back to the gathering hall, several farmers, including Boaz, Asher, and Caleb, were setting up the chairs for the day's services. His shirt and coveralls were returned, his shirt blinding white and his coveralls spot-free. He washed up at the pump and was dressed when the other wagons started pulling up.

The women all had the same dark coloring and severe looks as the farmers, and all regarded the newcomer suspiciously. The children whispered and giggled amongst themselves until they were cut off by a stern look from the pastor. Evidently Al's sandy hair and bright eyes were more amusing than the flying machine in which he'd arrived.

Sunday service was an all-day event among these people, Al was to learn at the agonizing expense of his numb posterior, broken by only two meals. The families, numbering just shy of two dozen people, murmured to themselves, but only the pastor addressed Al directly, and he did so infrequently. The day passed slowly, and Al's broken watch was no help. As the day wore on, the clouds got a little lighter, rain falling occasionally.

Al tried to appear reverent and patient while unable to tear his eyes away from the windows and weather conditions. The congregation sang hymns and listened to Bible passages, and everyone prayed, often with the petition that their Brother Aloysius got what he needed to be back on his way. Nobody amened louder than Al at those prayers. They followed with more hymns and songs, and a few times, Al was tempted to sing one of the songs he knew, which would've no doubt resulted in the roof caving in and Old Scratch himself appearing to lead all of their souls to perdition. The pastor gave another interminable sermon before the evening meal, which was accompanied by a heavy downpour.

After the prayers that followed supper, everyone stood to tidy up and put the gathering hall back in order. Al pitched in, taking down the tables and putting the chairs back into rows, always with someone following him and repeating what he had done, as if he'd done it incorrectly. The rain sounded to have abated.

As the families started to leave, Al called out, "Thank you all for the hospitality! Good night!" but nobody answered. In the dying light, Al fetched the blankets and spread them out.

Pastor David was the last to leave. He called out, "The Lord be with you, Brother Aloysius!" before shutting the doors behind him.

Another day behind, he thought as he bedded down. Another day of doom playing with him like a sadistic cat with a crippled mouse.

———

AL AWOKE LATER THAN HE'D expected to a quiet morning, the mist sitting on the wet grass but the sun in the eastern sky starting to burn off the haze. He walked out to the plane. He could see for at least a quarter of a mile, he reckoned, and the slight breeze indicated better conditions. He uncovered the DH-4's cockpit and untied the stakes that stitched her to the ground. He worked the fuel drain valve until he was sure there was no condensed water in the gas. Making sure the switches were in the OFF position, he pulled the heavy engine through a couple of rotations with audible grunts, making sure the Liberty was free and ready.

Al was ready to leave. He just needed a hand with the start-up. He went back into the gathering hall and put on his coveralls. Then he went quickly out the front door to the gravel road to see if he could flag anyone down.

Maybe if he got her started, they'd hear. He returned to the waiting airplane.

The chocks were in place, the prop swinging easy. He climbed into the cockpit and worked the stick and rudder, watching the ailerons, elevator, and rudder as he did. Before he climbed back down, he switched the left magneto on.

On the second forceful back-wrenching swing of the propeller, the engine coughed for a few seconds and with a loud backfire bang, sputtered to a shuddering start, blue puffs of exhaust shooting out of the long pipes. Ensuring that the plane wasn't lurching forward, he climbed back into the cockpit and turned on the other magneto, smoothing out the coughing and working the throttle slightly, bringing the engine to a rhythmic snorting patter. He watched the temperature gauge start to climb. If he got someone to pull the chocks for him, he'd be on his way. Then to find out where the hell he was and get back to the city to face whatever music awaited. His stomach re-knotted at the reality of his situation.

Looking aft, he saw a wagon pulling to a stop through the trees. It was Caleb or Asher, but probably Caleb, hopefully come to assist. The haze continued to burn off as the farmer made his way through the trees to the idling mail plane. Setting the throttle to the lowest idle he could without it cutting out, Al hopped out to meet him. Caleb kept a hand on his hat, obviously not caring for the blast of air or noise coming from the plane.

"Pastor David told me to help you," he shouted, as if to explain that it wasn't his idea.

"Great, thanks, Brother . . . Caleb? Yes?" Al shouted back. The farmer nodded. "Okay, Caleb, this is what I need. After I'm buckled in, when I'm ready, I'll wave my hands like this." Al demonstrated. "When I do that, you pull the chocks from in front of the wheels, okay? And when you have them both clear so I don't roll over them, you nod your head, and I'll know it's good for me to take off. I'll give her the spurs then. Okay?" Al asked, giving Caleb a thumbs-up. Caleb nodded. "I'm going to get my jacket, and I'll be on my way. Right back!" Al trotted away toward the building. Caleb stood there holding his hat and holding the rope.

Al went back to the gathering hall and once inside, put on his jacket. He looked out the front windows and saw no other wagons or buggies other than the one Caleb had rode in. They must have canceled the farewell parade. He made his way to the back door and caught himself just before he stepped out. He turned back around.

A minute or so later, he ran back to the plane and Caleb, zipping up his jacket.

"Caleb! What's the name of this road here?" he asked over the engine noise, wondering if this place was even on any maps.

"Ain't got a name. We call it Jericho Road," the farmer answered.

After climbing into the cockpit, Al buckled his harness and put on his helmet and goggles, giving Caleb a smile. Caleb didn't smile back.

Waving his hands, Al saw Caleb give the ropes a mighty tug, and the plane crept forward an inch or so as the farmer reeled in the pieces of wood. Al cracked the throttle, and the plane lurched forward. He went to wave at Caleb, but the farmer was already walking back to the wagon. The plane bounced and rocked down the meadow, Al pushing the throttle wide with a roar. Stick forward slightly, and the tail rose a little, and soon, the grass rushing beneath the lower wings became a blur and the bouncing stopped as the DH-4 climbed into the air and the silvery haze ahead. He pointed the plane south according to the compass. He checked the fuel gauge and noticed that his watch had started up again, reading 2:20. He'd have to reset it first chance he got.

For a few tense minutes, Al flew in zero visibility, the sun-bright mist all around him, but as long as the altimeter continued to wind upward, Al was confident. He was alive and headed home, with all of Taggart's whisky. No matter what lay ahead, he had blessings to count. He laughed at that thought.

When he broke out of the clouds at six thousand, the skies were clear to the west, and the farmland below was bathed in bright sunlight, the sun much higher than he'd expected. He was scanning the terrain for landmarks to navigate home when the river below on his left suddenly looked familiar. There was no way it could be the Mississippi; that would've put him hundreds of miles away from where he should've been. He spiraled down a couple thousand feet and spied a town on the river, hoping to catch sight of a name on the water tower near the center of the hamlet.

Clinton! *Impossible*, he thought, but he recognized the place. He was just about 120 miles away from Chicago. He'd be there in about an hour or so. How the hell could the weather have pushed him so far off course in such a short time? It had to have been a cracker of a storm. He pointed the nose east and opened the throttle a bit.

———

THE PASTOR PULLED HIS BUGGY up to the gathering hall and set the brake. Brother Caleb had told him earlier that the stranger was back on his way, praise the Lord. Entering the communal building, he looked around. Nothing out of place, everything neatly put back. He gave the closest thing to a smile as he'd been known to give.

He walked over to the bookcase and straightened the hymnals and Bibles on the shelf, pleased with the order and simplicity that God had restored to their little community with a sigh of relief. He picked up the old faded soda cracker tin and opened it. Inside, there were several county deeds, a small ledger book, the tithe envelope containing just over $7100, and a secondhand French Croix du Guerre.

"Hope the Lord provides what you need, Brother Aloysius," the pastor said out loud to the room, empty save for himself and his God.

———

Just before Al hit Joliet, he dropped to two thousand feet to navigate easier. Passing over the road where the transfer usually happened, he had to look twice. Were those the trucks from the scrapyard? Was Taggart expecting another delivery today? He dove and buzzed the trucks, waggling his wings, avoiding the telephone wires. Unmistakably, he saw his brother, Matty, leaning on a fender, puffing a cigarette, offering a rude gesture. Al circled and put the mail plane down on the road, leaving a dusty plume behind him. The trucks rolled up behind him through the gritty haze.

Al kept the engine idling as Taggart's boys came up and started unloading the crates from the cargo hold. Matty stepped up on the stirrup, squinting against the prop wash.

"I was givin' you maybe another half hour, and then we were leaving," Matty shouted into the cockpit.

"I couldn't get to a phone or telegraph. That idiot Heinz gave me bum gas! How'd you square it with Taggart?" Al shouted in his brother's ear.

"As long as we get it to him tonight, it's all jake!" Matty replied above the din.

"But what about the weekend? What happened?" Al shouted above the blasting air.

Matty shook his head. "I don't understand. I can't hear you, Al!" the younger Slattery shouted.

"I've been gone for days!" Al said.

His brother gave him a quizzical look. "You're crazy! Too much thin air, and you'd better not be helping yourself to Taggart's booze!" The boys were putting the dummy cargo back in the plane and closing the access panels. "We're done here. We'd better both scram!" Matty yelled, rapping the side of the airplane twice before jumping down and heading toward the trucks.

Al was airborne quickly and swung around to buzz the trucks again, seeing Taggart's men covering the precious cargo with scrap and debris to avoid detection and his kid brother offering a repeat of the earlier rude gesture. He opened up the throttle and roared off toward the South Side.

———

At 4:50 p.m. on Friday afternoon, Al Slattery touched the borrowed DH-4 down on the long cinder runway at Chicago Air Park, approximately 31 hours and 42 minutes from when he'd left the same airfield.

His watch was keeping perfect time.

FIRE

A PAIR OF HOT SHORTS:
FIRST AND LAST DAY ON THE JOB

As first days on the job go, this was pretty bad.

The lady seemed nice at first and genuinely interested in the charity for which I was collecting. I thought I was doing well.

Then she said she didn't think peaches could get alopecia, and even if they could, it wouldn't be much of a hardship for them.

So then I showed her the wretched specimens I had in a box just for situations such as this—evidence to melt even the stoniest hearts such as hers. She yelled at me that they were just week-old nectarines and that I was a chiseler.

I had no choice but to hit her in the mouth.

KENNEDY HALF DOLLAR

My grandfather was evidently quite the scholar when he was a young man. School was always kind of easy for me, and I think that was the basis of our special connection. We both had agile minds.

Granddad went to this really prestigious academy high school way back when. He really wanted me to take their entrance exam, even though there was no way we could have afforded for me to go to any other school but the local public.

I took the exam just to please him, and I scored very well. It wasn't easy. It was a challenge. Granddad couldn't have been prouder. I scored so high that there were even some grants available to me, but my family just didn't have that kind of dough.

Nevertheless, Granddad was thrilled. One day, he stopped by the house while I was still at school. He left an origami cube on my bed, on which he had written *Great job on the entrance exam!* Oddly, the cube contained nine bucks in Kennedy half-dollars.

I never spent those half-dollars. Those were the ones from Granddad. Those coins were the tangible ectoplasm of our special bond. No matter how tight the money got, no matter how many times I skipped lunch because I only had enough money for bus fare, I wouldn't part with them.

A few years back, when I was moving into this run-down apartment, the super mistakenly changed the locks on the doors twice. I was locked out when I tried to move in. A few boxes of my stuff sat outside the door for twenty minutes while I tracked the super down for the right key. I haven't seen the origami cube or those coins since.

Now *every* Kennedy half-dollar I get is one from Granddad.

REFLECTIONS

Even "unofficial" and clandestine meetings with the president seemed overly official and uncomfortable. Even if you had been a midshipman in the same class at Annapolis with the current commander in chief, as Dr. Ramsay had been, there was a majesty to the office that prevented him from not feeling slightly like a trespasser.

"Craig! Please, get in here now!" the president bellowed, sounding genuinely pleased to see his visibly rattled old friend. "Sit down, sit down . . . Jesus. I appreciate your coming to see me!" It was spoken as if Dr. Ramsay had had any choice in the matter. "Ernie, a Talisker on the rocks for the doctor, please," the president said to a white-coated steward. He turned back to his friend. "Bathesda said you checked out fine other than a bruised arm. I'm very grateful for that!" The president pointed to the hospital bracelet the scientist still wore on his left wrist.

Ramsay waited until he and the president were alone before asking, "Bob, just what the hell is this all about? Am I being gaslighted here?"

"Craig, I wish I could make sense of this for you. I chose you in particular in hopes that your insight might help *me* understand this matter. Please, fill me in from your perspective, start at the beginning."

"You mean from being abducted from my own goddamned office?" Ramsay queried, obviously irritated by the way the whole affair had been handled.

"Please, Craig, please," the president said softly, closing his eyes and using both hands in a calming gesture. "You of all people will recognize the need for secrecy. Certain protocols have to be followed . . . Even with one of the my oldest and most trusted comrades." The words sounded like the platitudes of a professional statesman but felt genuine. The president held up a finger as the door opened, and the steward returned with two whiskies in cut crystal glasses, handing one to Dr. Ramsay and setting the other down on the president's enormous desk on a coaster emblazoned with the seal of office. "Thank you, Ernie. That will be all," he said, dismissing the aide and waiting until the heavy oak door had shut behind him. "Okay, Craig. From the beginning, please . . ."

———

IT STARTED LIKE A CHEAP movie and seemed ridiculously excessive, even to someone as familiar with the daily workings of both the military and the state as Ramsay had become over his career. The two men in suits with very legitimate credentials had escorted him from his office swiftly, answered no questions, and merely assured him that all necessary arrangements, including informing his family that he'd been called away on urgent business for a day or two, had been made. They'd hustled him into a dark SUV with deep window tint that seemed to obey no traffic laws on its breakneck journey to the airport, where the two men in suits took him via service tunnels and nonpublic elevators to a waiting 767 with no markings save for its N-number.

He'd sat in a comfortable first-class seat that was curtained off from the aisle and other passengers. Indeed, it seemed as if most of the seating area was made up of these private cubicles. His in-flight entertainment was comprised of a selection of decades-old movies playing on the video screen at his seat and the contents of a manila folder marked with his name. It contained a brief biographical outline about him that included both official and private photos of him and his family, two pages of instructions regarding security, and two ominously worded NDA forms requiring his signature, of both the intellectual property and national security variety. The security instructions made it clear that in all interactions with the other participants of the meeting, every individual would only be referred to by their assigned number, even if the other individual was someone he knew. Save for a magnetic strip and microchip, the laminated badge he was to wear at all times had nothing but a bold black #9 on it.

Indeed, Dr. Ramsay had known a few of the other participants, who like he, deplaned at the end of the flight and were hustled onto a windowless bus in such a way to make it impossible to identify not only their location, but whether it was night, day, summer, or winter.

As the bus bumped and jostled them into the unknown, he recognized a junior colleague from the National Security Council fighting carsickness and wearing #3. Their eyes met, and they both nodded greetings. He also recognized the astrophysicist from Caltech and the highly respected surgeon known for her trio of books on ethics in medicine, among other scholarly works. There was also a fellow that Dr. Ramsay would have sworn was a minister who'd gotten famous on a series of lectures on religion before starting his own megachurch in Houston.

The bus slowed down considerably, and the numbered passengers looked to the other three occupants of the cabin of the bus, not including the driver: the man in the suit, who was obviously in charge, and the two security officers in dark fatigues with no insignia, who seemed to have been selected for their ability to remain as stoic and impassive as statues while simultaneously exuding a sense of menace and barely restrained violence. The three seemed completely uninterested in their human cargo, as if they were hauling cords of wood.

They barely even made eye contact. When the bus jerked back into swift motion, the engine noise changed considerably. They'd obviously entered a tunnel.

"Excuse me," #4 addressed the suit in charge, "certainly by now you can let us know something about what's going on?"

"I'm sorry. I won't have any answers for you." There was a shade of condescension in his tone. "What I will say is that when we reach our destination, Colonel Bartlett and Dr. Rudolph will fill you in with whatever information they feel you need."

"And who are they?" asked #8, the Caltech professor.

"I won't have any answers for you," the suit replied, slightly louder this time.

The feeling of apprehension was rising in the bus like a fog.

Accompanied by the sound of hissing brakes, the bus slowed and jockeyed in fits and starts to come to a rumbling stop. The group was prodded out into a huge subterranean space. Ramsay assumed he was deep in one of several ultra-secure bases that had been built in various locations under the Rockies, far from prying eyes and immune from conventional or nuclear attack. There were three buses parked, each with a handful of bewildered abductees led by a humorless functionary. They were processed through a security checkpoint, asked several personal questions, and directed to change into dark surgical scrubs and lab coats. They were not even allowed to wear their wedding rings into the briefing.

They were led to a large conference room, where an angry Air Force sergeant was directing a flustered and browbeaten airman to find another chair ASAP. The chairs were arranged around a long table. One wall had windows to the corridor; the opposite wall had a long mirror, which even a mongrel dog with dementia would have assumed was one-way glass. The wall opposite the enormous video screen held a counter with coffee, water, and an assortment of unappetizing sandwich rolls, and the corners of the ceiling held an array of security cameras. Once seated, they were subjected to another severe security lecture delivered menacingly by one of the suited gentlemen.

While it was apparent that the consultants had been summoned for a matter of extreme urgency, they rankled at the treatment and lack of answers they were receiving. It was as if an air of open hostility and malice filled the space between everyone. The sergeant scowled and muttered some invective under his breath as the sullen airman brought in the last chair. He then shepherded all of the lab-coated participants to take seats around the long table, leaving the end closest to the screen unoccupied to allow everyone a clear field of view.

Colonel Bartlett and Dr. Rudolph entered the conference room, and an airman closed the door behind them. Without fanfare, Colonel Bartlett began. "Ladies and gentlemen, we thank you for your participation in this important matter."

"Like we had a choice," #5 said sarcastically under her breath.

The colonel ignored her icily. "I'm afraid I cannot go into too much detail, but your government would like your input on a matter we're as of yet unable to understand. I ask for your attention and that you keep an open mind. As some of you will know, Dr. Rudolph is a top man in his field . . ."

"And what field would that be?" said #4, whom Ramsay recognized as a noted researcher in the field of particle physics.

"If you needed to know that, you'd know that already," the officer answered curtly.

So that's how it's going to be, Ramsay thought to himself. He noted that the colonel wore a covert earpiece, as did Dr. Rudolph.

"You will regard anything mentioned or shown during this meeting to be strictly a matter of national security of the highest priority. Any discussion will take place in this room and this room only. You are never to discuss the contents of this briefing with anyone else or even with each other in the future. I'm sure the NDA you've all signed made that clear." He gestured to his colleague and announced him with a simple "Dr. Rudolph . . ." before stepping to the side.

Dr. Rudolph seemed to be more enthusiastic than his military counterpart and smiled at the assembly around the table. Ramsay recognized him from several DARPA briefings, but otherwise didn't know the man.

"Ladies and gentlemen, I will do my best to give you the pertinent information without overstepping my bounds, so please bear with me." He paused and seemed to address nobody: "Am I allowed to outline the history of the project?" There was a high-pitched note that only a few seemed to notice, some of the younger members reacting as if they'd received a mild static shock. The only older person who reacted was #12, a kind-looking avuncular gentleman whom Ramsay did not recognize. Ramsay noticed the old man's eyes lingering on a fixture on the ceiling that could have been a smoke detector or something similar, where a dim red LED light flashed momentarily. The doctor's and colonel's attention were obviously taken by whatever instructions were being relayed through their earpieces.

"Okay, moving on . . ." Rudolph continued. "The need for newer and better security measures to counter espionage has led us to explore the technology involved with this program, which for our purposes today we will refer to as Monocle." Again, the red light and the faint whine interrupted the scientist. "Excuse me. Basically any energy— electromagnetic radiation of varying types used for communication and information exchange, for instance—can be passively intercepted and collected for intelligence gathering. For example, a simple conversation can be overheard from a short distance, but by using lasers from a long distance, the vibrations caused by the human voices can be detected by their effect on solid objects nearby, and these vibrations can be deciphered with amazing fidelity. Electronic data on a secure closed-loop system can be read passively just by getting a sensitive device close enough to react via electrical induction. Systems using fiber optics can be cracked remotely utilizing—"

The red light on the ceiling flashed again.

"Never mind," Rudolph continued. "What we are investigating

is the collection of data by analyzing any and all disturbances in the nearby space, audio, thermal, visible—the full spectrum, in fact, from radio and microwaves through the visible spectrum to ultraviolet, X-rays, gamma rays, and beyond. We then collate and analyze the data using three key algorithms."

The red light again. The two men listened for a bit before Colonel Bartlett took back over.

"So what we have is a novel approach to viewing activity in the spectrum and, using some sophisticated analysis, getting a more comprehensive view of the world around us from a security and intelligence perspective. Dr. Rudolph, please take us through the demonstration."

The lights dimmed in the room as if by magic. On the screen appeared what seemed to be security footage of a standard multi-person business office during operating hours. "What we have here appears to be the standard CCTV image." He let the footage play for several seconds. "However, using the most basic Monocle tools"—here, Rudolph manipulated a remote the size of a cheap desk calculator—"we can check on the data transmission volume."

The image changed, slightly at first, making everything electronic on the footage become alive. Computers glowed, as did power cords, the wiring within the walls. The doctor proudly adjusted the settings on the remote, and the visitors could see the throb of workers' nervous systems, the signals flexing their muscles, even a pacemaker installed on one individual. Several quiet gasps escaped from those assembled.

The woman who wore #5 spoke up. "This is potentially revolutionary for the medical field," she began, but the red light and shrill whine immediately claimed the attention of Bartlett and Rudolph. Ramsay wondered if the high-pitched whine was the source of his throbbing headache, which was starting to feel close to the start of a migraine. The pained and weary expressions on some of the other's faces mirrored his.

The colonel held up his hand. "That is out of the scope of this discussion. We will concentrate on the matters at hand," he said firmly, yet sounded as if he were merely repeating instructions he'd been given. Dr. Rudolph, though, could barely contain the urge to act like a proud parent.

The doctor held the control box with both hands. "Say for instance, you wanted to know how much cash this particular individual was carrying." The picture zoomed jerkily in on one man standing at a copy machine wearing a shirt and tie, then zoomed closer on his backside. As the image flicked through what seemed to be a series of filters, eventually the man's wallet and buttocks appeared in sharp focus. A few filters later, the anti-counterfeit strips in the folded bills became visible, as well as the magnetic strips on his credit cards, striped with their binary code. The strips in the bills seemed to have three different signatures. Dr. Rudolph pointed at them with a laser pointer on the screen. "There we have one, two, three, four twenties, two tens, three fives, and no singles!" he said, zooming the image back out and back to regular video.

"Is this a recording or real-time?" Ramsay asked.

"Immaterial," Bartlett barked without even acknowledging the questioner.

Ramsay felt his temples throb at the feeling of rebuke.

"Okay, one hundred and fifteen bucks and that man's Fourth Amendment rights!" said #2 with a snort.

Dr. Rudolph seemed to be immune from the insinuation, instead waiting for the man to turn from the copier to re-zoom in on the image and dial the filters again. He stopped when the image clearly displayed the man's key ring, three quarters and a dime, and a clear image of his penis.

"One hundred and fifteen dollars and eighty-five cents! And by the keys, we can tell that he drives a Chrysler and has Schlage locks on his house!" the doctor announced proudly, seemingly oblivious to the liberties taken with the man's privacy. He zoomed back out and went through a series of filters, some plainly showing the contents of desks and purses, and others revealing the worker's underwear beneath their clothes, then disappearing even the underwear, showing full details of people's bodies, including blemishes, scars, and hidden tattoos.

"Outrageous!" #5 hissed angrily. "Unbelievable!" she spat, slapping the desk in front of her.

"Ladies and gentlemen," the colonel said, a tone of reprimand in his voice, "you have been invited here to discuss technological matters concerning national security, not the Bill of Rights! That discussion is beyond the scope of this meeting!"

"Invited?" #4 quietly said sarcastically, which received some reactions of bitter agreement. The red light went on again.

"Ladies and gentlemen, we're straying off topic. Perhaps we can take a short break, collect our bearings, and resume in a bit," the colonel suggested, although Ramsay didn't believe it was the colonel's suggestion at all. The colonel and Dr. Rudolph stepped out of the room, and the lights got brighter.

"Can you believe this shit?" #4 asked of the room, which seemed too stunned to answer. A few people got up to stretch. Others grabbed coffee or water. Ramsay closed his eyes and tried to keep the headache at bay. He felt a warm hand gently brush his wrist. #12, seated next to him, addressed him softly.

"You seem to be in pain, no? Bit of a headache?" the man asked, kindness in his eyes. "If you'd indulge me: close your eyes, concentrate on relaxing your shoulders, and breathe deeply with me." The old man had a kind voice and a faint mid-Atlantic accent. "In . . . hold it . . . out . . . in . . . hold it for three seconds . . . out . . . Once again, in . . . and out. Now breathe normally." It may have been the man's calming voice or Ramsay's concentration on relaxation that helped to hold the migraine at bay; he really didn't care which. The atmosphere seemed unhealthy, the air thick with malice, even among the participants. Ramsay thanked the older gentleman, who seemed to be genuinely kind.

Ramsay's thought that #10 may have been a minister was bolstered when the man suggested that they all say the Lord's Prayer together.

"Oh please," groaned #11, rolling her eyes.

"Closed-minded fool," replied #10, though not directly at the woman.

"Maybe we should be keeping our personal thoughts to ourselves," suggested #1, an Asian-appearing woman in her forties with a California accent.

"I'm sure," #12 said softly, "that under these trying circumstances, we could afford to give one another latitude. I see no harm in allowing those who believe in prayer to pray, nor do I see the need for those who don't to be belittled." The man spoke his opinion as authoritatively as if he were chief justice, which he wasn't. Ramsay knew the chief justice.

A few moments later, the colonel and Dr. Rudolph reentered the room. The scientist dove right back into his presentation. "May I assume a number of you are familiar with Chladni figures?" There were nods of agreement from a few of the group. "For those of you who aren't, we're referring to shapes generated by certain resonant frequencies." Rudolph fiddled with a different remote, one that controlled a projector installed in the ceiling. Projected on the screen was a short clip of different tones being sent through a metal plate onto which sand had been sprinkled. As the tone played, the vibrating plate caused the sand to dance about until it had drawn a pattern, different tones casting different patterns. "Yes, see here, these are Chladni figures, which result from the particular mathematics of the waveforms generated, and of course, they aren't just two-dimensional." A few moments later, the scene changed to what appeared to be a black space filled with some sort of thick fog or smoke. Again, tones played on the audio track, organizing the vapor into definite three-dimensional patterns. "While Chladni discovered this phenomenon, the mathematics behind it were unraveled by a woman named Sophie Germain, who unfortunately—"

"Doctor," the colonel interjected.

"Yes, excuse me," the scientist continued. "Anyway, you all have some appreciation for Monocle's passive capabilities. The system can also be used actively."

"You don't consider that active?" #2 snorted derisively.

Dr. Rudolph chuckled a little smugly—it seemed to Ramsay—at the man's lack of understanding. "What is meant here in the technical sense is something akin to radar or sonar. A radio receiver can *detect* radio waves, a microphone can *detect* sound waves, but radar sends out an electromagnetic pulse and then detects how it is reflected by objects. Same with sonar, which emits an audio 'ping,'" the doctor explained, using air quotes, "that is reflected by objects it encounters. Part of the problem, perhaps with Monocle as well, is that these 'pings' can also be used to detect the source through triangulation, which—"

The red light and piercing whistle again. There was silence for several seconds as both the doctor and the colonel listened to whatever was coming through their earpieces, the colonel nodding faintly. Dr. Rudolph looked at the colonel, as if to plead for directions.

The silence was broken by all hell breaking loose. The lights in the room snapped off, and automatic shutters rolled down along the windows as red lamps became the only light source in the room. A loud Klaxon sounded, along with a recording broadcasting, "WARNING. ACTIVE SHOOTER," over and over. The colonel seemed jolted into action and hectored the group to shelter beneath the table. More than a few of the group cried out in panic.

"Down! Now! Under the table! Everybody!" he shouted, authority in his voice.

———

THE PRESIDENT, LISTENING TO RAMSAY, his index fingers steepled to his lips, nodded. "Yes, Craig, I heard. Unfortunate business . . ."

"What unfortunate business, Bob? What kind of theatrical bullshit was that?" Ramsay demanded. "Why were we being treated to that dog and pony show?" President or not, his jangled nerves made him dismiss the courtesy due to his friend's office.

"I assure you, Craig, upon my honor, no theatrics occurred," the president stated firmly but calmly. "The unfortunate business, preliminary reports inform me, may have involved one security officer using his service weapon to murder another airman. It may have been over the spouse of one, but details at this point are murky."

"Does vetting not happen anymore, Bob? How many loose screws do we have wandering around high-security facilities? Under arms?" There was real edge in his voice that bordered on insubordination, which the president chose to ignore, or he at least chose to give his over-stressed friend extra latitude.

"Craig, I assure you, we're looking into it. As sketchy as the details are at this point, it's looking like the soldier in question may have been suffering from delusions. Could I get you a refill, Craig?" the president said solicitously, making a move for the call button.

"I'm fine, Bob. I'm fine," Ramsay said, trying to moderate his mood.

"Please go on, pardner," the president urged, trying to sound like one midshipman encouraging another.

As soon as the loudspeaker announced, "ALL CLEAR, STAND DOWN. ALL CLEAR, STAND DOWN," the regular lighting clicked back on and the red light extinguished. Ramsay assisted #12 back to his feet as the rest of the panicked group also climbed up from the floor. After a few minutes, the shutters on the windows to the hallway rolled back up, and a master sergeant wearing the ubiquitous blue beret knocked twice before entering. He seemed to ignore those assembled with the sole exception of the colonel.

"Sir, are we okay in here?"

"Yes, Sergeant, we're fine. Thank you." The red light and whine again. He dismissed the sergeant with a wave. "That will be all. We'll continue, please, ladies and gentlemen. Let's collect ourselves like professionals." Quiet grunts and growls seeped from the agitated members. "Dr. Rudolph, please continue."

Dr. Rudolph seemed to still be a little stunned by the harsh interruption but quickly collected himself, straightening his clothes. "Yes, well, Monocle's active capabilities . . . to use the musical analogy, and with the concept of the Chladni forms in mind, try to imagine a combination of pulses in the electromagnetic spectrum, a 'chord' of energy being sent out into the surrounding area and detecting the resulting echo. Our first attempts proved very interesting, maybe even revealing . . ."

The damned red LED again and the annoying whine. Whatever came through the earpieces, it seemed to make Dr. Rudolph redden in the face a little.

Colonel Bartlett stiffened and scanned the faces around the table. He glanced at the mirrored glass and gave a curt nod. "Ladies and gentlemen, I'm asking you on behalf of your nation to keep an open mind and not jump to conclusions about what Dr. Rudolph is about to show you . . . Dr. Rudolph, please walk us through the examples."

The scientist stood for a few moments, nodding his head slightly, obviously taking in instructions being relayed through the earpiece. When he straightened and faced the group, he again manipulated the remote for the projector. "During the course of development, certain anomalies began to show in the data," he explained. "Of course, this was to be expected with prototypes and experimental technologies, not to mention certain initial flaws in the computational algorithms, several of which turned out to—" The red light and whine cut him off.

"The voice of God again," sneered #6 in a stage whisper, which earned a chorus of soft tones of agreement.

Dr. Rudolph continued, "Please observe." He clicked the remote. On the screen appeared film of two men on a street corner, seemingly shot from some distance. They shouted at one another with animated faces and wild gestures. They both displayed the unmistakable body language of hostility that bordered on violence, malice between them like dry tinder waiting for the spark. "Now watch carefully as Monocle is tuned." The image seemed to flip through a series of filters, showing the same image in different versions. The filters flipped and then settled on a grainy version with washed-out color, except the two men were cocooned in a dark haze, like an aura of dark smoke.

"Not the sharpest of images that you've shown," #8 commented.

"Keep watching, please," urged the scientist.

The man on the left seemed to grow more agitated and looked to be furious. He was obviously yelling, spitting as he talked and motioning toward the other man with his hand like a vertical blade rising and falling in rhythm to whatever he was growling. His dark aura grew darker and larger the more forceful he became. The other man's aura flared as well, momentarily, before seeming to pale and shrink. There were gasps of realization from some around the table.

"Curious, no?" Rudolph said, continuing to stare at the screen.

As the more aggressive man's dark cloud became denser, the other man started to back away. There was a brief flicker, like a pale lens flare, right before the man lashed out explosively, cracking the retreating man in the jaw with a strike that sent him staggering and reeling, lifting his arms in a defensive gesture that came too late.

"What the hell?" #6 blurted out.

"What the hell indeed!" Dr. Rudolph agreed.

"Fakery," #11 said skeptically, shaking her head.

"Oh, I assure you, while we're not sure *what* we're detecting, there is no fakery, manipulation, or deception involved. We have more curious examples, but we'll press on . . ." Rudolph paused, seeming to wait for instructions that didn't come. "The next image," he continued, clicking the remote, "is a very short clip, but also interesting." The screen showed a crowded public scene, perhaps a park or a zoo or similar venue, with groups of people walking around in several directions. "Nothing much here, yet Monocle . . ." the scientist teased.

The image ran through a series of filters again, changing brightness and hue along with clarity, before settling on the same pale grainy look of the previous clip. Most of the auras were lighter than the ones that appeared during the argument and seemed to be no more than a slight blur on the image. The scene played for several seconds, with people drifting in and out of frame.

"Right edge of the screen," Rudolph said, his gaze also locked on the video. A faint wisp at first, then a pale image, roughly person-shaped, drifted into the scene with no person within it. The shape moved through the crowd, seeming to navigate between the other pedestrians, unacknowledged by any of the passersby. The clip ended, and Dr. Rudolph scanned the faces at the table, his eyebrows slightly raised as if in question.

"More fakery," declared #11. Dr. Rudolph smiled. "I'm waiting for the footage of Sasquatch or the Loch Ness Monster you're going to try to sell us," the woman added.

#8 spoke up. "An artifact? Some optical fault or glitch in the analysis system?" he offered.

"Our thoughts at first," he addressed the fellow scientist. "However, a full analysis of both the data and equipment has revealed no faults as of yet, and then there's more. As we continue . . ." Rudolph clicked the remote again. "Focusing on the . . . settings?" he seemed to ask the mirror. After a brief flicker of the red light, he carried on. The screen showed another busy street scene. "We'll say that focusing on the system settings that gave the previous images led us to capture this . . ."

The busy street scene played, footage of a busy intersection in a metropolitan area. The image went through the familiar shuffle of filters, altering color, brightness, and clarity before dialing in on the washed-out look of the other clips. Pedestrians all showed the aura effects seen previously, some more intense than others, mingling with the enhanced look of the vehicle exhaust, which the filter revealed more prominently as well. The group watched the scene silently play for a few seconds, until it captured the image of a bicycle messenger speeding through the intersection against the light. A city bus slammed on its brakes to avoid hitting him, but a taxi driver in the next lane, his view blocked by the halting bus, had no time to react, violently striking the cyclist. The messenger flew up in the air like a rag doll, coming back down on the rear driver's side quarter panel of the taxi to flop lifelessly to the pavement. Traffic swerved and braked madly to avoid the broken body on the pavement. The bicycle was lodged firmly under the decelerating taxi, throwing a wake of sparks rendered even more vivid by the filter. There was a thin chorus of gasps from around the table, with participants adding:

"Damn!"

"Oh my!"

"Mercy Lord!"

"How awful!"

A few more similar reactions quietly sounded around the room.

The group exchanged looks before someone drew their attention back to the screen. The aftermath of the accident naturally drew a crowd, some auras darker than others, the cab driver's noticeably dark and diminished as he clasped his hands in front of him in tragic response. A traffic cop with a large aura took charge of the scene, barking orders and gesturing to onlookers as he simultaneously directed traffic, occasionally keying the mic hanging from his shoulder.

"Look at that!" #2 blurted out. There, among the crowd of gawkers, stood a faint aura with no accompanying person, stone still as the rest of the milling crowd talked to one another. Dr. Rudolph, remote in hand, sped up the footage. As the scene played out, all the eyes in the room stayed glued to the solitary shadow standing at the corner of the intersection. It barely moved as first responders tended to the crash victim, taking the body away in an ambulance. It stood like a sentinel for a while, and then as traffic eventually started moving again, the shadowy figure began to drift down the sidewalk, fading slowly before gently sublimating away.

"I'll be damned!" #7 exclaimed over the gasps of some of the others. "Is that real?" the participant politely demanded of the colonel. The question seemed to bruise the scientist's pride in his project.

"As I've assured you before, sir, no fakery, manipulation, or deception was involved in the production of any of the examples presented. Nor will there be," he assured the group.

#10 spoke up. "I think it's obvious that you've discovered a way of detecting and proving the existence of the soul! Mankind has inherently known about his divine nature and true substance since time immemorial, but this proves beyond doubt the true spiritual nature of life! This will end the endless debate from the doubters and those who refuse to see!" He shot a glance at #11, who'd displayed her skepticism from the beginning. "This is historic! Wonderful and truly miraculous!" His excitement was met with silent mixed reactions from those assembled. If what he said was true, Ramsay wondered about the implications and ramifications for the gentleman's chosen profession of ministry.

"Ladies and gentlemen, we ask that we not get ahead of ourselves with our assumptions at this time. The fact is, we don't know what we're observing at this point. I cannot stress that enough," Colonel Bartlett cautioned sternly.

"Come now, Colonel!" argued #10. "If you're insisting that what you're presenting is true and factual, then you cannot pretend the implication isn't obvious. It would be sinful to deny that your little program has discovered proof of what mankind has hungered for since the beginning, and—"

Bartlett cut him off sharply. "Sir, while the evidence *is* true and factual, it is also true that nobody can say for certain what the phenomenon we're experiencing is or what it represents. Also, in the interest of helping all of you maintain an open mind, I will remind you that no one at this table is privy to all of the facts and background of this project. However, I can guarantee that the most well-informed and knowledgeable minds on the project do not know for certain what they're encountering."

#12 turned to #10, smiling kindly. The younger man obviously felt unfairly chastised on some level. "You know, my friend, it occurs to me that if the existence of the Lord—or of man's immortal soul—could be detected, proven, and measured by some gadget"—the avuncular man cheerfully waved a hand in the air—"a simple toy of man, what value would faith hold, then? Faith, perhaps the most precious and truly rare commodity in life, might be rendered completely unnecessary and lose its value. That would be truly ghastly, wouldn't you agree?"

#10 smiled slightly, pondering the man's words.

Dr. Rudolph's face flashed a brief expression that reminded Ramsay of a bride at a reception encountering a prettier guest wearing a prettier dress. He stifled his laugh to a swift inhale through the nostrils.

"Beliefs and mythology aside, Monocle's sensitivity also gives us other strange views. Observe . . ." Rudolph manipulated the remote. An image appeared of a park in winter, snow on the ground, trees quite bare. A few people, bundled against the cold, walked swiftly through the well shoveled paths. Rudolph switched remotes, and the shuffle of filters commenced, settling on an image paler than the original but with the faint aura visible again and the pedestrians' vaporous breath rendered more vividly, down to the swirling fractals of the disturbance in the air. Rudolph adjusted the remote, announcing, "I will pause the image. Watch . . ." All movement on the image halted, the people appearing as meandering blurs through the scene. "We have the paused image, and if I further alter the settings," he continued, "we encounter this. It will help if I zoom in a bit." He manipulated the zoom feature to concentrate on a copse of trees in the distance. As the filters changed, the naked branches on the trees gradually gained the ghostly images of leaves in full maturity. "Pretty fascinating," the scientist proclaimed proudly.

"What on earth?" #2 declared in astonishment, saying out loud what most everyone in the room was feeling. They looked at one another, on the verge of conversation, but then the shrill whine and red light interrupted, and the earpieces stole Bartlett's and Rudolph's attention.

Within several seconds, another alarm sounded in the room. Much less harsh this time, it consisted of four ringing chimes repeated three times. A recording of a calm feminine voice alternated with the chimes, declaring, "Level Four Incident, Active Stations. Level Four Incident, Active Stations."

Bartlett took front and center, one hand up to his earpiece, the other held up in a calming gesture. Randomly, pairs of security guards double-timed past the windows, the shutters staying up this time. The red light extinguished, and the colonel announced to the group: "Nothing to worry about, ladies and gentlemen. This is a common drill for certain minor maintenance issues. I assure you there is no danger. There may not even be any incident per se, but rather, it may be a precautionary measure taken before certain tests and experiments on the schedule."

It sounded plausible, but equally could have been more subterfuge—a thought shared by quite a few members in the room, Ramsay included.

––––––––––––

"So, Mr. President, were we lied to there?" Ramsay asked the commander in chief, who was leaning back in his chair, listening intently as his gaze stayed fixed on a portrait of Thomas Jefferson. The president swiveled his seat to face Ramsay directly.

"Of that, I'm not sure, Craig. You have my word that I'll get back to you on that. There was an incident several levels down, I'm told. Mechanical or accident or something, evidently pretty big. There's a possibility that a couple of lives were even lost. I have yet to get a definitive picture. At this point, I'm not sure that there were fatalities due to the accident or if they all occurred later."

Ramsay pinched the bridge of his nose between his closed eyes to help relieve the tension wracking him. "Did this accident have anything to do with what I witnessed after, Bob?" he asked the president.

"Not sure of that either, Craig, as aggravating as that's going to sound. You can understand that we're still getting bits and pieces of information, not to mention casualty lists. But when we do have a better picture of the sequence of events, I have no intention of leaving you too much out in the cold. I'm sure you'll want some answers for personal reasons. That being said, Dr. Rudolph went on to demonstrate the results of the active feature of his ungodly device, the damned Flashbulb, is that right?" the president prodded.

"Oh yes, the Flashbulb . . . He showed us that. Like a proud father showing his kid's latest crayon masterpiece," Ramsay said sourly.

———————

AFTER ANOTHER BRIEF BREAK WHERE the participants were allowed to stretch and use the restroom but were instructed not to discuss the proceedings, Dr. Rudolph continued. He showed the group several more examples of shadowy figures and unexplainable apparitions showing up on images collected by Monocle, some only appearing briefly for a few frames of the footage. There was footage of what appeared to be a babbling homeless woman, her aura quite distorted, surrounded by a dark cloud that darted around her. Another scene showed a mother holding a child, yet the infant's aura seemed to be cradled by another aura much larger than its mother's. A brief clip taken from what Rudolph claimed to be the inside of a hospice ward revealed a thin cadaverous patient writhing on a hospital bed. When the image was adjusted, her aura was revealed to be large but fuzzy, as if made of television static, as no fewer than six shadowy figures surrounded her. Ramsay felt deeply moved by some of the images and noted that the demonstration seemed to affect everyone in the group deeply in different ways, yet nobody made the first move to open discussion. His head throbbed.

"All of the imagery we've seen so far has been collected using Monocle's passive array. Now to go back to the radar and sonar analogies: our next phase of the program involves an active version. Like the radar signal or the sonar ping, we've constructed an emitter." Rudolph paused here momentarily, seeming to wait for the red light to speak to him, then hearing nothing, continued. "The details of which I'll omit, but which we refer to as the Flashbulb. It can send a pulse through the spectrum, many in fact, emitted like an arpeggio or chord of energy, to put it in musical terms. We can do this omnidirectionally or in a focused manner." This phrase seemed to draw the ire of the red light.

"Anyway, these pulses acting harmonically emanate into the ether, and any returns can be picked up by the passive Monocle array." Before the scientist could continue, Colonel Bartlett jumped in to cut him off.

"Thank you, Dr. Rudolph." The officer took charge again and addressed the room. "And here we get to the crux of the issue, the phenomenon about which we'd like your thoughts." He scanned the faces around the table. "In clip one, we've degraded the image somewhat for security reasons and blurred out several of the components so we could show you people. This is footage of the third test of the Flashbulb apparatus. Dr. Rudolph, clip one please."

All eyes were transfixed on the screen as Rudolph worked the remote. The scene showed footage that looked to have been taken from a high vantage point in a room the size of a small aircraft hangar. There were racks of electronic equipment and banks of computer displays around the periphery, stout cables snaking around the floor anchored by gaffer's tape. A few lab-coated individuals moved about like worker bees, their faces blurred. Indeed, many of the terminals and devices were similarly blurred, as was the clock on one wall. Whatever was in the middle of the room—a tall structure like a nine-foot-tall architectural model of a skyscraper—was completely obscured by a gray smear by the censor. It appeared as if a small tree were being hidden by a vertical oval, vaguely shaped like a surfboard, hiding all but the phalanx of stout cables radiating from the base like roots and disappearing out of frame. A light flashed three times, the source not visible in the image. That seemed to be a signal for the technicians to move swiftly out of the room. When the room looked to be clear of people, a small counter at the lower right corner of the screen started ticking over much faster than before.

"We'll jump ahead several minutes here," Colonel Bartlett explained. "Please keep watching." *After the unbelievable things we've been already shown, who here could look away?* thought Ramsay. His headache was quickly building to a migraine. He could feel the beginnings of accompanying nausea.

After several seconds, the counter on the video returned to its previous rate, prompting Bartlett to announce, "Here."

There were several flashes on the image, one or two bright enough to temporarily wash the image out on the screen, with the exception of the tall gray oval, obviously added later. After another bright flash, there was a brief pause before three shadowy masses drifted swiftly into frame. Two appeared to be roughly the shape of the dark auras they'd witnessed earlier, the third a black amorphous cloud that swirled and darted around the censored structure. It jetted about in fits and starts, sometimes obscured by the gray censorship shape, moving much quicker than the other two shapes. Suddenly, the image went completely dark, the gray oval remaining alone on the screen before snapping off.

"That, ladies and gentlemen, wasn't the end of the clip. That's where the monitoring system and telemetry failed for a brief period," the colonel narrated, still watching the black screen. Eventually, the screen showed static and distortion for several seconds, the counter and gray oval reappearing before the scene gradually came back on as before, with the addition of technicians with blurred faces who were rushing about chaotically. Light smoke swirled around the top of the image, and two technicians milled about carrying fire extinguishers at the ready, while others stood in front of monitors, some screens dark and others winking back to life. Several operators talked animatedly into telephone handsets.

"Colonel, do you have a cause for the—" #7 started to ask.

"Unknown at this time and possibly out of the scope of this discussion," Bartlett snapped before the question could finish, his harsh replies doing nothing to ease the almost unbearable tension in the room. "Dr. Rudolph, proceed to clip number two, please." The scientist obediently worked the remote. "Flashbulb test seventeen, different vantage point," Bartlett announced.

Headache or no, Ramsay's analytical curiosity spurred him to hazard the colonel's wrath. "Colonel Bartlett, are the anomalies detectable on single cameras or all of them?" Ramsay waited for the stinging rebuke that didn't come, though he was ready to remind the Air Force officer with all courtesy to remember just who Ramsay was. Instead, the red light on the ceiling appeared to direct Bartlett to answer once the whine ceased:

"I can confirm that the phenomenon is corroborated by multiple sources from multiple vantages, and no system glitches have as yet been found. Dr. Rudolph . . ."

The scientist with the remote hit play. The image on the screen was from a lower angle and direction, with the central structure and many items of equipment censored as before. A few technicians in lab coats looked to be adjusting settings while standing at control panels. Their tasks complete, they all walked swiftly out of view. Then came the three flashes, their source a light high on the wall visible from this different angle.

Once more, the counter on the screen sped up crazily for a few moments before returning to its original rhythm. The image stuttered for second, looking as if the filters were changing. Power surges and fluctuations in the equipment, now rendered visible, seemed to morph animatedly, and eventually, several shadowy auras began to drift aimlessly through the scene. A series of bright flashes that again briefly washed out the image blinked in irregular succession, and this time, when the picture returned with any clarity, the shadows stood still for a moment, some fading slightly, before they all started moving again, now drifting toward the obscured structure in the center of the room. Then the screen went dark, replaced with the phrase *SIGNAL INTER-RUPTION* before it, too, faded to black.

"Looks like you've gotten someone's attention!" #7 stated ominously.

Colonel Bartlett didn't jump on the comment this time as it hung in the air like cigarette smoke. Bartlett cleared his throat to speak. "We can as yet only speculate as to what we're detecting on the array, and the investigation is still in the preliminary phases. Finally, there's this . . . Clip three, please, Doctor," the colonel instructed the scientist, whose upper lip now appeared to be sweating. Rudolph fingered the remote. "Flashbulb test number thirty-two, same vantage point," Bartlett announced.

The clip started just as the last—the fiddling technicians with blurred faces working on the fuzzy images of equipment and monitors, the tall structure obscured by the vertical gray oval. Just as before, the three flashing lights, the personnel clearing the room, and the counter speeding up wildly for several seconds. When the counter resumed its previous rate, the image again stuttered as if going through a series of filter changes, like an optometrist dialing through different powers during a visual exam. When the image settled on one filter, there again were a few shadowy auras drifting through the scene—not as many as the last clip, but in this version, one or two seemed to drift into view by passing through solid objects, one blowing into the frame right out of a bank of electronic equipment. Again came the series of dazzling flashes that temporarily washed out the picture, and when some clarity had been recovered, the shadowy auras seemed to be temporarily transfixed. This time, there was what appeared to be a small nimbus cloud of unreal black pulsing just to one side of the obscured structure in the middle of the room. It started to grow slowly before violently exploding into a mass of blackness that seemed to strike the screen and the viewers as if it had substance.

The indescribable black flash stabbed Ramsay's eyes, building the pressure in his head as if to make his skull explode. He heard a sharp groan of pain escape his mouth as his hands went reflexively to his head, shielding his eyes from the terrible black image. It caused pain—*real* pain—and left a faint pink-and-green static in his visual sense while Ramsay's eyes were clamped tightly shut. And something else, something terrible . . .

Ramsay smelled vomit before he heard the commotion around the table and listened to the cries and moans for several seconds before he could dare to open his smarting eyes. #11 had pushed partially back from the table, head down, body convulsing as she retched uncontrollably between her feet. Several members held their heads in their hands in much the same way Ramsay had. #2 stared in horror while covering his mouth agape with shock, pointing at the now blank screen. Ramsay wanted to shut his eyes, but the image behind his eyelids was more unbearable than the misery around him. Tears streamed down the cheeks of three or four of the participants, and un-stifled sobs were heard. Bartlett and Rudolph stood with their eyes shut, the scientist with one arm steadying himself on the wall, Bartlett leaning with his hands on the table as if to hold himself upright. Ramsay instantly realized that they'd both known better than to look at the screen at the end. He felt a tightness in his chest and a searing pain in his lungs. It was difficult to inhale.

"What did you see?" asked #12 softly, his calm voice a life preserver in an ocean of wretched chaos.

"Nothing," Ramsay croaked, it being painful to talk.

That had been a lie. Ramsay knew damn well what he saw behind his closed eyes. The ugly terrifying figure of Harry the Hat.

Over twenty years ago, when Ramsay's son, Adam, had been only four, he'd gone through an awful period of being terrorized by nightmares. Most kids do, Ramsay had told himself, but the child's life was being upended by the torment he was suffering in his dreams. The poor child would torture himself in attempt to keep from falling asleep. Ramsay and his wife often acquiesced and allowed him to sleep in between them. Still, the agonized child would wake up shrieking, his convulsing little body sweaty and clammy, his heart racing alarmingly. Ramsay and his wife, unable help their child grow out of this unpleasant phase, eventually turned to an eminent child psychologist, desperate for help.

After several agonizing sessions with the doctor, Adam finally opened up and shared his night terrors—bad dreams with a foul mean monster the child later named Harry the Hat, who would torment the helpless child with grotesque threats and unbearably frightening imagery. When the boy was eventually coaxed into drawing his impression of the character, Adam produced a scribble of an ugly ghoul with dark rings around his eyes, scraggly black hair, a vicious gaping mouth full of pointed teeth, wearing some sort of top hat and dark frock coat, prompting the moniker.

Ramsay, in an effort to help his child conquer his dark nighttime fear, also began drawing a version of Harry the Hat, this time a small silly pathetic character. He told Adam fanciful stories in which Harry the Hat would try to do bad things and cause mischief, only to be thwarted by Adam's bravery. This went on for some weeks before the nightmares became fewer and further between, the child eventually outgrowing the phase. Whether or not this was due to the efforts of Ramsay and his wife, aided by the professional, or just through natural maturation as Adam grew, Ramsay didn't know. In fact, he often thought that Adam had lost all memory of the terrible episode.

After the black explosion struck his consciousness, the terrible image burned into Ramsay's mind, one of raw fear, malice, and evil, and he could only describe it to himself as Harry the Hat. And in that instance, Ramsay lived a hundred years of the child's fear and helplessness, his every nerve scraped raw with real unimaginable terror.

"Nothing," he repeated to the older gentleman. "It just pushed my headache over the edge."

"Ladies and gentlemen," Bartlett began, attempting to regain control and ignoring the misery happening around the room. "I think before we continue, we'd better—"

A ground-shaking rumble, like a nearby rocket launch, shook the facility. A brash deafening alarm wailed through the loudspeakers, accompanied by an earsplitting announcement of, "Emergency! Evacuate Immediately! Emergency! Evacuate Immediately!"

"Shit!" Bartlett cried before taking charge. The room—indeed the entire complex—erupted in chaos. "Everybody out now! Now! Now!" the colonel shouted over the confusion, shepherding everyone out of the room as fast as possible.

Ramsay tried to dash toward the door but stumbled and fell over the chair #6 had sent flying as he, too, darted for safety. He fell heavily against the floor and wall, cracking his elbow painfully.

"Follow the lights, people! Follow the lights!" Bartlett instructed forcefully as other panicked participants accidentally kicked and trampled Ramsay, who writhed on the floor as they exited. He was helped to his feet by #12, who ushered him gently to the corridor, now filled with smoke and running personnel. Yellow safety lights in the baseboards pulsed in the direction of the exit like runway lights.

"To the right, my friend, to the right. Quickly!" #12 encouraged, his hand on Ramsay's shoulder. Klaxons blared, and Ramsay was jostled heavily by soldiers and technicians who moved much quicker. Ramsay lost track of #12, who seemed to be the last one out of the conference room with the exception of Colonel Bartlett. The choking smoke made Ramsay cough harshly as he followed the pulsing yellow lights through corridors, some marked with placards reading *NON-SOLO OCCUPANCY ONLY - DEADLY FORCE AUTHORIZED.*

He eventually moved with the chaotic mass of evacuees into the cavernous room where the buses were parked idling under flashing red emergency lights, soldiers packing the civilians on board swiftly as the military personnel sprinted in two lines down the sides of the exit tunnel. The choking Ramsay, his eyes smarting from the smoke, was maneuvered to the open door of a waiting bus, where a security sergeant pushed everyone aboard. Ramsay strained his eyes to see if the older man had made it out to safety, but before he could focus, he was firmly manhandled up the stairs of the bus.

As the coaches began to pull out down the large entrance tunnel, the door to the one Ramsay found himself on snapped shut and lurched into motion. It was chaos on the bus, with people coughing and crying out in shock and pain, the careening bus throwing the standees on top of those who'd collapsed into the seats. Ramsay held his throbbing elbow as he leaned on one of the seat backs, trying not to fall onto those seated. Up ahead, he could see a bright half circle of daylight as they approached the entrance to the underground facility, weaving between the two lines of sprinting soldiers. There was palpable relief among the passengers as the bus exited the tunnel into harsh natural light, hurtling past gathered throngs of military evacuees on either side of the road. The bus showed no sign of slowing or stopping, when a woman toward the back exclaimed, "Oh my God!" drawing everyone's attention to the rear window.

Dense black smoke billowed from the tunnel, withering the scrub that grew on the mountainside above. A blinding flash, followed by a wall of flame, shot out of the tunnel, followed seconds later by a tremor in the ground that caused the bus to swerve violently from side to side. The sound of the explosion followed, raising the dust from the ground and deafening the occupants of the bus for a moment. The cacophony of cries continued as the bus, one of at least seven in the convoy, hurtled through the checkpoints and double security fence of what appeared to be the rear entrance of an Air Force base.

Before the stunned Ramsay could collect his bearings, he found himself sitting on a triage gurney, a muscular African American medic checking his pupils with a flashlight and addressing him by name. "Dr. Ramsay," the medic asked firmly, "do you know where you are?"

Ramsay had to chuckle grimly with gallows humor. "Of course I don't, you nitwit! Read the NDA!" Ramsay croaked, giving the medic a brief lopsided grin.

———————

THE WHITE HOUSE STEWARD FRESHENED their glasses as Ramsay and the president sat silently. Several seconds after the door had shut and they were again alone, the president leaned forward and spoke.

"Craig, I cannot tell you how grateful I am that you're back in one piece. When the casualty list came in, my heart about stopped."

"What do we know so far, may I ask?" Ramsay asked.

"At least two dozen confirmed dead, dammit. Bartlett among them. Went down with the ship. Rudolph is still MIA, but things aren't looking good. As far as your group goes, they're mostly fine, with the exception of Dr. Nakamura's broken wrist and Dr. Wilson's wrenched knee. General Phipps, Mr. Howlett, and Judge Campbell all got some cuts and bruises, more minor than yours."

"Bob, I have to ask . . . I don't know who #12 was, but please tell me the old man made it out okay."

The president held Ramsay's gaze for some time before speaking. "About that, Craig," the president began, clearing his throat, "one of the more troubling things about this whole mess—I don't know how to broach this . . . There were only eleven individuals invited to that conference. There was no #12 . . ."

Bullshit, Ramsay wanted to say, but he kept that to himself.

THE ADDICTIVE SOUNDS
OF CANNIBAL SALAD

The bands got loyalty from teenagers that was normally only seen given to a nation in wartime or faith under persecution. Arena stoner rock and roll was the neighborhood tribe, although metalheads and punks were welcome as long as they behaved. The kids didn't know that country fans under sixty years old even existed. If you went to a party and two groups of teenagers came into contact, the band logos worn under their flannel shirts were a strong early indicator of possible violence later.

Rory's awakening to his favorite band was a respectable one: listening to his older brother's copy of perhaps their most influential album, their sound straddling the subgenres of both progressive rock and psychedelia. In fact, though, what drew Rory to it was the iconic cover of the light beam hitting a prism and splitting into the spectrum. The image was a sigil among true fans, predating the crossed marching hammers of their magnum opus released six years later. Some guy in the neighborhood even had the prism image painted on his van. It was beautiful.

Rory read the magazine articles and the books and collected all of their albums, always checking the import bin for obscure foreign pressings and older cutouts. There were still a few good record stores nearby, as well as the chains in the mall, but Rory was lucky enough to live less than a mile from the music and rare record shop to which many people traveled long distances to leave their money. The store was great.

It had been a large grocery and hardware store back in the old days, and the storefront and first third of the shop was a traditional music store, selling sheet music, guitar strings, reeds for the school bands, double reeds for the pipe bands, and a respectable line of good-quality beginner instruments, from drums and guitars to saxophones and French horns. Through a hallway that passed by an office, one passed into an enormous collection of racks and shelves containing tens of thousands of records, albums, 78s, 45s, and the recently introduced compact discs. The wooden floor creaked with every footstep, and under the hum of the fluorescent lights, the faint musty smell of basement and second-hand treasure hung in the air as if wafted by a senser. And after a bike ride on the hot pavement on a summer afternoon, there were few things as fine as standing in the cool air conditioning flipping through the stacks of records looking for undiscovered treasure. The music shop had been in operation since the fifties. The record department was added in the midsixties, and since then, the original proprietors had passed the business on to their two easygoing sons. One focused on the front of the shop and the other the back, so Rory had more dealings with the hippier one who handled the records.

If rare and obscure records were your thing, there were also the huge swap meets that happened a few times each year, usually in the conference rooms of some local chain hotel. Those could draw in vendors from several states away. These were incredible places to find hard-to-find pressings and the first place Rory had heard the term *Cannibal Salad*. He'd heard one collector ask one of the larger vendors if he had any Cannibal Salad behind the table. Rory had just assumed that the collector was looking to buy drugs. The vendor replied that he'd never heard of that band, but upon reading the scrap of paper the collector handed over, invited the customer behind the table. Had to be drugs, Rory was sure.

There were some bootleg records that you'd only find if you asked a vendor that trusted you. There were some really high-quality recordings of concerts floating about and records cut from studio masters of outtakes and alternate versions that didn't make it onto the commercial albums. Naturally, the publishing companies who owned the rights to the music but didn't see a dime out of the studio acetate pressings and illegally cut vinyl had a vested interest in eradicating the clandestine trade and often sent representatives to root out the pirated material. This material was the gold a true fan was always hoping to strike. Often, these bootleg albums were listed under obscure names the famous bands had before hitting it big, so you also had to look for albums by the High Numbers, the Quarrymen, the Warlocks, or in Rory's case, the Abdabs, for the obscure pieces one desired.

Rory had nearly forgotten the Cannibal Salad exchange when he next heard the term on a cassette recording of an interview two members of the band had given on one of the illegal pirate radio stations that were so important to rock music in Britain and Europe for over a decade. Toward the end, the interview got a bit acrimonious as the prickly DJ and the moody guitarist known for bending the notes perfectly started to butt heads over some dumb point and the guitarist shut the DJ down sharply, refusing to continue the matter. That's when the DJ—on his last broadcast from the pirate station, as it turns out—asked the musicians if they had ever recorded any Cannibal Salad. The guitarist's reply was, "We're done here. Cheers!" The recording ended with the DJ asking the departing rock stars if they knew who Rabbi Shazaam and Hambone were, and did they deny recording under those names?

It could have just been bizarre English radio theater, or it could have been a clue to something greater. Rory was determined to find out. He replayed the banter three times to make sure he was hearing it correctly, then wrote *Rabbi Shazaam and Hambone* on the back of a slip of paper with his class schedule that was in his wallet way past its original usefulness. He made a mental note to ask the guy at the music store what the hell *Cannibal Salad* meant.

In fact, Cannibal Salad was the most underground of all music genres. For some time, some of the top musicians in the industry had been doing wild collaborations in private, pushing the boundaries of music experimentally. It started in the late sixties, when four of the top guitarists from the Second British Invasion wave got together with a marimba player, a well-known French chanteuse, and a respected Caribbean steel drum quartet and recorded a twenty-two-minute mini opera based on the life of a German serial killer from the twenties. The result was never to be released because of the conflicting contractual obligations of the artists involved but was of such dynamic beauty of sound that bootlegged reel-to-reel recordings secretly circulated among some of the most open-minded musicians.

This secret genre gained the name Cannibal Salad from this first sonic outing, and soon, other daring musicians were furtively making recordings and collaborations that would shock their most loyal fans. Before there was punk and grunge, there was Cannibal Salad. Cannibal Salad out-progressed prog rock, out-jazzed jazz, and made heavy metal seem only fit for elevators and commercials. Because the publishing houses and management companies weren't able to make any money on these endeavors, Cannibal Salad would never officially see the light of day. In the industry, it was outlaw stuff.

Among true musicians in the know, it wasn't how many platinum albums one sold or how many arenas one sold out, but on the merits of one's Cannibal Salad compositions and experiments that marked one as a true genius. Furthering the mystique was the tremendous secrecy surrounding the subgenre—originally a fire lit out of legal necessity but since hyper-oxidized by the allure of a rock and roll secret society, known only to a few inside the business and damn fewer outside. Its adherents acted as if blood-oath-bound to secrecy.

As Rory was to find out just a few weeks later, one of those adherents was Jackie, the guy at the music store.

It was on an afternoon in autumn on a day off from his part-time job that Rory wandered into the music store on his way home from school. Jackie was in and happy to talk about the merits of Rory's favorite band before and after the departure of their original composer, an iconic victim of his own mental issues and eventual acid casualty.

"Hey, that reminds me," Rory asked Jackie, "ever hear of Cannibal Salad?"

"Nope. What is it, a punk band? They local? Local bands are over there," Jackie replied, gesturing with an old Fats Waller record.

"Never heard of it?"

"Nope," Jackie replied.

Rory fished the piece of paper out of his wallet. "Ever hear of Rabbi Shazaam and Hambone?" he asked the proprietor, just in case.

Jackie paused and regarded Rory closely. "Where'd you hear that, kid?"

"Bootleg of an interview from pirate radio," Rory said, trying to sound as in the know as possible.

"Radio Iona?"

"Yeah, that's it."

"Come back on Saturday afternoon, if you can. One o'clock-ish. And bring money!" he said with a laugh, returning to his work.

———

THERE WERE FOUR DOORS IN the music store that were marked *Employees Only*. On Saturday afternoon, Jackie led Rory through the one closest to the one marked *Toilet* and down a creaking wooden staircase to a large room in the basement with exposed rafters and a Persian carpet on the cement floor. The walls were a treasure trove of black light posters, and the chairs and couches were well worn and tatty. Down here, the musty basement waft was augmented by the musky aroma of south-of-the-border agriculture. A huge redheaded brute Rory recognized as a neighborhood fellow that had graduated from the same high school Rory currently attended a few years earlier sat talking to a thin smiling man in a rumpled suit with bloodshot eyes and a voice raspy from cigarettes.

"Who's this?" the smiling older man asked Jackie.

"Tell them what you're looking for," Jackie prodded Rory.

"I'm looking for Cannibal Salad. Rabbi Shazaam and Hambone," Rory said to the amused men.

"Doesn't exist!" said the big fellow, squinting his blue eyes.

"Someone's pulling your leg, kid. Where you hear that stuff?" the older man said, sounding like he was gargling asphalt.

"Pirate radio interview. Heard a tape of it," Rory answered.

"We're done here. Cheers!" the ginger said in a passable imitation of the famous musician who'd said it on the tape. Jackie and the older man laughed. Evidently, they'd all heard it.

"Kid, you're about to have your mind blown!" the old man rasped. "What's your name?"

"Rory."

"Rory, I'm Walt. This is Shock O'Kelly," he said, hooking his thumb at the big man, who nodded at him.

"Hope you brought money, Rory," Jackie said pleasantly. "First taste is free . . ." which brought chuckles from the other two.

"Ain't that right!" Walt said. "Probably be cheaper to go with heroin! Turn back, kid! Turn back now!" He cackled.

"Sit down here. You're going to get an eduma-cation," Jackie said, motioning toward a comfortable rocking easy chair. The sound system in the room was on a rack just behind it. Rory was handed a high-quality set of headphones, thickly padded with independent volume controls.

"Okay, so *Rabbi* Shazaam and Hambone were one of the acts on this album here. It's kinda a compilation album, and it's a really good place to start. There's about a half dozen collaborations on this one. Check this shit out." Jackie handed the album to Rory. It was a plain ivory jacket with crudely printed titles on it. The front merely stated the album title, *Satan, Beelzebub, Lucifer, and Gladys, Live at the Club Foote*, while the back listed song titles attributed to assumed names, including J. Arthur Plaguemuffin, Giggles Hitler, and Sunny Gertrude, the Hamster of Death.

"Check out the record," Jackie said.

Rory pulled out the paper sleeve and carefully slid the disc out a few inches. It was pressed on heavy custard-yellow vinyl, the bright pink label displaying only the image of a hand flipping the bird on the first side and a similar image of the same hand giving the up-yours two-finger gesture on the other. Jackie took the disc from him and placed it on a top-of-the-line Bang & Olufsen system with racks of components and a strobe-timed turntable.

"Getting a beer!" Shock said, ducking under the ductwork to retrieve cans from an ancient refrigerator in the corner.

"How old are you?" Jackie asked.

"Seventeen," Rory answered, knowing that Jackie was aware he was still in school.

"Ah, not old enough to drink. Pity."

The huge fellow came back with four cans anyway.

"You go ahead and listen to the headphones. We'll have it on in the background, so if you want to say something to us, don't scream like an idiot. We can hear you fine." Rory put the heavy headphones on. "And away we go!" Jackie said, gently easing the needle into the custard-yellow groove.

It was sonic fireworks inside of Rory's head.

He recognized some of the musicians from just their sound. Some of the most hair-raising examples of virtuoso playing combined with thought-provoking and intelligent lyrics laid on with a tectonic clash of styles and arrangements using instruments from around the globe, strange and familiar. Cannibal Salad was the some of the most satisfying music ever conceived. Rory almost cried in front of those strangers.

At the end of side one—or at least the side with the bird on it—Rory took off the headphones like he was exiting the baptismal font.

"Whaddaya think, kid? Dig the whorl of those grooves?" Walt wheezed.

Rory took a gulp of beer while Shock and Jackie exchanged an amused glance.

"My God, that was excellent!" Rory declared. "That was the best stuff I've EVER heard!" He laughed with joy at the aural rush.

"Well, son of a bitch! Give it time. It grows on you," Shock said, laughing, while Walt coughed and cackled away.

"You haven't heard the other side yet. 'Ska Tissue' is going to knock your socks off," Jackie teased.

"I don't get it. Why is this a secret?" Rory asked.

"More fun this way!" Jackie said. "But we take it seriously. If I think anyone is passing this stuff around, you're barred from the shop, got it? From here on out, you keep your trap shut, deal?"

His silence would be a pittance to pay for those glorious sounds, he decided.

Unfortunately, Walt was right; heroin would have been cheaper. He had to have *Live at the Club Foote*, which unfortunately was about three times the cost of the most popular albums out at the time. Later that afternoon, he biked home and back to raid the rest of the cash he had stashed in his sock drawer. Jackie had offered him a deal on that record and two more sublime recordings:

Unravel Your Cardigan and Crimea River was an ambitious three-disc musical retelling of the Battle of Balaclava in 1854, composed by a trio of the most well-respected bass players in rock and roll, playing along with, among others, perhaps *the* master Romanian pan flutist, a mariachi orchestra, and a choir of Tuvan throat singers. The recording was noted for its complex rhythms, the historical accuracy of its lyrics, and its deep vibrating low end that had been noticed to relieve constipation in some listeners. It was considered to be one of the pillars of fine Cannibal Salad works.

Sexual Harassment Suit and Tie was a more mellow work from the late seventies, performed by Smokey Laphroaig and the Loch Pickers, a tribute to Robert Burns, with flamenco guitar and didgeridoo complementing the bagpipes, banjos, and array of Moog synthesizers. More classical than klezmer, though still both, it was known among the community for its beautiful musical passages and the fact that no fewer than four of the contributing musicians died within a year of its recording, one of them drowning while behind the wheel of a Rolls-Royce Corniche at the bottom of the swimming pool of a five-star hotel in Lake Tahoe.

Just those three albums cost Rory all his cash on hand, plus a penny from the sidewalk. Jackie had insisted on the penny. He claimed that that way, he wasn't selling the underground records; he was trading them for a numismatic collectible plus the cash difference. If there had been a receipt, Rory was sure Jackie would have made him eat it just to be safe.

———

THAT WAS OVER TWO YEARS ago now. Home from college, Rory was at a record swap out in the suburbs. They seemed to be getting smaller every time. Jackie was there at a dealer's table, and he ran into Walt as well. Rory picked up a video recording of the bass player from his favorite band from his last tour after he left the group, but not much else. What he was really looking for were Volumes III and IV of the five-part opus *Sepia Swirls in the Porcelain Vortex*, probably the most ambitious Cannibal Salad project ever, a rock opera depicting the many lives of a reincarnated apple who gets eaten and digested by ten of the most influential mathematicians in the history of science. The rhythm of each piece of music was derived in part from some principle attributed to the subject, and nearly eighty of rock and roll's most famous and accomplished musicians contributed. Volume IV was a particular bitch to find, but the transition from Gauss to Ramanujan played on the glass organ, cello, and taiko drums was reported to be completely worth the effort.

Unfortunately for Rory's ears and fortunately for his finances, he wouldn't be finding either one at this swap meet. It was slim pickings at this one, and it wasn't even memorable, save for the one exchange he had with a preppy-looking guy going through the stacks of CDs next to the rack of imports Rory was combing through. They shared some comments about the recent auction of the Strat that Jimi used to play "The Star-Spangled Banner" and the lineup at the Knebworth Festival. Then at one point, the preppy guy asked him, "Ever hear of something called Cannibal Salad?"

"Never heard of it," Rory answered a little too quickly.

The vendor behind the table gave Rory a respectful nod.

TRIBUTE

Lissa plugged in the microphone and turned the sound system on. She'd brought her best guitar, a beautiful Martin, and tuned it in the dark church, the acoustics of the room and instrument seemingly made for each other. She'd barely slept but showed up extra early to ensure that everything was just right for the last time she'd play that song.

She strummed the jauntier version like the one recorded by the big Hawaiian fellow on the ukulele. Gary loved that version. The well-crafted guitar rang through the barely lit space.

It wasn't a bad song, but she hated it—screw the fact that it was a classic. She'd hated the movie as a kid so much that she wasn't done hating it as an adult. Just the fact that the mean old woman threatens to have her dog destroyed was traumatic enough to see, but learning that the authorities might actually kill someone's dog on the testimony of a mean old bitch was worse. Lissa could never see the charming fantasy angle of a house getting destroyed by a tornado, the creepy preternatural "friends" she made along the way, or violent flying monkeys for that matter either. Throw in a Technicolor witch and drunken munchkins, and you had a two-hour nightmare.

She still hated the movie after having to read the book in high school and learning that it was actually an allegory about fiscal policy or some equally dry bit of trivia, yet she watched it at least twice every year. Her brother, Gary, insisted on it. It was his favorite. Lissa tried to get him to read the book too, but he had no interest. If Gary read any book, it was about serial killers or Hollywood scandals. The movie couldn't be topped for him.

Gary was five years older than Lissa and a tremendous big brother. Lissa and Gary were close out of necessity. There was no way they could have survived being latchkey kids stuck in the middle of their parent's acrimonious relationship without each other. Their mother was crazy, no doubt about that, but only psychologically dangerous. Lissa's mother knew that she'd deserved much better than the life, husbands, and children fate had given her and could do little to hide her displeasure.

Their father, mostly absent, was less crazy but self-centered and a bit of a narcissist. An attractive athletic man, he had little time for Gary, especially as he grew into a chubbier, introverted, nerdy, effeminate version of himself. Gary seemed to be a disappointment for the vain man. And if Gary was a disappointment and difficult for their father to deal with, Lissa was maybe a thornier issue. Despite what her birth certificate said, Lissa's brown eyes, jet-black hair, and typical Mediterranean features settled any question as to their mother's fidelity. Lissa wasn't very old before she'd already gotten an inkling that her appearance in the family heralded the end of her parent's marriage, not that it was any major loss.

Gary and Lissa took refuge from a stormy homelife mainly through the radio and the VCR. After Gary got a job mopping floors and shoveling French fries into paper cartons, at least three times a week they'd be up at the video store renting science fiction and horror movies, which their mother despised, and occasionally old musicals, which she didn't. But she was disappointed that it was her teenage son bringing home the Rodgers and Hammerstein fare. Gary loved horror—the lower the budget, the better. Right when he left high school, he started helping plan and build the Halloween spook houses up at the park every year. That might have been his calling, instead of ordering frozen burgers and closing out cash registers.

Gary had always looked out for his little sister; in fact, he was quick to defend any outsider or outcast. With his gentle nature and general awkwardness, he would have been an easy target himself, save for his size and his ability to make friends among the social pariahs, who surprisingly could be marshaled into action if one of their numbers were threatened. Honor among dweebs, maybe.

It was Gary that started calling her Lissa, since she hated being called Mel. It was Gary that convinced their mother to let Lissa give up the piano and let her take guitar lessons, and that was no small battle. People commented on Lissa's long fingers even when she was small and would suggest she should study piano, and Lissa's mother was determined to make a classical pianist out of her. Lissa enjoyed music, enjoyed playing, but never was the prodigy her mother would have preferred. When she was twelve, her mother found a new tutor, a stern old bitch whose method of motivation was a sharp slap on the wrist with a wooden paint stirrer. After two sessions, Lissa didn't return. That put their mother in a vile mood for quite a while, and whenever she came upon Lissa listening to the radio, she'd snap it off angrily and declare, "Since you don't like good music!"

Around this time, sick of these outbursts, Gary started telling his mother about a co-worker at his fast-food job that was taking classical guitar lessons up at the music store—how this kid was applying for scholarships to study music at some university and how far he was going to go. Over the course of a few weeks, Gary had laid it on thick enough that their mother finally relented. It was much more than a minor victory for Lissa. It did cost her, however, as Gary made her play "Somewhere Over the Rainbow" for him. She vowed it would be the last time she played it.

To Lissa's knowledge, Gary had never had a boyfriend, but he didn't come off as straight. He had a softness about him that was unmanly and a theatricality to his manner and gestures to match. He did have several girlfriends, all either over or underweight and all social outcasts themselves, asexual and neurotic. Their mom didn't care for them either. She didn't like his weird friends, his apparent lack of ambition, his juvenile sense of humor, or the fact that he smoked, although never in the house. For all Lissa knew, she and Gary disappointed the bitter woman to death.

With Gary to thank, Lissa took to the guitar like a zealot. One of the middle-aged hippies that owned the music store gave guitar lessons and on seeing Lissa's aptitude and enthusiasm, made their mother a very good deal on a thirdhand Ovation that he'd restored for much less than it was worth. With the years of piano practice she'd already put in, she was an eager and advanced pupil, if a little shy about playing for strangers. The music store became a safe haven for her—and an ideal place of employment during her last years of high school and summers home from college.

But a few years before she started working at the music store, she had an experience so profound as to set the course of her life in stone.

It was a Saturday, and their mother insisted that their father, whom she only referred to as "the Cheap Dutchman" these days, spend some time with them. By this time, their father had remarried, this time to the daughter of the owner of tile-and-countertop outlet where he'd gotten a job as sales manager. It was her second marriage, and Lissa's father had moved in with her and her two kids, both slightly younger than Lissa and both spoiled by moderate wealth and indulgence. They had no interest in their stepfather's kids from some shabby neighborhood who appeared to be losers by their standards. Nobody would have admitted any relationship other than purely accidental. They had a wonderful large house in a much more affluent suburb, with an in-ground pool that Lissa and Gary couldn't use and game room in the basement that was too loud for Lissa and Gary to play in. However, in the vast garage, the older one had an electric guitar with a real amplifier. Lissa asked him if he played.

He was taking lessons, was the answer, though he thought he was going to switch to drums. Lissa asked him to play a little, to see what it sounded like. Sensing an opportunity go get one of the losers in trouble, he let her play it.

It was a new experience, hearing the notes come through the amplifier, and the guitar badly needed tuning, but she could get it pretty close by ear. Then she placed her three fingers to make a D chord and strummed. Her notes traveled from the strings to the amplifier to her spine. It made her laugh.

"Do it again!" her dad's stepson said, cranking the volume at just the right time without her realizing it, so loud it would guarantee an angry outburst from his mother toward the unwelcome visitor. It worked.

But that chord, a sound of her own making, blocking out everything else, changed her. She could feel the legs of her corduroy slacks vibrating against her skin, the sound traveling from the soles of her feet to the follicles on her scalp. Her fingers went straight to an F chord, and she strummed again, changing to a C, then to a B flat, the power of the volume making her feel like a laughing giant. She couldn't help but grin, even as her dad's wife bellowed and railed at her. It was a glorious day. For the first time ever, *something* made sense.

It was one of the sticking points that led to seeing their dad less frequently. His wife didn't want Gary and Lissa over, and that was fine with Gary and Lissa. Whenever their mother insisted that the Cheap Dutchman see his children, their dad would pick them up and drop them off at the movies, which made a fine day out for everyone. That only lasted for a while though, since Gary left high school as soon as he had enough credits and spent most of his time either working slinging burgers or hanging with his weird friends. After that, if Lissa made the excuse that she was too busy with schoolwork, that seemed to leave them both relieved at not having to face the lack of relationship.

Lissa was in high school when Gary moved out. The same burger chain offered him an assistant manager position at another location, and he found a garden apartment that he shared with two of his misfit girlfriends not far from there. That neighborhood was changing, and the local crime statistics were rising quickly, but it was a fun place to hang out and get away from home for a bit. Gary took the bus to work. He'd gotten his license but was a nervous and inept driver, so he left driving to others. After Lissa got her license, she could finagle the car out of her mother by using the excuse to do the shopping for her and, while she was at it, swinging by and picking up Gary to take him too. They'd cruise around, sometimes with one or both of his housemates but sometimes just the two of them, and Gary would make her drive past houses that had hosted sensational murders, haunted buildings, and fly past the cemetery on Archer looking for the elusive Resurrection Mary. Gary had a head full of the local lore of hauntings and ritual sacrifice. He should have been a tour guide, as long as it didn't interfere with his haunted house creation duties. Sometimes, he'd ask Lissa to bring her guitar and play for them at the apartment. She was everybody's kid sister there.

In the late winter of Lissa's sophomore year, Gary inexplicably quit cigarettes, which made him even more nervous and quite a bit chubbier despite working longer hours. He'd smoke one offered by one of his harem, but he stopped buying them. Lissa tried to give him as much encouragement as she could, glad that he was looking after his health, but the real reason for his temporary foray into clean living became apparent on the Thursday afternoon in May when Lissa came home to a Gibson Melody Maker guitar just like the most badass woman in rock played and a Fender amplifier. Her mom and Gary were both at work, and Lissa's book bag was still on the floor where she'd dropped it when her mother came home. Except for calling Gary at work to thank him, she'd spent all afternoon playing *loud*.

When she talked to Gary on the phone to tell him that she loved him, he told her that the guitar came with a price. It only took Lissa a beat to figure out what the price was.

For a Gibson, she could make an exception and play it again, if only just the once. The handful of square pegs at Gary's apartment made her play it twice though.

That was the Gibson she played at the school talent show two years in a row. It was the Gibson she played in her first college band, the first time they passed the hat and actually went home a few dollars richer than when they'd arrived. Her scholarships meant she could easily get by on the money she made giving guitar lessons and tutoring math.

Their mother's cancer took her quickly, and there was much left unsaid between her and her children, but as bad as it made them both feel, the world seemed less turbulent without her.

Gary had moved a couple of times by then, one of his housemates replaced with another one just as awkward. Lissa listened to Gary's phone calls and offhand references to armed robberies and casual violence and was worried for him, but as nervous as he was, he wasn't timid or a worrier. He was excited to hear about her life, finishing up school and playing in the band and playing solo at folky cafés around campus. He was proud when she graduated, thrilled at the great IT job she'd landed, and was her most enthusiastic supporter when he came to any of her performances, whether there were three or seventy people in attendance.

And now she was making the chords of the song she dreaded to play for the last time.

The doctors said that he never regained consciousness after the beating and was dead within six hours. According to the police, the savage bastards that jumped him had robbed him of all eighteen dollars he had on him at the time. The news said that the three youths, one of whom was only sixteen, had had lengthy arrest records already.

She was warming up her best guitar to play it one last time for him, the guitar she'd bought with her second check from the IT job he was so proud of her for landing. She'd contemplated bringing the beloved Gibson, but the Martin suited the venue and the song much better.

And as long as this was the last time she was going to play it, she owed it to her brother to make it as perfect as possible.

No matter how much she disliked the song, she gave it her all at the close of the service. There wasn't a dry eye in the church, least of all Lissa's.

THERE WERE MERCIFULLY FEW DETAILS to take care of. Gary owned almost nothing, owed almost nothing, and left few entanglements. His insurance took care of most of the arrangements, and he didn't have much to dispose of, save for the photographs that Lissa kept, his collection of DVDs that rightly went to the housemates, and his clothes that went to St. Vinnie's.

With one significant exception: Gary started buying company stock as soon as he became an assistant manager in his late teens and had continued to do so while maintaining his frugal lifestyle.

Lissa used some of it to have his ashes interred in Resurrection, just in case he'd get the chance to hang with the spectral Mary. He'd like that.

She also used some to buy a custom Guild Traditional top-of-the-line slim-necked acoustic guitar and several hours of studio time to make her first CD. You can buy them at her performances.

"Somewhere Over the Rainbow" is track #13.

ARS LONGA, VITA BREVIS

ordon MacWhorter's body of work, far loftier than run-of-the-mill "movies" and certainly worthy of the label "great cinema," might be more precisely referred to as "moving pictures." His images, far more than theatrical production or lofty storytelling, seem to be the focus of his art. Indeed, there are famous scenes in his films made up entirely of frames, any single one of which could have been a Life *magazine photograph of the year.*

Bob Lamphier finally had the opening of his seventh book on the electronic page. First step taken.

This was to be an investigation of the genius of Gord MacWhorter, the celebrated director. Bob knew MacWhorter's films inside and out, loved them, and this would be a joy of a project. A dozen DVD cases were stacked to one side of his desk, the core of the director's work, to play on one of his monitors for reference and inspiration.

MacWhorter's films were epic, no matter how basic the story. Take his classic CinemaScope *Sudan*, a tale of three British soldiers. The scene where Cyril Crosbie's Sergeant Archer wanders off into the desert—a full four-minute shot of the crazed man walking away until disappearing into the shimmering heat, his image blurring into a small bright formless streak at the end of the trail through the sand—would never even be filmed today, replaced by a quick shot or an expository reference. But MacWhorter makes the viewer viscerally feel the anguish of the other two foot soldiers, knowing they'll never see Archer alive again. Just setting up the beautiful shot had to be an agonizing clockwork of planning and execution.

On his left-hand monitor, *The Rising of the Moon* played, an epic MacWhorter shot nearly a dozen years later. Although a box office flop, the film was highly praised for its brilliant cinematography. The heart-rending scene that sets up the tragic ending where the local guerrilla captain, played laconically by Brien Cullen, strides heroically up from the beach toward the looming uprising and his certain doom will be studied in college film classes for decades to come. The image of the love triangle, with ingenue Carol Wiltshire's Molly watching Cullen's character through the rain-spattered window, her face barely reflected in the glass, and in the distance on the beach, Merideth Kelly's melancholy Mrs. Aylmer watches him also, her skirt and shawl and hair whipping in the wind. The viewer knows both women are praying that the captain will acknowledge her, perhaps even abandon his suicidal obligations and chose them and life above duty, but Cullen's granite expression and determined stride lets the viewer know that no happy ending will come with tomorrow's sunrise.

The genius of the scene is the fourth yet most powerful character in the image: the rugged Atlantic shoreline itself.

The foamy crashing of the gray water upon the rocks on the beach, the cauldron of storm clouds blowing in from the ocean, the unreal greens of the fields, and the spatters of wind-whipped rain are of such beauty that the viewer cannot tear his gaze away. What an amazing scene. From the camera set up inside the cottage where Molly is hiding, over her shoulder, to blocking Merideth Kelly's walk on the beach to stop on her mark at just the right moment and the timing of Cullen's marching gait, all at the mercy of the weather and the sunlight. How did MacWhorter get it so perfect?

Bob clicked to an alternate audio track on the disc to listen to commentary by Carol Wiltshire recorded years later. She recounted how sick with pneumonia MacWhorter had been during the filming, too sick to get out of bed for much of the filming. According to the actress, much of the technical direction and the direction of the actors was done by notes passed via assistants. In the commentary, she claimed that Gordon didn't even know what he'd gotten until he was able to view the rushes.

Wait, what? Bob's brain glitched. Gordon MacWhorter wasn't even present at the filming? How was that even possible?

He reached for his phone and immediately phoned Gail Hornsby, his close associate and legendary encyclopedia of movie history. Gail, in love with movies since childhood, knew almost nothing else. In fact, her entire resume was movie related, starting as a video store clerk, then as a projection operator at a theater chain, now a data librarian at a distribution company. She was Bob's best hope at learning the truth.

"Oh, hi, Bob," she said in a droning greeting, her nasal voice enhanced by a constant vocal rip. "What's new with you?"

"Gail! You have a minute? I'm working on the MacWhorter book, and something is puzzling me."

"You know Gord had a twenty-year affair with Marjorie Allain? He was only married once, and they were together until he died, but he supposedly bopped a slew of young starlets and kept seeing Marjorie even when she was married."

"Yeah, I've heard that, Gail,"

"Putting it in the book? You should."

"No, this is just about his films, not his schmeckle."

"From all accounts, it wasn't much of a schmeckle, but he sure used it a lot." Gail's knowledge of Hollywood lore extended far beyond the technical and wholesome.

Bob cleared his throat. "*Anyway*, I was listening to the commentary on *The Rising of the Moon*, and they're talking about the scene where Brien Cullen is walking up from the beach—"

"Fabulous scene, Bob. I could have sex with that scene."

"Great to hear, Gail, but anyway, Carol Wiltshire said something to imply that MacWhorter wasn't even present at the filming! He was bedridden at the time!"

"Yeah, Gordon was really sick. I've heard that. He almost worked himself to death on several films."

"How the hell could he direct such a scene without even being there? That's unbelievable!" Bob exclaimed.

"Yeah, the story is, he had all the ideas in his head and got production notes to everyone every morning. Gloria Hand did the costumes. She passed on the instructions to the actors. It was in Merideth Kelly's memoir."

"So who set up the shots? The AD? I don't see MacWhorter leaving that up to an assistant director!"

"Yeah, that's weird Bob. I'll look into it."

Great, he thought. If anyone could uncover the story, Gail would.

———————

Gail's email several days later was disjointed and stream of consciousness as usual, involving an argument with another woman at her job concerning a parking space, an emergency trip to the vet for her German shepherd who'd ingested a feminine hygiene product dug from the garbage, and yet another unsuccessful attempt at veganism. But buried in her meandering text was what she'd deduced about the setup of the scene in question. It was done by a lowly camera assistant named Roy Hopewell, on whom MacWhorter was oddly reliant. The name didn't even ring a bell for Bob, but he did find Roy Hopewell's name buried in the credits of many of MacWhorter's blockbusters, always as some sort of assistant. Despite being Gordon's right-hand man on such a pivotal scene in one of his most monumental works, Roy Hopewell didn't warrant more than a passing minor credit.

Bob searched the standard internet sites for a list of Roy Hopewell's credits. This presented quite a problem because there was obviously more than one Roy C. Hopewell working minor jobs in movies since before the golden age of Hollywood. The positions were never ones that commanded any respect, but the movies on the list were truly epic. Some Roy Hopewell had worked under Hugh Deacy, a man responsible for making the American Western an art form of its own. An R. Hopewell worked on several early pictures done by H. Stephen Cousins, master of shock and suspense. There was a Roy Hopewell mentioned in the credits of several films of Salvatore Arpetti, who brought a gritty realism to so many big films of the seventies and into the eighties.

Bob continued to add to the MacWhorter book, but more and more, Roy Hopewell tickled his curiosity. Just how common a name was Roy Hopewell in Hollywood, anyway?

"Oh, hi, Bob," Gail answered the following week.

"So, just how common a name is Roy Hopewell in Hollywood anyway?"

"I know, right?" she moaned in reply.

"Any chance this is one of those fake names in the business, like Alan Smithee or George Spelvin?" he asked, referencing the fake names used in movies by persons who'd rather have their association with a particular project forgotten.

"Not that I ever heard of, and nobody ever thanks an Alan Smithee or a George Spelvin in their autobiographies, but a few of the really big guys have thanked a Roy Hopewell in theirs," Gail reasoned.

"An unknown Hollywood dynasty? Four generations of Haddows doing makeup in films, quite a few children and grandchildren of Allan Alfred doing musical scores and jingles—that kind of stuff?" There was a pause in the conversation before Bob added, "If so, the Hopewells didn't seem to get the success of the others. Always assistants."

"And not even assistant cameramen, just credited as camera assistants and such, like they lugged cables and carried film canisters," she added.

"Like nobodies like us?" he asked.

"Yeah, precisely. I'll keep looking," she promised.

Bob thanked her and hung up.

—————

"How's it coming, Bob?" his literary agent inquired, his tone friendly.

"On schedule, not much meat left to write. Layout guys are sending me pics on the reg for captions. We're full steam ahead."

"Good to hear. So you're solid on first draft by end of next month?"

"Solid. Hey, as long as I have your ear, I may have a new project . . . Might involve a family of laborers in the film industry, and although none of them were anyone notable, many were actually present during the filming of some of the most iconic scenes in movie history."

"So far, it sounds tough to sell."

"Thanks for the support!" Bob said sourly.

"Finish the one we've already gotten checks for, then write up a proposal for your carny idea."

"They work in movies. They're not carnies!" Bob insisted.

"Sounds like they are."

—————

Amazingly, the next day, one of the photographs the layout people sent him for captioning contained an image of Roy Hopewell himself. There in a candid taken by the studio during the filming of McWhorter's *Hand of the Raj* was Gordon and Director of Photography Al Mirscheimer conferring during a shot setup. Several technicians in the process of setting up equipment were plainly in view. Luckily, every person in the photo had been labeled. Looking slightly shorter than average and lean, the man identified as "R. Hopewell" sported a checked shirt and a neatly trimmed mustache, with a part in his short hair that seemed laser straight. He could have been anywhere between his early thirties and midforties. As *Hand of the Raj* filmed in 1958, that was at least a starting mark to determine which Roy Hopewell credits might be his. Bob took a screenshot of the file and emailed it to Gail, typing *Photo of Roy Hopewell* in the subject line.

The following morning, he got a reply titled *SEVERAL Pictures of Roy Hopewell and the Plot Thickens…*

Gail had abandoned her typical meandering communications to open with the question: *3 generations???* and a collage of images snipped from various sources, all of Roy Hopewell from behind-the-scenes and candid photographs. One showed the same Roy Hopewell leaning to speak with Hugh Deacy, who sat behind the wheel of his white Auburn Boattail with Hollywood legend Les Masters in his costume from *A Dawn's Hanging*, dating the photo to twenty-three years older than the one of MacWhorter. The men were identical and could only be related, most likely father and son. Gail had sent photos of what seemed to be the same man from the sets of a dozen classic and easily identifiable movies, many showing him in conversation with some of the most revered names in cinema history. One of the most recent snapshots showed Roy Hopewell with a light meter during the shooting of Sal Arpetti's Vietnam war epic *Madness and Glory*, the film that had almost cost the young director his own sanity. So there was Roy Hopewell in the jungles of the Philippines in the mideighties, no older or younger than any of the other Roy Hopewells in the other photos. Either every Roy Hopewell looked identical or the active-looking man in the jungle photo was at least in his seventies. Both were impossible.

Bob recognized the set from the *Madness and Glory* shoot. He'd studied it extensively when he wrote a well-received article praising Arpetti's labors bringing the terrifying war film to life. In the article, he'd compared the composition of the scene to works by the sixteenth-century Flemish painters; the long continuous shots followed the tense action, but the background was filled with dozens of little vignettes, each a story in itself. The little details were set up with extreme care, no matter how out of focus they appeared or how quickly they passed by in the final shot. It was brilliant painstaking filmmaking. And Roy Hopewell was there.

Two days later, he received a text from Gail in all caps imploring him to *CALL ME RIGHT AFTER WORK TODAY.* That kind of urgency was rare from Gail unless she was trying to score concert tickets. Bob knew she worked until 4:30 p.m. as a rule, and his afternoon dragged as he sat in front of the computer ignoring the MacWhorter project until then.

At 4:22, his phone chimed. It was Gail, talking a mile a minute.

"Okay, Bob, you've got me down a rabbit hole! You won't believe what I've found."

"Spill it!" he commanded excitedly.

"You know how Hugh Deacy shot all of those westerns in the same place?"

"Yeah, Bent Fork State Park in Utah. Everyone knows that."

"Well, Deacy was from New Hampshire and hadn't seen much of the West. The story is he found the place by accident when he was intending to scout at a place closer to Nevada. His assistant got them lost, and Deacy was furious. He was going to can the assistant and leave him in the middle of nowhere when they came upon Bent Fork!"

"Okay, and . . .?"

"Roy Hopewell was the assistant!"

"Wow, I wonder if Deacy kept him around as good luck."

"That's not all. Hopewell may have pointed out Les Masters to Deacy when Les was still Leonard Merrie and moving props at the studio!"

"You're saying Hopewell discovered Les Masters?" Bob said, incredulous. "Where are you getting this?"

"The Bent Fork thing is from the notes in Deacy's autobiography. The Masters bit is from a tell-all Masters's second wife wrote. Not the showgirl, the dyke."

"Wow, and we've never heard the name before?"

"Oh, Bob, it gets way weirder." Gail's nasal drone is made worse with the edge of excitement.

"All right, lay it on me."

"You know all of Cousins's phobias and crap?"

Bob grunted in acknowledgment. H. Stephen Cousins was known as one of the great masters of terror and suspense—and also known for his psychological hang-ups. He was notoriously afraid of heights, yet made the thriller *The Steeplejack*, a film with such dizzying scenes filmed around the tallest cathedral spires in London that it famously made many moviegoers ill. He was also afraid of animals, blood, closed spaces, and the dark, and he was credited with devising some of the most terrifying scenes in movie history as a way of facing his dark and relentless fears.

"Well, apparently," Gail continued, "he couldn't even watch the filming from the ground without losing his tea and crumpets, and you know who set up the shots?"

And Bob *did* know. It would have been legendary Director of Photography Norman Tate.

"It was Hopewell!" Gail screeched.

"Calling BS on that one, Gail. No way Norman Tate would allow anyone to screw with his shots!" Bob said confidently.

Norman was a noted perfectionist and had a reputation for being an unyielding tyrant on the set. One oft-repeated story held that Norman, rankling under a famous director's demand to do a second take of an elaborate scene Tate felt complete, had the whole take reset and reshot for the director without a single inch of film being loaded back in the cameras.

"It's in Norman's camera assistant's notes! He wrote that word came from Cousins to extend the scaffolding above St. David's, and

Hopewell and a crew worked all night to have the setup done by morning. Tate came in the morning, checked the light and angles, and never made a fuss!"

"I don't believe it," he told her.

"Save it, Hemingway. I'm just getting started. You got me *deep* down the rabbit hole! Cousins evidently used Roy to set up several scenes that disturbed him. Know how in interviews he said he couldn't even watch a lot of his stuff? He couldn't *film* them either. Hopewell did it!"

"We don't know that it's the same Hopewell," Bob reminded her.

"I'll send you all the pics I found, Bob. You can't tell me it's not the same guy!" Gail was adamant. "I don't know how, but it's the same guy. Maybe he's got the best plastic surgeon in California."

"That would be quite an accomplishment, because he'd be in his eighties if he was still working with Sal Arpetti on his last film," Bob reasoned. Gail had included a photo of Hopewell and Arpetti on location at the Jersey docks during the filming of *Union Dues*.

"Then call it his early 120s, because there's still a Roy Hopewell listed on the team over at the Tumbler Group," Gail informed him.

"Tumbler Group? What do they do?"

"Script doctors. Some of the best. The big movie and cable studios all use them. You've seen hundreds of their projects. Sows' ears get sent to them, and they send silk purses back."

That would make a great company motto, Bob thought. *They should pay Gail for that if they weren't using it already.*

"The Tumbler Group were the ones that did the screenplay for *The Vault*. It was their decision that you never know for certain if they kill the kid or not."

"Well, that was pretty brilliant," he opined.

"Hey, Bob, I just sent you a link. It's going to blow your mind. Start watching from the time stamp. It's going to take the top of your head right off!"

"Yes, cranial damage, I've been warned."

"Blow your mind, I'm telling you!"

"You said."

"Look, Bob, I have a contact at the studio that I might be able to ask to get in touch with someone at the Tumbler Group and sniff around for Hopewell. His info isn't on their website, but I have someone who may also be able to track down a number or something if he's really still alive and in the LA area. Gonna cost you," Gail warned, yet seemed eager to see answers to the questions.

"Like cost me what?" Bob said warily. She already got thanked in any book she helped research that he got published.

"You know what I really want," Gail droned.

Bob knew exactly to what she was referring: his beloved Harley Knucklehead, sitting polished and well locked up in the shed.

"Right!" He snorted in laughter.

"C'mon," she whined, well aware that she might as well have asked for the moon.

"How about I will it to you if this pans out?"

"Promise me you'll die soon, then?" Gail pleaded in a monotone rasp.

The video clip at the URL Gail sent *did* blow his mind. At the 2:26:15 mark of the rough cut of an unreleased documentary on modern dance was a segment filmed in the late fifties at a colored retirement home in Georgia, the lighting harsh and the audio quality poor. Clarence Saint, one third and probably best remembered of the legendary Saint brothers, sat in a wheelchair like a reedy skeleton carved out of walnut. His lap covered in a blanket and his thin hair in a hairnet, the once superhuman and athletically gifted hoofer gasped and croaked, quietly telling tales of the old days touring with his brothers.

Gail had discovered Clarence Saint telling the story of the filming of the most gripping scene in the early thirties gangster picture *It Ends at Wabash*. The scene that sets up the violent climactic machine gun duel in the alleyway was an amazingly innovative shot, where the camera follows the heels of Saint's tap shoes as he takes to the stage of a speakeasy jazz club, the only soundtrack being the sound of the tap dancing and the riotous jazz music. At one point, Saint performs a twirling leap, and for the split second he's airborne, the camera refocuses past the stage to where we see the gangster boss's moll being passionately kissed by his wheelman before Saint lands gracefully and continues his choreography. The next twirling leap and quick refocus reveals the gangster boss recognizing his daughter on the arm of the crooked alderman at the bar, the actor's reaction caught just in time before the wingtips descend and block his face. At the third twirling leap, the shot angle has altered again, just enough to see the hired assassin creeping up through the tables of the club toward the boss.

As the gangster's world comes tumbling down from all sides, the camera remains focused on the shoes performing maybe the most blistering and energetic tap dance solos ever caught on celluloid. Clarence Saint's chattering tattoo on the stage had to be witnessed to be believed.

It was hard and a little heartbreaking to believe the frail fragile old man reminiscing in the harsh bright camera lights was once the virtuoso dancer he had been, and although his voice creaked and sometimes failed him, his mind and memories seemed as sharp as a butcher's slicer. An off-camera voice asked the old gentleman about filming the brilliant scene.

"Oh, yes, well, that was just an experiment Mr. Haskell tried one day," the elderly man said, referring to Victor Haskell, the director of *It Ends at Wabash*. "We shot the scene the original way too, with me doing the first routine we'd worked out shot from the floor of the club, and all of the other shots needed, but we all had to be there for the wide angles. When Haskell was done with the original version wide shots, he left the set, and an assistant named Roy brought out this experimental rig he'd built that ran on roller skates, see? On this rig, the camera pointed straight down at a mirror at the bottom that was angled back so that the camera shot from the eye level of a garter snake, you see? And this Roy had me do basically the same routine but told me to really jump high at the right spots in the music while he operated the focus. As hard as I was working, Mr. Roy was working just as hard, wheeling that rig around just right behind me, pulling the focus, all the while tugging on fishing line that ran under the stage out onto the floor. You see, this fishing line was tied to the actor's ankles so they knew when to do their reactions at just the right moments, you see? Can you believe we did it all in two takes? Nobody was expecting it to turn out the way it did, and after they showed the rushes next morning, word spread around the whole studio about what Mr. Haskell had pulled off. He had carte blanche with the studio from then on, I can tell you!" the old man croaked animatedly, still obviously proud of his contribution to the fabulous segment.

Wait, was Gail saying that the Roy who worked on *It Ends at Wabash* was the same Roy Hopewell? That a man had contributed to such majorly memorable scenes in cinema for almost a century and nobody knew his name? That he wasn't even mentioned in the most in-depth film classes or discussions? Impossible.

"IMPOSSIBLE," BOB'S AGENT DISMISSED THE idea. "Anyway, I don't do fiction, and you don't either, but like I said, write up a good proposal *after* you finish the Gordon MacWhorter book, and I'll pretend to humor you."

"I'm not talking about fiction," Bob corrected firmly.

"Yes, you are. End of this month? Complete first draft?"

"Yeah, on time, like I said. In fact, it's nearly done, but I'll use all the time allotted to make improvements, not that I foresee many," Bob said confidently.

"Trying to think if I have any clients that *don't* think they're Tennyson, but I will say, you do produce," the agent said in a rare display of charity. He usually seemed to feel that if an artist needed more praise than what was printed in the box on the checks, they should volunteer at a soup kitchen. "As long as we're on schedule for proofing and checking, we're not losing money, and all's right with the art world."

———————

"OH, HI, BOB," SHE BEGAN, her nasal rasp not improved by the voice-mail recording. "Well, I've pulled off the impossible. I've emailed and rung the Tumbler Group, but nobody will forward a message or put me in touch with Roy Hopewell. It's just a recording about submissions. Apparently they only take stuff from select clients. He does have an office there, but there's no indication of regular hours. But my friend at the LAPD got me an address and phone number, and I looked at the place on the net. Little Spanish bungalow surrounded by apartments owned by the studio, kinda small. No Hollywood royalty type stuff. You won't believe this. The cop searched the records—place has been owned by a Roy Hopewell since the early thirties! I sent the address and phone number to your email. And hey, Bob, I really didn't mean to—" The voicemail cut her off. The voicemail often cut her off, but as long as she got to the point early, it was never an issue.

———————

"HELLO, MR. HOPEWELL. MY NAME is Bob Lamphier, and I'm following up on an article I wrote on Sal Arpetti's work a while back. I was wondering if I could have a few moments to get your thoughts on some things. Please let me know. I look forward to your call."

———————

"GOOD EVENING, MR. HOPEWELL. IT'S Robert Lamphier. I left a message last week. I did an article on Sal Arpetti, and since then, I've come across a great photo of you and Sal on location for *Union Dues*. Is there any way I could get in touch with you? I'd love to hear any memories you may have of working on that film. You can reach me at . . ."

———————

Dear Mr. Hopewell,

My name is Robert Lamphier, and I'm just finishing a book on the films of Gordon MacWhorter. I'm writing about the scene where Brien Cullen is walking up after landing on the beach to assemble his column on the road. I'm sure you recall the one. Cullen passes between Carole Wiltshire in the foreground and Merideth Kelly in the far distance—one of the greatest scenes in the history of cinema. Merideth Kelly mentioned your involvement in her memoirs, and I would like to know if you have any recollections of the on-location shoot.

I would be delighted if you could spare any time to chat. You can contact me at your convenience at . . .

Bob almost didn't answer the phone when he saw it was his agent. He was nearly done, ahead of schedule, and didn't need any browbeating. On the fourth ring, he answered out of guilt.

"On time for chrissakes!" he barked.

"Good, glad to hear it. Wondering *how* well you're doing on time? Enough to give up a couple of days for some really easy money?"

"Let's hear it. *How* easy, and *how* money?" Bob asked warily.

"A couple of grand for a couple of hour's work. Not that it'll be work for you."

Bob was waiting for the catch. "What's the story?"

"A panel discussion on the history of science fiction films. They had a big-name guest speaker drop out, and they need someone for the panel. You go up there, talk robots and rubber dinosaurs and crap, then get paid!"

Bob was still wary. "What's the hook?"

"It's at some virgin and dork convention in LA. Business-class airfare, room for two nights, meals, and they pick you up from the airport. Yeah, the travel will be a pain in the ass, but it's almost free money!"

"*Two* tickets and *two* passes?" Bob pushed.

"I could wrangle that. Not even worried."

"In!" Bob jumped. Maybe he could track Roy Hopewell down himself *and* give Gail a mini vacation for her help. Two birds, one virgin convention.

BOB AGONIZED OVER WHETHER TO drag Gail along while he stalked Hopewell. On one hand, the presence of a woman could help lower any barriers to talking to the man; on the other hand, she could wig out and start spraying film trivia all over the afternoon like a broken fire hose and scare the old gentleman off for good. Leaving Gail to leave her money with the collectibles dealers at the convention center, he took a cab to the address of Roy Hopewell, merely seventeen minutes away via the 101, which only took him fifty-three minutes.

For some reason, mounting the three steps in front of the well-kept but small Spanish-style house gave him the kind of butterflies he'd gotten before a first date as a teenager. Bob was about to ring the bell for a second time when the arched wooden door opened, and through the glass, he saw the man from all of the studio photographs, unmistakable and utterly unchanged. Bob found himself tongue-tied.

"Ah, good afternoon, sir. I hope you'll excuse—"

"I'll bet you're Bob Lamphier!" Hopewell said with a smile and a laugh, bobbing his index finger in Bob's direction.

"Yes, Mr. Hopewell! I hope I'm not intruding . . ."

"It's Roy. Come on in. You're quite welcome, Bob. May I call you Bob?" he said throwing the outer door open and gesturing for Bob to enter. "You've come at a perfect time. It's a bit early, but I was going to have a brandy. Would you like a brandy, Bob? It's very good!"

Bob stepped into the small foyer as Roy closed the door behind him. One wall contained framed publicity photos of about thirty of the greatest leading men. The wall opposite was similarly decorated with almost double the number of famous starlets. The wall between them was a who's who of directors, producers, screenwriters, and technicians. Above the doorway into the rest of the house was a plaque reading *ARS*

LONGA, VITA BREVIS. For some reason, Bob was almost speechless taking it all in. When he did find his voice, he horrified himself to find that he was just reading the motto out loud.

"Yes, art takes time, but life is short . . . But you'd already know that, wouldn't you, Bob? I mean, you *did* take Latin in high school, correct?" his host said cheerfully. "But what about that brandy? You will join me, won't you? Don't force me to insist!"

"Sure, Mr. Hopewell. That's very kind."

"Splendid! But of course, it's Roy, Bob!" he said, sounding genuinely pleased at the visit. "Know what I call these walls?" He gestured at the foyer while backing into the front room, leading Bob along. "Gods, Goddesses, and Titans! That's my domestic tribute to Hollywood mythology! Sit down, sit down, please get comfortable!" Roy said, motioning toward the comfortable leather couches.

The interior was Spanish ranch style, with books on the shelves and a few odd trinkets displayed as art, both elegant and warm. It was timelessly tasteful and wouldn't have been a shock at any time during the twentieth century or later. Indeed, even Roy seemed to favor a classically tasteful style—pleated trousers, handmade leather loafers, and a silk sports shirt—his fashion extremely hard to date.

"By the way, Roy." Bob was not quite yet comfortable with the informality. "I did in fact take Latin in high school," he said for some reason as Roy carried two generously poured snifters from the sideboard.

"In Chicago, wasn't it? I think I'm correct there," Roy said, baffling Bob further. Had Roy Hopewell been researching *him*? *Wouldn't that be funny*, he thought. "And now you're in town for a sci-fi convention, am I right?" He handed Bob one of the glasses. Bob nodded at the question, but before he could ask his, Roy raised his snifter. "Well, Bob, here's to art, the flickering lights, and the kids necking in the dark!"

Bob chuckled at the toast as Roy touched his glass to his with a chime.

And it was good brandy too.

"Roy, I have a million questions for you, but I have to ask, when did you start? You have to be about my age!"

"Not important, Bob. What's important is what you want to work on. What's *your* art? Not what you do to pay the bills. What are you inspired to do?" Roy said avuncularly.

"Well, to be honest, Roy, your story has been what's on my mind. What's your deal? How were you able to do what it's clear you've done? And why does nobody know it?"

"Oh no, my story isn't important. It's the stories that are important. I'm not an artist, Bob. I'm a midwife for art!" Roy gave out a genuine laugh before taking a long sip of the smoky liquor, smacking his lips slightly after the swallow.

Bob laughed too. "C'mon, Roy, you're telling me you make your living as a muse?" He liked the charming fellow but was nearly done with the leg-pulling.

"Oh no, no, not a muse," Roy said, seemingly serious. "I don't inspire artists. I merely help them. I'm an assistant." He looked Bob in the eye as if this would add any clarity to the riddle he was giving as an answer. The writer paused in exasperated silence.

"I'll put it this way, Bob. Art exists. It's out there." He pointed to the ether all around and raised his eyebrows. "Sometimes you get an artist, and he's like a cosmic antenna; he brings the art into the world. The art needs to be made manifest, and the artist needs to make that happen. I help where I can. It's an important job, but no more glamorous or noteworthy than the ball bearings in a piston arm of a mass-produced engine. I hope that helps," he said, draining his snifter. "Come, let me show you some of my stuff, things you'll appreciate."

Bob thought it best to back off his line of questions for the moment and spent the next amazing hour with Roy showing him props and artifacts from some of his favorite films. Western six-shooters, fencing swords, a bird statue cast in lead, original scripts, and sheet music, all hidden around the charming little house that also contained an Auburn Boattail in the garage. The collection could have been in a museum and probably should have been insured for the national debt.

Bob was declining a third brandy when he noticed the time with a jolt. He hadn't much time left and would have to call a cab now to make sure he was on time for the event that was paying for this encounter.

Before he could even offer his apologies, Roy announced, "I've really enjoyed your visit, Bob, and it's a shame you have an engagement to attend to, but I assure you, we'll speak again!"

"I hope so, Roy. I can't thank you enough for your hospitality. I really think I'd like to write your story."

"Alas, no, Bob. That's not in the cards. Anyway, my story isn't what's important. What's important is the art you want to do," he replied stubbornly, gracefully bringing his index finger close to Bob's chest. "Oh, before you go, please allow me to give you this." He dug a box out of a desk drawer and handed a large silver brooch to Bob, who recognized it immediately. It was the clan brooch worn by Nigel Hollister's highland swordsman Alistair MacKenzie in the rousing swashbuckler *Highwayman of the Heather*, Bob's favorite old film when he was a child. "You know what that is, right?"

"*Highwayman of the Heather*! That's one of my all-time favorites! Wow," he said, then after a pause, handed it back. "I couldn't possibly, Roy."

His host closed Bob's hand around the large badge. "I insist, Bob. That's the real one. Lifted it from Hollister's trailer myself!" He laughed, walking Bob toward the door. "Consider yourself a friend, Bob, and we'll see each other again."

"So, Roy, as long as we're friends," Bob said slyly, "let me ask, how old are you?"

Roy let out a laugh, opening the door to find the cab pulling to the curb. "Do you know the pictures of the antelope in the caves of Lascaux? Well, if the clever fellow with one eyebrow couldn't think of anything other than boobs to draw, I would have been there to help him!" Roy crossed his eyes, stuck out his jaw, and bared his lower teeth, pulling a silly childish caveman face. Bob had to laugh along.

"Okay, have it your way, Roy," the writer said, dying to get the real story out of the elegant gentleman. "Thanks again!" He stepped out onto the porch.

He would definitely have to tell the Roy Hopewell story, of that he was certain. Sliding into the cab, he repeated the destination to the driver, adding, "Behold the Highlan' Riever, the swordsman from the gates of Hell itself!" while brandishing the clan badge. It was one of Hollister's best lines.

———————

"So, where is it?"

"I still have four days," Bob said firmly to the agent. "Four days, and I'm going to use them!"

"Well, I'm getting nervous," the agent replied.

"Relax. It's nearly finished. In fact, I'll probably be finished with the proposal for the next book by then as well. This one is going to be different; this guy has a hell of a story!"

"The carny?"

"He's not a carny, you ass."

———————

The deadline came and went with no word from Bob. Four days later, as the result of a wellness check, Robert Jules Lamphier, 42, was found dead in his house of a sudden brain aneurysm. The only file on his computer open at the time of his passing was the manuscript for the Gordon MacWhorter book. The manuscript was complete and only needed minor tweaks, making it to press on schedule. It outsold all of Bob's other books on cinema history.

In the printer tray, however, was the 110-page draft of the screenplay titled *Hearts of Iron*, a love story between two young Métis mothers, both widowed during the Red River Rebellion in Canada in 1869. The stunning film that resulted won multiple awards in Hollywood and Cannes some six years later—and immortality for Robert Lamphier forever after.

WATER

A WET-WORK SHORT:
YOU'RE DEAD

In the surreal period between a deep warm sleep and awakening, he noticed that she was no longer beside him, but the panic didn't register until minutes later. The house was eerily silent. Mid-stretch, it occurred to him: the mission and its consequences. The realization gave him a dose of adrenaline.

Where the hell was she? He slid to the edge of the bed and stood up as quietly as possible. A glance at the clock told him it wasn't yet 8:00 a.m. He quickly donned his boxers retrieved from the floor. He had no time to look for other clothing. He grabbed his pistol from on top of the dresser and tried to silently slide the patio screen door open, just enough for him to squeeze unheard into the yard. The morning was bright and sunny, and the dew was pleasantly cool on his feet as he tried to avoid being seen through any windows.

The garage. The back garage door was probably unlocked. With luck, he could reenter the house and flank her position. He could circle in behind her trap.

His pulse was quietly droning in his ears as he made his way to the hallway where he found her. Slowly, he crept close enough to the baseboards to mask his approach, breathing through his mouth and keeping his weapon trained on her. He tried not to laugh. She was wearing only his undershirt, on her knees, left hand using the hallway wall for cover. She kept her gun trained on the bedroom doorway around the corner, waiting to blast him as soon as he stepped through. Treachery, for which she would pay.

Even presented with an easy head shot, the temptation to shoot her right in the bare ass was too undeniable. He squeezed the trigger.

He missed the proverbial bull's-eye by a measure of centimeters, his first shot hitting her in the left cheek and sending her into terrified convulsions with an earsplitting shriek. Her body jerked onto her back, and he kept firing.

"Dammit!" she bellowed, pulling the T-shirt down to her thighs, her feet drumming a tantrum tattoo on the carpet. She moaned in defeat.

"Checkmate," he croaked his first words of the day, chasing them down with three quick shots from his ruby-red squirt gun, molded in the shape of a German Luger. He walked in triumph toward the bathroom. "And the world's most dangerous assassin will be having French toast and bacon for his breakfast, thank you!"

Two squirts from her lime-green Colt water pistol went wide left as he closed the door behind him.

"You know what?" she yelled from her back. "Next time . . . you're dead!"

JELLY'S DAY IN THE COUNTRY

Just do your job, you stupid bohunk!"

Augie Jelinek wanted to punch Sal right in his big dago nose, show him that he wasn't so tough. If Sal's uncle hadn't been the boss, Sal would've been nobody. Let's see how he liked it then.

"Sal, c'mon . . . It'd be easier if I do it after the kid gets out of school. I could tell him I need help looking for a lost dog or some shit."

"Jelly? You a mongoloid or something?" Sal sneered, squinting one eye. Augie hated that name, and what was worse, it was Sal that started it. That's how clever Sal thought he was. He thought it was real funny. "Do just like you were told, asshole. On the way to school, between the house and the bus stop. Don't make a commotion, dummy." The boss's nephew waved his hand at Jelly dismissively. Some of the other guys chuckled. God, Sal needed a punch in the nose.

On his way to the back door out to the alley, Moe the Jew motioned to Jelly. "Look, kid, you want to avoid being seen dragging a screaming kid off of the street. On your way home, you need to stop at the department store. Weather's going to be nice tomorrow . . ."

WITH THE SUN JUST COMING up over the neighborhood, Jelly put a dime in the payphone in front of the liquor store and dialed the club number. Richie answered.

"Richie, it's Augie. I'm about to go."

"So go, Jelly," Richie said tiredly.

"Okay, so we're still on, then."

"Goddammit, Jelly, yes! Now go do it! For Christ's sake!"

"Okay, and then I'll call at one."

"Don't cock this up, Jelly! Just stick to the plan. Sal's right, you know. You couldn't pour piss out of a boot if the instructions were stamped on the heel. Now don't be late, you dumb bohunk!" Richie hung up.

Man, if they made him boss, he'd make some changes around the crew, believe it.

And nobody'd call him Jelly anymore.

IT WAS ALREADY GETTING TOO warm for his jacket, and he thought about taking it off as he sat in his car down the street from the house. Any minute now. Jelly's .380 was in his jacket pocket; he didn't want to put it in his trouser pocket. He'd catch hell if the bosses knew he was out carrying, but the way Jelly saw it, they weren't in the nice guy business, right?

There! Jelly could see the housekeeper seeing the little brat out the door, paper-bag lunch and books under his arm. He leaned over and rolled down the front passenger window before putting the car into gear. Give the housekeeper time to shut the door.

Jelly pulled over abreast of the kid about a block later.

"Dicky! You Dicky Pope, yeah?" The young boy nodded. Jelly put on his friendliest smile. "Hiya, Dicky! I'm Mr. Johnson, and I work with your dad. You know, at the bank."

"Do you know Coral and Mr. Andrews?" Dicky asked.

"Oh yeah, I know all them guys. We all work together," Jelly assured him.

"I've never seen you before," Dicky said, looking Jelly in the face.

"Nah, I work in the back, see? I only go to your pop's office when he has a special job for me. And hey, that's why I'm glad I caught you. Your dad's got a surprise for you today!"

"Yeah, what?" Dicky asked, edging closer to the car door.

"He's taking you fishing! He was supposed to come get you, but he has some very important papers to sign at work, so he told me to come get you. We'll go out to the river, and he'll meet us later. C'mon, hop in."

"But what about school? Won't they be mad?"

"Don't worry about that, kid. Your dad'll explain it to them. C'mon, let's go!" Jelly said enthusiastically, gesturing to the fishing rods and random outdoor gear in the back seat. He leaned over and opened the door. *Come on, you little pansy. Don't make me grab you off the sidewalk in broad daylight.*

The kid peered into the car. "My dad didn't say anything about going fishing . . ."

"Yeah, that's why I told you it was a surprise, see?" Jelly said, his exasperation rising.

"My dad never took me fishing before," the kid said softly.

"Well, he was gonna today, but if you're going to be a sissy about it, you're going to get *me* into trouble!" Jelly barked. The kid's eyes welled up a little; the words stung. *Goddamn sissy*, Jelly thought. He was going to have to drag this little prick off kicking and shouting for the whole neighborhood to witness. *Thanks a lump, Moe.*

"I'm sorry, but my parents don't like me talking to strangers. I don't want to get anyone in trouble."

"Yeah, well, I ain't really a stranger if I know Andrews and Carl and all of them guys at the bank, and your pop trusts me enough to take you fishing so he can come join us later, right?" *C'mon, kid . . .* Jelly didn't want to go to plan B.

"I guess not," the kid reasoned. His resolve was breaking, even if he didn't know anyone named Carl that worked at his dad's bank.

"That's it, pal! Use your head. Your pops said you was pretty smart, that the nuns said you was a good kid." Jelly gestured him in. "Hop in, Dicky! We're going to have a great time!" He smiled wide. Dickie piled in, pulling the heavy car door shut. *Thank fucking Christ.*

THE KID WAS QUIET FOR the most part, real bookworm type. It suited Jelly just fine as he repeated the plan to himself. Sit on the kid, keep him occupied, call the club at one, and Sal would say where to drop him off—easy. Nice and slick. The kid's old man would play ball.

"Hey, that reminds me, second game of the series is on today. Got rained out yesterday. Maybe we'll catch it on the radio this afternoon when your pops comes to join us."

"The baseball game? My dad doesn't care too much for baseball," Dicky answered.

Figures, family of stuck-up sissies. Jelly snorted to himself.

"C'mon, pal, you gotta like baseball, and it's the series. Same as last year though. Goddamn New York hogging the spotlight."

The kid blushed crimson. "Mister! You said a swear!" He giggled like he had just walked into the ladies' changing room. Jesus, what a sissy.

"Yeah, the nuns and your ma probably don't want you talking like that, but we won't tell them nothing, will we pal?" Jelly said with a fake laugh. "Well, I'll listen to the game, and you and your old man can fish. Got a bundle on Brooklyn again."

"Will we be in a boat? I don't think I like small boats. We should have those life vests if we do."

"No, we ain't going to be in no boat." Jelly sighed. "We're just going to fish from the shore like the shines do." *You yellow sissy*, he wanted to add. Imagine being trapped in a rowboat all morning with this little pain in the ass.

The city gave way to the neighborhoods on the fringes, then the tracts of prairie and the occasional farm. God, there's a lot of nothing once you leave the city. He almost missed the turn. Not even a stoplight, and Jelly barely remembered the directions. He'd no sooner started recognizing the area than a sign on a country filling station caught his eye: *BAIT*. Oh yeah, better pick up some worms.

The tires whined briefly as Jelly swung into the lot of the gas station, stopping in front of a Coke machine. "Look," he said, shutting off the ignition. "You stay put. I gotta go in and get some worms. Stay quiet, and I'll get you a Coke to have with your lunch. You can eat it picnic style while we're fishing."

"My mom doesn't let me have soda with lunch. The sisters give us milk."

"Well, your ma don't got to know. You can tell her you had milk. I don't give a crap. A pop ain't going to hurt you anyway." Jelly slid out into the bright sunlight. Summer was hanging on. The leaves were starting to change, but the day was warm. He walked into the filling station, the little bell ringing above the door.

"Morning," the thin old man said, less than friendly. He peered out the window and spied the city registration sticker on Jelly's windshield. He hadn't pulled up to the pumps or to the maintenance doors, so he was just another city slicker looking for directions for free.

"Yeah, I gotta get some worms. Don't need a lot," Jelly said, looking to move on quickly.

"Going fishing?" the old man asked, growing a little friendlier.

"No, Pops, I was raised by pigeons and I'm meeting them for breakfast, for Christ's sake!" Jelly said. Unbelievable how dense they grew them out in the sticks.

"Okay, young man. Crawlers are fifteen cents a carton. Of course, you have your fishing license?"

"Fishing license?" Jelly said in disbelief. "I don't need no fishing license. We ain't going after red snapper or nothing." Fifteen cents for a cup full of worms and dirt . . . This coot was a class A rip-off artist, he'd give him that.

"Oh, sir, you'll need a fishing license!" the old man said, smiling.

Go ahead and get smart with me, city slicker. "If the DNR catches you without a license, the fines are pretty steep!"

Just what I need, a shakedown, Jelly thought. *The last fucking thing I need is this old bastard bringing some local law out here to poke their nose in my business.* Jelly gave an exasperated huff. "Yeah, and how much for a license?" he asked.

"Two dollars."

Two fucking bucks to put a hook in the goddamn water! *All the real criminals wear badges, that's for certain,* he thought. He should slap this mutt around a little and teach him some proper customer service. He could feel his angry blood rushing to his face, but Sal had been very clear: don't make any waves. Nice and quiet. Fucking Sal.

"Okay, better get me one of them licenses, and let's make it quick," Jelly said, peeling three singles from his pocket roll. The old man got out his book in comically slow motion. *Just to piss me off,* Jelly thought. He could tell.

"We just have to fill out this form here, mister, and I have to check an ID," the old man said slowly, knowing that every second more out of Jelly's day was another victory.

Jesus Christ, he'd have to thank Moe the Jew for this when he saw him next. Jelly really didn't want this old bastard writing down his real name and address. He whipped out his wallet and proffered the ticket he'd gotten last week. Just then, the little bell over the door tinkled. It was the kid.

"Didn't I tell you to wait in the car?" Jelly said a little too loud, his irritation evident.

"I just wanted to see what was taking you so long," the kid mumbled. He looked around the shelves in curiosity at the lures and bobbers and pliers and hunting knives hanging on the pegboards. "Hey! They have comic books!" Dicky said delightedly, hopping over to the rack.

"We ain't here for no stupid comic books, kid. We're going fishing," Jelly said, suddenly *very* annoyed. Now this gyp artist had seen him with the kid *and* had his name and address. Jesus Christ, this could get messy. Sal would hit the roof if he had to send some guys out here to keep this old man quiet, and Jelly'd never hear the end of it. Goddammit. "You'll just have to read the comic books you got at home, kid," Jelly said, trying to sound pleasant.

"My parents don't let me have comic books, Mr. Johnson. They think they're a waste of money," Dicky explained.

"Johnson?" the old man said, eyeing the fishing license he had just filled out for an Augustus Jelinek suspiciously.

"Yeah, I let the kid call me that," Jelly growled. "Can't pronounce my name too good. Is there a problem?" His blood was beginning to boil. Supposed to be an easy job, nice and simple. Why couldn't he catch a damn break? "C'mon, let's go, Pops. We're on a schedule." Jelly tapped the booklet of licenses.

"Some of the other boys get comic books. Sometimes they let me read theirs," the kid said, spinning the wire rack and making it squeak. "I like *Superman*."

The old man tore the license out of the book and pushed it across to Jelly with his traffic ticket, scooping up the three dollar bills with the other hand. Jelly wadded both pieces of paper up and stuffed them in his shirt pocket. He took the carton of night crawlers and thrust them at the kid's chest.

"Here are your worms . . . and Superman's a fairy," Jelly announced. "C'mon, get in the car." He took the change from the old man and shot him a dirty look as a warning. "Only a fairy would wear a cape," he said to nobody, striding out the door.

———

THE RIDE TO THE SPOT on the river was done in silence, the kid clutching the bottle of Coke from the machine. As soon as Jelly saw the railroad trestle, he knew he was in the right place: nice spot behind an old grain-loading station right next to the river. He parked the car on a patch of cracked pavement that was losing the fight against the tall prairie grass that sprouted from every crack. The river shore was all broken rock, with some tall trees across the moving water. Nice out-of-the-way spot.

"Okay, kid, this is the place."

The kid sat in silence for a bit, looking out toward the river. "I don't think Superman's a fairy. I think he's pretty neat. He fights for truth, justice, and the American way."

"See? That's what I mean. If anyone with half a brain could do what Superman can do, they'd go grab all of the gold out of Fort Knox or something. Don't tell me that if you was Superman, you wouldn't be using your X-ray vision to look through some pretty dame's clothes just to see some tits and ass."

The kid turned beet red as he hid his open mouth behind both hands, stifling a nervous naughty giggle. "Mr. Johnson, I can't believe you talk like that!"

"Yeah, well, the nuns ain't around, kid. Now go take a pole over to the water and catch a big one. I'll stay here and wait for your dad." Yeah, this kid should wear a cape. The kid's parents were right about comic books. The only books that weren't a total waste of money were the ones kept by real bookies.

The kid got out of the car and opened the back door, retrieving a fishing pole and net, holding the carton of worms gingerly. He looked over toward the river but stood still. "Aren't you going to show me how, Mr. Johnson? I've never been fishing before."

"Jesus Christ, kid! What's there to it? You've seen it in the movies, ain't you? You put a worm on the goddamn hook and put it in the water!" The kid just stood there, frozen. "Ah, for Pete's sake, kid, you're killing me!" Jelly swiped the net and pole from the kid. "C'mon! Bring the worms and the tackle box!" he commanded, striding over to uneven rocks that led down to the water.

The sun was bright, and the long weeds sang loudly with grasshoppers. The river hissed and gurgled, and the loose rocks gave way under his feet as he picked his way to a nice flat piece of concrete that tilted toward the water that would be good to sit on.

"This is a good spot," Jelly said to no one, as the kid was far behind, cautiously navigating the rocks. "C'mon, kid!" he moaned as he pulled the small hook from where it had been stuck in the cork handle. He had the line and bobber untangled by the time the kid made his way to the concrete slab and sat down. "Finally, slowpoke. Dig me out a worm." Jelly gestured toward the carton.

The kid prized the lid off and stared at the damp soil where the night crawlers writhed. He poked the black dirt with a finger and instantly recoiled as if it were red-hot. "Mr. Johnson . . ." the kid whispered.

Oh, you have to be kidding me, Jelly thought. He rolled his eyes. "Here. Take the damn pole," he barked. He snatched the carton from the kid and dug out a curling worm. The kid stared at it in disgust. "Hold it still. Don't put the hook through my goddamn hand!" Jelly commanded, trying to grasp the fishing line dangling from the waving pole. The kid winced as Jelly took the hook and threaded the coiling worm onto its point.

"Doesn't it hurt the worm?" the kid said sadly.

"Who cares?" Jelly said before seeing the kid's eyes well up again. *Oh, for fuck's sake.* "No, it don't hurt them. They don't have any feelings." *When this shitty day is over, tell your old man to buy you a cape*, he thought.

"How do you know that?"

"Ah, for Pete's sake, kid! Worms don't have feelings, okay? They don't got arms or legs or eyes, and they don't have feelings! That's what makes them worms, all right?" Jelly grabbed the pole. "Here. Watch." He cast the line about a dozen feet from the rocks on the shore, the red-and-white bobber riding the ripples. "Now you sit there and watch that bobber. When a fish comes for that worm, he'll take the bobber under. Watch for that. When that happens, reel in like hell. Got it?" He handed the pole back. "Got it?" he repeated.

"Got it," the kid replied. Clearly, he didn't.

"Good, then," Jelly said, heading back to the car.

JELLY SAT IN THE CAR, eyes closed. The insects in the grass buzzed loudly. He looked over toward the kid. The pole lay on the slab next to him as he threw rocks into the river, watching the splashes. God, this kid. What a piece of work.

He looked at his watch. 10:20. Not much longer. At one, he'd call Richie, find out that the kid's old man was cooperative, and learn where to drop the brat off. Simple. He closed his eyes again. Brooklyn would take it again this year, and he'd make enough to maybe tear up the town some night. He smiled.

He had no idea how long the kid had been standing there when he next opened his eyes. It almost made him jump. "Yeah, what?"

"When is my dad going to get here?"

"Not until after lunch, he said. Don't worry about it." He grabbed the kid's brown bag lunch from the stack of schoolbooks on the seat. "Here, why don't you take your lunch and eat while you fish."

"And the Coke too?"

Jelly let out an exasperated moan. "Yeah, and the pop too," he said, handing the warm bottle through the window.

"How do I open it?"

Jesus Christ, kid, you are one helpless ballbuster. "Here. Give it back," he growled, looking around for something to open the bottle. "Dammit," he said in annoyance. Nothing in the glove box, no pocketknife. Finally, he settled on using the corner of the glove box door to pry the cap off with a foaming hiss. "Aw, son of a bitch! It's getting all over!" He thrust the sticky foaming bottle back at the boy, getting sugary drops all over the seat and his clothes. "Ah, dammit," he said, dabbing at the spills with his handkerchief. "Go and eat your lunch."

He had just closed his eyes again when he heard the glass breaking and the rising moaning cry of the kid. *What now?*

The clumsy little sissy had taken a tumble on the uneven rocks, smashing the bottle and sending his lunch flying. He wailed like a pig in the slaughterhouse and clutched his knee. *God, this day just gets better*, Jelly thought as he sauntered over to the crying child.

"What's wrong?"

"I fell on the rocks!" the kid moaned between sobs. "And the bottle broke!"

"You cut?" Jelly asked, looking the blubbering kid over.

"I hurt my knee!"

The knee of his trousers had an L-shaped rip in it now, exposing a barely scraped knee. "Ah, you're all right," Jelly told him in a tone intended to stop the crying. Jesus, this kid was a pantywaist.

"My mom will be mad that I tore my pants!" The eyes started to well again.

"Don't worry. I'll fix it with your dad," Jelly assured him. *Your parents got bigger problems than a torn pair of pants*, he wanted to say. *When your old man finishes his business with Sal, they'll be happy enough just to see you again . . .*

"And all the soda spilled," the kid mourned.

"Well, too bad. You ain't getting another one. Good lesson in being careful," Jelly said, picking up the lunch and standing the kid up. "You're fine. Go over and eat your lunch . . . quietly. You're probably scaring the damn fish."

———

It was almost time. Jelly whistled the kid back to the car. "C'mon, Dicky! We gotta go!" The kid cautiously wobbled his way back over the rocks and to the car with the rod and tackle box. "Okay, c'mon, get in."

"My dad hasn't come yet."

"Yeah, I know. I have to make a call. I'll find out where we're meeting your old man. Get in."

"I still have to get the net and the worms," the kid explained.

Jelly motioned to the kid. "Forget them. We're leaving. Hop in," he said impatiently, starting the car.

The kid looked back toward the worms and gear left on the cement slab and then to his torn and dirty pants. He decided that he didn't like fishing; he'd rather be in school with the nuns.

Jelly took a different route back. He needed a payphone, and in the first little town, he found a drugstore on a corner. They'd have a phone in there. He parked the car.

"I gotta go in and call the office. I'll be right back. Stay put this time. I mean it!" he admonished the kid as he stepped out of the car.

Inside, it was cooler, and it took a few seconds for his eyes to adjust to the indoor light before he spied the two wooden phone booths near a rear entrance. Jelly walked through the aisles and closed the bifold door behind him, fishing a dime from his pocket. He checked his watch: 1:12 p.m. He dropped the coin and spun the dial, listening to the hollow clicks every time the dial spun back.

Richie answered after six rings.

"It's Augie."

"You're late, Jelly," Richie barked.

"Yeah, so, what's the plan?" Jelly asked impatiently. He needed this day to be over.

"Son of a bitch won't play ball. He's being real cute."

"So what do I do?" Jelly pleaded. There was a pause on the other end.

"So you do your job, you dumb bohunk!" Richie hissed in a condescending tone.

"Richie, c'mon . . ." Jelly implored. "What—"

Richie cut him off. "I said you do your fucking job, you stupid bohunk."

The line went dead.

Several minutes later, Jelly walked slowly back to the car, carrying three comic books and a bottle of Coca-Cola.

THE NUMBERED DAYS
OF JULIAN CALLENDAR

This was the second time in his life that Julian Callendar had seen Death. This was not to imply that he was in any way courageous, foolhardy, or that he lived a life marked by even the slightest bit of risk or excitement. In fact, Julian was known to be a stunning bore. He kept that one interesting fact about himself—the fact that as a child, he'd actually seen the Grim Reaper in the putrid flesh, so to speak—a complete secret.

He was eight when it happened first, already an unremarkable child. One early spring afternoon, he was being driven to his grandmother's house by his parents, and he saw the Grim Reaper standing on the porch of the old woman's house. His child's mind, too unformed and dull to be terrified by the vision, was merely repulsed and didn't even question it. The tall figure in the tattered black robe holding a scythe had vanished by the time the family car parked on the street in front, and in his revulsion, he dragged his heels, joining his parents who'd already entered the home. He'd only made it to the porch when he heard his mother cry out, causing him to freeze until his father came jetting out of the front door and swiftly guided Julian back into the car, where he was told that everything was all right.

Sitting on the chairs of the funeral home at the wake, Julian could only wonder if the old woman now lying dead in her casket had seen what he'd seen as the other mourners pronounced her passing as *sudden* and *unexpected*. From then on, even more than before, Julian put his efforts into avoiding risk and danger, preferring to keep the Reaper away. For decades, his strategies worked to perfection, although work it was. He watched what he ate, shunned red meat, alcohol, tobacco, drugs, casual sexual entanglements, and adventure. He kept active while avoiding anything strenuous or stressful, and the numbers he presented at his biannual physical seldom wavered. He worked his way into a position at the bank's main branch, a dull monotonous job in the rear offices where few people knew what his actual function was. Too dull to be happy, Julian Callendar was content.

Until this morning, when waiting for the bus, Julian Callendar spied the unmistakable figure of the Grim Reaper across the boulevard and down a side street, standing in the shadows of an old oak. His mind flashed back to that afternoon more than forty years ago, and he wondered whom the Reaper was there to see.

Several blocks into his bus ride into work and before he could start properly reading today's newspaper's concerning stories, Julian noticed that the tall hooded figure was now sitting on his very bus. A thrill of terror shot through his body, unpleasant and unwelcome and very foreign to someone so usually and successfully careful. He forbade himself from looking back again, lest the figure move even closer.

As the bus slowed down and bucked slightly at the stop in front of the bank, he almost rose to get off when he noticed the Reaper standing near the large doors of brass and thick glass, looking in Julian's direction. The sight froze him in his seat, and for the first time in his life, Julian broke routine and stayed on the bus. He was too nervous to worry about calling into his boss or what attendance protocols he was currently violating; he kept the spectral figure in his peripheral vision as the bus pulled back into traffic.

Julian's heart raced. Had he gotten away?

He rode for miles contemplating his next move when the bus approached the end of its route near the rapid transit station. There, standing by where the next outgoing bus was taking on early passengers was the Reaper again, waiting for him. Since he had to disembark before the terminal, Julian reluctantly made his way outside but decided to try to hide in the crowd of commuters heading for the elevated trains, leaving the Reaper back at the terminal.

Julian paid his fare and slid into one of the remaining seats of the first outbound train, not caring where he was going as long as it was away. He spotted the Reaper again at the third stop the train made, waiting on the platform. Julian was ready to bolt out the car door at the last moment if he saw the Reaper step on, but the hooded figure stayed put. So did Julian.

The Reaper was also at the next stop and the next, keeping Julian hostage in the car, until a couple of stops past the downtown interchanges, the train pulled into one stop where none of the dozen or so waiting on the platform were hooded or carrying ancient agricultural tools. Julian made his break and fled down the unfamiliar streets. He found himself near a side entrance to the zoological gardens and noticed the figure of death waiting for him a half a block up the sidewalk, so he dashed into the park to again attempt to hide among the crowds.

He occasionally caught glimpses of the Reaper, but so far, he was successful in eluding him, flitting from one crowd of zoo-goers to the next, doing his best to be elusive prey. His unaccustomed nostrils were rudely tickled as he watched the gorillas and orangutans laze in their fake jungle enclosures, and he laughed at the antics of the penguins in their ersatz Antarctic display. As soon as any dark shadow entered his vision, Julian would be off to wherever the next crowd was, using the safety-in-numbers tactic that might have saved some of the exhibits from winding up so far away from their original homes. He was standing listening to a pair of walruses gorp and blow spray in the air and walrus flatus bubbles in the water when he spied the Reaper approaching from afar. Julian made for the nearest exit.

Once out of the zoo, Julian realized how close he was to the lake. If he went to the lakeshore, he'd limit the number of directions on which he would have to keep watch, so he walked in that direction with purpose, passing through the pedestrian tunnel that emerged in the park next to the water. He kept a close watch on the joggers and strollers that populated the park, keeping watch for the Reaper. As he got closer to downtown, the park included sandy beach, so he took the opportunity to remove his shoes and socks—completely inappropriate for the fast hiking he'd been doing—and allow his feet the relief of walking on the soft sand. The sensation was only slightly tempered by the worry of impaling his feet on hidden broken glass, so he didn't remain unshod for long. When he saw the Reaper up ahead near the end of the beach, Julian, completely out of character, decided to cross the eight lanes of traffic that stood between the beach and the buildings of the city, his thumping heart nearly drowning out the sounds of honks and squeals as he sprinted across.

He found yet another large crowd to hide among, a loud and colorful gaggle that spoke a language Julian could only guess at. He stuck with them, keeping his head on a swivel for his otherworldly tail, all the way to the amusement park pier that was their destination. Julian was eager to go to where he might get a view of the beach he had just fled to see if he'd been successful in eluding the Reaper. As he made his way along the north side of the pier farther and farther out for a better view, his hopes were dashed first when he realized that his view of the beach was blocked by the water filtration plant and then even devastatingly more so as he plainly caught sight of his pursuer at the end of the pier.

Julian changed his direction in mid-step and ducked into one of the buildings of the indoor mall. Seconds later, the figure reappeared a hundred yards in front of him, standing in the wide covered avenue between the shops and attractions. Julian ducked into the first dark entrance he came across and found himself watching a loop of Charlie Chaplin and Laurel and Hardy shorts in a dark room with a bunch of kids squealing delight in Spanish and laughing at the old films. Julian watched too, realizing that as iconic as the old stars were, he'd never really watched them. He was lost in this realization until the loop started over, replaying what he'd already watched. He found himself disappointed that they didn't show some Buster Keaton as well. Exiting the little theater, he checked for the Reaper in both directions and, finding the coast clear, made his way back outside to leave the pier.

Just beyond the entrance, toward the parking lot and the city streets beyond, there the black figure stood. Julian turned on his heels and headed back into the amusement complex, occasionally checking over his shoulder. The most ridiculous and fanciful thought occurred to him: from the top of the Ferris wheel ride, he could plainly keep watch on the Reaper that waited for him.

He spotted him eventually standing like a statue just beyond the entrance and lost sight again as his Ferris wheel car dipped to ground level momentarily, Julian's view obscured by the crowds. On his third revolution upward, Julian froze to realize that the Reaper had disappeared again, causing him to scan the crowds in a futile panic. When the ride stopped, Julian found himself back in the middle of the promenade, wondering which way was safe to go. The figure hadn't reappeared near the entrance, and the coast seemed to be clear, so Julian made his break for it.

He made his way through the park downtown, searching for his pursuer among the thriving city, not finding the Reaper anywhere in the vicinity. His senses were on high alert as he made his way back toward the train lines. Perhaps it was safe to head home, he thought while for the first time walking through downtown without actively ignoring it.

Once on the elevated train in a mercifully Reaper-less car, he started making his way toward home again, where he'd be able to relax. His relief was cut short when he noticed the Reaper getting on the car in front of his at the stop by the baseball stadium, and at the last minute, Julian dashed off the train, eager to make his escape again. He almost jogged to catch up to a large throng of people heading into the afternoon game, and seeing the value in hiding in yet another crowd, he bought a cheap ticket at the box office, always keeping a paranoid eye out for his stalker.

The seating area he was in seemed unnaturally cool as a result of the constant shade it received from the second deck overhead, but the game was in bright sunlight. The crowd around him buzzed and rumbled and occasionally erupted in shouts of triumph or peals of displeasure. Words of encouragement, criticism, or disfavor sometimes floated oddly clear above the din. The game hadn't made it to the seventh-inning stretch yet when Julian caught sight of him on the jumbotron of all places. Nobody else reacted. Evidently Julian was the only one who saw the ghastly image on the enormous video screen, but see the Reaper Julian did, prompting his hasty exit from the ball field.

Once back out on ground level outside the park, Julian continued to hear the cheers and groans of the crowd and the occasional crack of the bat as he made his way back to the train. He checked every street, every shadow, every figure, determined to make his getaway. He was almost in a sprint heading toward the next train to pull away and was breathing hard, listening to his thumping chest as he scanned the platforms and the seats for the relentless specter. As the train pulled away, heading back south, he breathed a sigh of relief to have the car to himself. He felt like he'd made it and, in his exhaustion, closed his eyes. He didn't doze off; his ears still took in every squeal and thump the rumbling train made, and his eyes snapped open at every stop, making sure the Reaper didn't join him when the doors hissed open and shut. Once moving again, he allowed himself to feel the relief of relaxation.

He didn't know what caused him to snap to attention, but when he did, the jolt of realization that the Reaper was sitting just beside him made his breath freeze in his lungs. He was trapped between the buildings streaking past the window on his right and the Angel of Death blocking his exit on his left. The blood drained from his face.

"Relax, Julian Callendar," the surprisingly gentle and kind voice said.

Julian tried to scream, but the air would go no higher than under his throat.

"I have something for you. You'll love it," the Reaper said, handing Julian a flimsy plastic bag. "Try it." It was more of a respectful request than a supernatural command.

Dumbfounded, Julian retrieved from the bag a fried dough confection, dusted with cinnamon and sugar and dipped in chocolate. As helpless and confused as a child, he obediently took a bite. It was glorious and brought a smile to his face and a delighted tear to his eye.

"Wow! You know, I've always seen these, but I'd never tried one before. It's wonderful!" he declared before swallowing and taking another bite.

"Julian Callendar, did you have a good day?" the Reaper asked, his voice full of kindness.

Julian paused, then in full realization, answered, "Why yes. Yes, I did!" giving a small chuckle after.

"Are you ready?" the Grim Reaper asked.

"I suppose I am," said Julian Callendar fearlessly, closing his eyes as the train rumbled off toward home.

LESSON LEARNED, MRS. AVERY

Mrs. Avery taught sixth grade, and in those days, that meant teaching everything. Math, science, English, history, geography—the whole shebang. But I think she felt that her greatest duty was teaching us something more, how to be a citizen, a member of society, and in that, she excelled. She had a fairly even temperament but was known for being strict and unbending. That was no doubt the secret to her success at riding herd on thirty or so hyper children, school year after school year, for almost forty years in a row.

Her punishments were legendary. The slightest infraction would win you a pink slip of paper that your parents would have to sign, outlining your transgression of the law and the punishment you had incurred, usually in the form of metatarsal-crippling essays of Homeric length. Late to class once, one thousand words, fifteen hundred for every subsequent offense. Chewing gum, two thousand words. And really unruly behavior would earn you an exhaustive dreaded five-thousand-plus-word punishment. We were all to learn how to be good citizens at the peril of our digital mobility, that's for sure!

It was the first time I had been back to the neighborhood in years, and while some of the changes made me marvel, the way some of it hadn't been touched by time at all made me wistful. I drove up and down the streets with my cousin Annie, reminiscing about our shared childhood, the playgrounds, the haunts, the little candy stores now converted to residential houses. Where there had been stretches of prairie where you could play soldiers or cowboys all day long, there were now patches of nearly identical modern convenience housing. Ah, the march of progress. Where did the kids play cowboys now?

As I turned down Hickory Drive to make the final mile or so to Aunt Maggie's house where Annie had grown up, she pointed to a small familiar well-kept cottage. A caricature of the American Dream, far too small for today's housing market but pristinely kept and manicured, with flowers and an anachronistic picket fence strategically placed. The house just screamed *Occupant knows the value of good-quality doilies!*

"Did you know Mrs. Avery still lives there?"

"You've got to be kidding!" I laughed. "She's got to be a million by now. I'm pretty sure she voted for Grover Cleveland. Hell, it's been about twenty-five years since we had her, and she was old then! No way she's still around."

Annie snorted when she laughed, covering her face in embarrassment at the porcine reaction. "No, she's still around. Probably in her nineties, but my mom says she still gets around. Sees her in church most Sundays and up at the grocery store now and again."

"No kidding. It's weird; I was thinking of her recently because of a book I'm working on."

"Really? Maybe you should stop by and say hello."

"I just may." I knew I had to.

I *HAD* THOUGHT OF MRS. Avery recently. In doing research, I had read a biography of a man who had been in prison in England during the fifties. He described the punishments the prisoners received and spoke about how sometimes, the wardens would put off their punishment for days or even weeks and how that had made it much worse, since they never knew when the reckoning was coming. And that was a tactic Mrs. Avery used with finesse.

Sometimes a student would cross the line and realize his fate, but lo and behold, three fifteen would come, and the bell would ring without the appearance of the dreaded pink slip. *Did she forget?* he'd wonder, or was all forgiven? His head might swim with the endorphins of relief and gratitude for having dodged a bullet, only to have the fantasy crash down on him days later when he wasn't expecting it. During reading hour or right after lunch when all was quiet, she'd walk past his desk, almost unnoticed, and grandly place the folded pink slip on his desk. Then she'd walk back to the front of the class with a satisfied smile, knowing from his fallen face and slumped shoulders that the lesson had been taught: reckoning passes by no man. Perhaps she had read the English criminal's book. More likely, she'd taught it to Her Majesty's Prison Service.

I had several reckonings, but mostly for minor offenses like tardiness or talking in line. Sometimes the pink slip came on the day, sometimes on Friday afternoon, just in time to wreck a homework-free weekend. She'd place the slip on my desk, and I'd groan at the snickers of some of the other children. I'd look up at Mrs. Avery, and she'd say sweetly, "You didn't think I'd forget, did you?" and that would get a quiet laugh from the class.

The worst part was having to get my dad sign the pink slip. If I showed it to him as soon as he got home from work, I'd catch holy hell. The best way to deal with the situation was to forgo playing ball in the afternoon with my pals and get straight to working like a crazed scribe for the hours before supper. That way, when I went to my dad with the note after dinner, I had a finished punishment essay to also present to show my contrition. Then, if I was lucky, he'd just sigh loudly through his nose in exasperation and mutter something unintelligible under his breath as he signed. After that, I just had to endure the few final hours before bedtime being spoken about in the third person as if I weren't there.

The worst one I ever got cost me a whole three-day weekend fishing with my uncle and cousins. I can't remember why Russell Fraser and I were at odds that week, but that's how it started, and as it was spring, I would hazard a guess that it stemmed from something that happened during a baseball game. If it had been autumn, it would have been football, or winter, a snowball fight. Anyway, it was on a Thursday, and for some reason, the fourth-grade teacher was away from the classroom for a few hours and had asked Mrs. Avery to watch her students as they copied out of workbooks.

Mrs. Avery assigned some reading and a few pages of questions to us and informed both classes that there was to be no talking under *any* circumstances. Well, that was easy enough, as we were given enough work to do, but the story is easier to understand if you realize what a complete terror Russell was in the best of times, and when he was feuding with any other kid, he was a complete bastard.

I was maybe a page or two into the reading when—*WHACK!*—something hit me in the temple. What the hell was that? I looked around to see Russ Fraser glowering at me, ruler in hand. He had a huge gum eraser and was tearing fingernail-sized bits from it. He then held one at the end of the ruler, drew it back like an archer at Agincourt, and—*WHACK!* right in my shoulder from clear across the room. His marksmanship was remarkable, as the US Marines would find out nine years later. He got medals for it and everything. Had they only asked me, I could have saved them lots of time and bullets. Russ was gifted.

I could only read the chapter with one eye, as I was forced to keep the other out for projectiles from Russ's direction. I held my notebook up to use as a shield and successfully deflected probably 95 percent of the barrage. When Mrs. Avery returned to look in on our class, I had to quickly put the notebook down, and Russ had to stash the ruler and eraser on his lap to avoid detection. I guess I could have put my hand up and told Mrs. Avery, but being branded a snitch was far worse than taking a million gum-rubber projectiles. I just had to endure and pray that she caught Russ in the act. Revenge would be mine. Or so I thought.

After about ninety minutes of shelling, I'd reached my breaking point. Mrs. Avery had just checked on us, and I knew that I had at least several minutes to retaliate. But before I rose, the school principal walked in the door, looked around, and said, "Where's Mrs. Avery?"

Several children talking in unison sent him to the fourth-grade classroom. If he was going to chat with Mrs. Avery, that would buy me extra time. Now was my chance. I grabbed the heaviest textbook I had handy—science—and made a beeline for Russell. He was frozen in indecision or disbelief as I brought it down hard on his melon. *THUMP!* Faces turned toward us, and I struck again for good measure. *THUMP!* I raised the book again to deliver the coup de grâce when I heard a quiet "Ooooohhhhh" travel through the class.

Standing in the door was Mrs. Avery. Best laid plans, Burns had said.

"Timothy Kelsey back in your seat!" she shrieked.

I could feel my face burning. I walked back to my desk with all of those eyes on me. I wanted to give my testimony, but I knew better and swallowed my words. I sat down and stared at the words in the book, eyes not focusing. I knew the reckoning was upon me.

Three fifteen came and went, but I knew not to take it as an omen. Sure, Mrs. Avery knew Russ was a problem child and no doubt deserved every clout and more, but there was no way I was going to skate on this one. Then Friday came and went, no pink slip. Tuesday of the next week, all was forgiven between Russ and me, and he picked me for his dodgeball team during gym class. Still no pink slip. Wednesday, Thursday . . . Friday, certainly the boom would be lowered. Nothing. It had all been forgotten. Or she had seen the eraser bits on the floor and was onto Russell's game. Whatever it was, I thanked God.

The following weekend, my uncle invited me to join my cousins and him for a fishing trip to Shale Lake, where they occasionally rented a cabin and boat. It was a three-day holiday weekend, and sometimes, if the fishing was particularly good, my uncle would make it four days and keep the kids out of school one extra day. It promised to be glorious, and I was too excited and preoccupied daydreaming of the lake to act up at all. The week dragged on, and in my anticipation, Friday was just a blur. The clock could not make it to three fifteen fast enough. I watched it all afternoon.

Right around three o'clock, I was gazing out the window at the bright sunshine and blue skies when the dreaded pink slip appeared on my desk. My heart seized, and I gulped audibly. I opened the paper to read the words: *Timothy Kelsey. For misbehavior, specifically striking another student with a textbook, ten thousand words. To be turned in before class on the next school day and signed by parent.* I was speechless. There was no way my parents would let me go fishing now.

I looked up at Mrs. Avery. She was smiling coolly.

"Did you think I'd forget?"

No man escapes reckoning. Lesson learned.

———————

I SAID GOODBYE TO AUNT Maggie and promised to phone Annie as soon as I'd made it home safely. I had a couple of stops to make before I headed to the airport and home. My last errand was at Johnston's Bakery, which still made the strawberry tarts I knew Mrs. Avery always relished.

I parked in front of the little well-kept cottage and walked up to the door with my surprises behind my back and rang the bell. It was the old kind you had to twist. Two cats watched me from the windows.

After a geriatric pause, a wizened Mrs. Avery opened the big door. She looked up at me. "Yes, may I help you?" She was older and thinner, but still spry and sharp. She wore a blinding white crochet sweater, buttoned at the top button only, over a floral dress with a large amber necklace. Not a hair was out of place from the snow-white bun on her head.

"Mrs. Avery? It's Tim Kelsey. Remember me?"

"Oh my, Timothy! Why of course I do!" She beamed and opened the screen door. "Come in, come in, Timothy! Mind the cats."

I slipped carefully around the door.

"Why, how long has it been, Timothy?"

I smiled warmly at her as she reached up to give my shoulders a friendly squeeze.

"What do you have?" she asked slyly.

I produced the bag from Johnston's. "Strawberry tarts. I remember they were your favorite." I handed the bag to her.

"How kind and thoughtful!" She clapped her hands together. "What else did you bring?" she asked, nothing escaping her notice.

"I think it's a handle for a sledgehammer. I got it at the hardware store," I said, holding the piece of ash out for her to see.

"What's that for?" she asked with genuine interest, leaning her head slightly.

"Ah, just for this—" I grasped the wood with both hands, drew it back like a horizontal golf swing, and laid the old woman a good clout along the jawline with a soft crack.

"Oof!" She crumpled sideways in slow motion. I aimed four really good kicks right at the same spot on her hip. She groaned at the first one but was quiet for the others. She'd have to live another ninety years before those bones knit, I made damn sure.

"Well, good day to you!" I said, putting the handle on my shoulder. As I walked out the door, I was almost tripped by three or four cats darting out into the sunshine. As the door whooshed and clicked closed behind me, I had to chuckle.

Did she think I'd forget?

FLOTSAM AND JETSAM

The rush and sigh sounds of the ocean mixed with the crackle of burning wood. The fire was in full flush, yet only occasionally betrayed the palm fronds above on the moonless night. The sacred Storyteller shuffled lazily around the light counterclockwise as was his custom, keeping his left hand toward the flames. When he spoke, he spoke loudly, partly because of the importance of his words, but mostly to be heard clearly from behind the carved wooden mask that was the badge of office. It was made from rippled wood bleached gray by age and sun and decorated with bits of shell and dry grass.

He stopped where the fire was directly between him and the center of the island, the flicker illuminating his gaunt frame and grotesque mask against an impossibly black backdrop of ocean and starless sky. He raised his arms dramatically, the wind fluttering his ragged sleeves like prayer flags, and spoke the opening words:

"Hear me! I have come from afar, and I have brought a story to tell!" His voice boomed to the congregation. He paused for the traditional response.

I was the congregation that night. We took turns. And out of my deep reverence for the office of the sacred Storyteller, I responded, speaking the correct reply in a clear stentorian voice:

"Oh, Storyteller! Tell those assembled how that shit went down!"

"Well, since you're willing . . ." he began. "A long time ago, in the time when our fathers were young, the world was at howling war. And off in a camp one day, a new prisoner was added to the sorrowful souls kept like animals behind barbed wire. This new unfortunate was a proper Englishman, an aviator, and his name was Chrichton—"

"Crittendon," I said, admittedly out of turn.

"Chrichton," the Storyteller insisted.

"No, it was Crittendon . . . Dr. Bombay, Malcolm the Englisher."

"I fucking well know who Bernard Fox is, douchebag!" the Storyteller spat loudly from beneath the mask. "And by the way, just which one of us is wearing this fucking thing?" He pointed first at the mask and then in the general direction of the ledge of rock where the tribal laws had been inscribed using a broken piece of outboard motor propeller as a stylus.

He had a point; I was out of order. Our code was literally written in stone. Never mind that he was off his goddamn rocker. I'd seen that episode a million times. Eddie had too, but he was obviously remembering it wrong. Chrichton, for Christ's sake. Maybe the strain of being stuck out there for so long was making his synapses smoke and sizzle a bit. Or even some weird parasite eating his frontal lobe; we had to be teeming with them. There was a muddy pond of questionable but fresh water farther inland that hadn't killed us yet. We boiled everything we drank, except for stuff we tried to ferment, the results of which might be what was taking care of our internal parasites. Externally, we were covered by bites and scabs.

Jesus, at that point, I had no real idea how long we'd been stuck. Years obviously, but somewhere along the line, we'd stopped counting. With no real seasons to speak of here other than delirium-inducing heat or torrential fire-hose downpour, there was nothing to break the time into discernible increments. I'm sure the girls we'd gone down to

Costa Rica with all that time ago had wasted no time getting on with their lives without us.

And fuck the both of them too. It was their goddamn bright idea to go to the time-share presentation. Eddie and I wanted no part of it, and we'd made that clear. However, intoxicated by the lure of free stuff, they were both of mind to barter with us for our capitulation. I'm not going to lie; I'm a weak-willed individual. Eddie maybe trebly so.

So winning the fishing excursion as one of the door prizes was their fault, but the two of us were determined to salvage something of our manly dignity as we sat through the endless time-share pitch. Both of us blew our gaskets when we discovered buried in the fine print that the fishing excursion wasn't free but half off and not redeemable during the time we were down there. We had wasted a day of our vacation. It was unacceptable. We required justice.

It's easy to say now that all of the rum and mescaline was most accurately *my* fault, but there's no denying Eddie had insisted that because he'd spent his summers driving his dad's speedboat on the lake, he was perfectly qualified to pilot the craft we eventually liberated from the marina where the fishing excursion boats were. If they could put time requirements on our prize, so could we, and we chose 1:30 a.m. or thereabout.

We were only successful in that we made it out of the harbor undetected. The keys to the boats were carelessly kept hanging on a board in an office with a broken window right next to the door latch, so we borrowed a key and a wad of paper towels for my bleeding knuckles. We made it way the hell out to sea, way beyond the point where you could spot land when you were on top of one of the swells. And sweet baby Jesus, there were swells. The subject of Eddie's shortcomings as a seafarer hung unspoken in the air like the smoke after a grease fire in a small kitchen. It still hadn't been acknowledged when the storm blew up.

Eddie and I were being gangbanged by Poseidon, Neptune, and Davy Jones all at once, while the mescaline and rum pummeled us from the inside. All we could do was hang on, which we barely did, for most of the day. The homicidal sky was black apart from a smear of sapphire blue in the west when the God Almighty bang happened. I thought we'd come down on some shallow point in the middle of the ocean because it felt like the boat had been dropped on rocks from a twenty-foot height. As things unfolded, I now believe it was some form of jetsam just under the surface—maybe a cargo container that got loose from a freighter in similar conditions sometime in the past. The collision happened at the stern, destroying the prop and driveshaft and putting a decent crack in the transom. We slowly took on water all night. Luckily, the storm eased up during the night, turning to light drizzle, and even the waves went easier on us, morphing into a rough chop that still flexed the crack in the back of the boat, sending pulses of water to add to the slow seep.

We drifted like that all through the night, slowly sinking. By this time, we were both wearing at least two life vests each, and several had been lashed to the industrial cooler and a bag full of anything we thought may be useful, come what may. If there was a life raft on board, we certainly didn't find it, and it wouldn't have been for lack of looking. Neither of us wanted to be trapped inside the cabin if the boat suddenly went down, so we sheltered in the overhang just aft of the cabin, ocean water and occasional islands of puke sloshing around our shins.

The storm blew up again in the morning, the rain so thick we had no visibility as the waves threw us around. We'd been taking that beating for hours, unable to even talk to each other above the roar, when we heard an awful scrape, followed moments later by a sudden molar-shattering crash that momentarily froze us at an awkward angle before we were lifted again, followed by more scraping. It sounded as if the boat were being torn apart, and we were frozen in our panic, wedged into the opposite corners where the cabin met the gunwales. We could feel the surge of water that poured into the hull below us before feeling a sharp thump, and then the boat started to yaw violently, throwing Eddie, the cooler, and the rest of the string of crap we'd lashed together right on top of me—hard. The life preservers cushioned the impact, but the force of it all knocked the wind out of me, and I took the cooler so hard to the forehead—luckily the flat top and not an edge or corner—that my mind went all calm and peaceful for a while.

When I returned to the program after a word from our sponsor, the soundtrack was loud with the howling wind, pounding surf, and Eddie's gurgling schoolgirl shrieks as I sat in sloshing water up to above my navel. Eddie clung to the ladder to the flying bridge as he screamed and squirmed against the gentle rise and thump the boat was now doing. Our vessel sat a little low at the bow, listing slightly to starboard, and seemed to be loosely spindled in place. The sky had lightened a bit, though we were continuously battered by stinging spray, and Eddie eventually got his legs under him enough to pull himself up into a standing position at the ladder.

"We're back! We're back!" he yelled hoarsely, but I only knew what he was yelling by lip-reading.

Once I got used to the rhythm of the rise and thump of the deck, I was able to slide myself upright against the cabin to periodically view a low green cliff and black rocks no more than a couple hundred feet away. I laughed with relief.

Eddie made his way over to me, grinning. "We're back. We just have to make it to shore and then find a road and get back to the hotel!"

He made his way gingerly along the gunwale and to the transom. Before I knew it, he'd slithered over the back by the diving ladder and disappeared below. I slipped and slid my way back to watch him and his three life vests alternately swim and half paddle, half crawl over the jagged rocks to shore. There were bits of debris and flotsam all along the shore: rusting jumbles of cargo containers and bits of watercraft of different sizes smashed to pieces and decaying. I grabbed a bottle of rum out of the cooler, wrapped it in a damp towel I'd wrung out, and took it with me as I followed Eddie, collecting bruises and scrapes on the sharp and slippery rocks. I found myself still crawling long after I would have been able to awkwardly walk.

When we finally met up on a fairly flat piece of beach, Eddie was having a smoke and I broke out the bottle. After two wordless passes, Eddie pressed on to the edge of the vegetation as I stood there partially emptying the bottle and fully emptying my bladder.

I was about to start off to join him when he called, "Joe! Joe! It was only supposed to be a three-hour tour! A three-hour tour!" Fucking hilarious.

———————

WELL, OF COURSE WE DIDN'T find a road, and of course we weren't back. Of course we were screwed. We were marooned on an island pummeled by surf and garbage. What we learned quickly was that the island wasn't all that big. It was doubtful it had even four miles of coastline. From the highest point on a clear day, you still couldn't see anything else on the horizon. There was a muddy pond in the depths of the thickest part of the vegetation. We wound up setting up our shelter on the lee side of the island with a gentler beach, using scraps of corrugated metal, wood, fiberglass, and whatever else could scavenge—and we had plenty to scavenge.

There were small lizards in the wooded area and seabirds and rats everywhere. I jumped three feet when the first one I saw leaped out at me as I went to move some piece of junk in the weeds. Later that night, as we sat in the firelight, I clubbed one that ran across my foot to death with a piece of driftwood.

"God, I hate those bastards," Eddie said sympathetically, using a metal rod to flip its carcass into the fire. "Wonder how long it's going to take to kill them all."

Four days is the answer, but not to Eddie's question. Four days is how long it took for rat to become our staple protein for our duration in paradise. That was also the second day since Eddie's smokes had run out. It was a grim day. His company had gotten so prickly that had someone offered me a cold root beer in exchange for his life, I would have bashed his brains in while giggling. That's not a good situation on a postage stamp-sized island.

To break the tension, I asked him, "Remember when Mr. Drysdale found out that Granny kept all of her savings in cash and spent the episode trying to convince her to deposit it in the bank?"

"Yeah," he replied, "and it turns out all of her dough was in Confederate script, so it was worthless for deposit."

"Uh-huh . . . So how goddamn dumb was Milburn to not recognize that the historical value would only increase?"

"Oh, he was an idiot, all right. Jane Hathaway was the real brains, but her career could only go so high."

"Because she was a woman in the sixties?" I asked.

"No, because she sexually assaulted Ellie Mae at a cement pond party that got out of hand. It cost the bank dearly to keep Jed from going to the cops or taking the law into his own hands."

"The hell you say."

———

EDDIE AND I HAD USUALLY worked well together since high school when we both had jobs at the liquor store, and true to form, we were in a fairly regular schedule keeping busy. We had cleared a rectangle of vegetation down to the rocky soil near the top of the high point on the side of our arrival and had spelled out *HELP*. Initially, this was spelled out in dark rocks in letters about six feet high, but several months into our residency, the letters were redone about three times larger, rendered in a mixture of black rock and soil and all manner of trash and detritus deemed useful for nothing else, especially if it was brightly colored. The larger letters were also positioned above a shallow trench that underlined the letters filled with combustible material that could be set alight as a beacon if we spotted potential salvation.

Along the path from one side of the island to the other, we had a small clearing containing the Mini-Mart—sorted piles of goods and scraps of material that may be of use in the future. We'd devised about a half dozen different rattraps of varying efficacy that had to be checked daily. There was scavenging to be done among the rocks when the surf allowed, and there were dumb brown seabirds to attempt to sneak up on and thwack with a board, etc. The seabirds tasted awful, but it was a change from the rat, and the fish seemed to bite on the bird guts more so than the rat guts.

Every so often, something new would wash up, but most often it was crap we couldn't use, like four gross of sandals in kid's sizes decorated with cartoon frogs—cruel shit like that. The island had plants with huge waxy leaves that we called taro and may have really been taro, because we pounded their roots and ate it with the rat, lizard, fish, and dumb brown seabird chowder. Some of the trees had small sour green fruits that we sometimes added as well. In our scientific exploration of our new home, we dried and attempted to smoke every sort of flora and two kinds of lizard that the island provided. The only thing we learned was that there were little round wrinkly-leaved plants that would make your heart race like the bejeezus and close your throat quicker than a strip club that refused to pay protection.

The booze salvaged from our boat was strictly and carefully rationed, so we finally ran out and sobered up around day three. Once in a great while, a crate of cheap mouthwash would wash up on the rocks, and on more than one occasion some broken-masted and snapped-keel wreck of a sailboat came within our reach with high-end bar contents still intact, twice with quantities of very respectable schnozz candy as well. But these sea-falls were few and far between, and monotony was the main enemy, as we were very lucky to be surviving well enough to experience monotony. What we wouldn't have given for a crate of smokes for him and root beer for me to wash up one day, but we were always disappointed in that regard. When we got on each other's nerves, we just wandered off and worked elsewhere alone, sometimes for a couple of days. In the case of the Spat, nine months at least.

The Island Religion of the Story formed organically and rather quickly. We worked to feed our bodies, and so too did we work to enlighten our souls through the sacred and holy tradition of passing on the wisdom and stories of our people. It may have been born out of desperation. One night early on, as we ate our evening slop out of two children's beach pails, several dozen of which would eventually polka-dot our *HELP* sign in garish color for some time, I went on a rant.

"Eddie!" I said, louder than necessary. "This is too much. Know how it's better to tape something on TV so you can fast-forward through the goddamn commercials? I'd walk through fire to watch a couple of hours' worth of bad commercials!"

"Why the bad ones, Joe? Eh?" Eddie said, suddenly calm with the mantle of inspiration. He put his bucket down deliberately in the sand and rose to his feet. Taking a deep breath, he began: "Hot dogs! Armour hot dogs! What kind of kid eats Armour hot dogs?"

He was inspired. He was an antenna linking us to our culture through time and space, living Americana adrift on the globe. "Fat kids! Skinny kids! Kids who climb on rocks!"

Maybe it was the beginnings of malnutrition dining on our frontal lobes. Maybe it was the mental strain of the reality of our situation, but nevertheless, it revealed itself to both of us then and there, a truth we did not discuss yet was clearly expressed between us, that the culture was alive and within us.

"Tough kids, sissy kids," I joined in, a congregation assembled, "even kids with chicken pox!"

Amen and selah.

I HAD JUST ABOUT PERFECTED the nylon strap arrangement that kept the Storyteller's wooden mask comfortably in place. I continued to address the congregation: ". . . and as the door shut behind him, someone told him to put on a mask. Slowly and sadly, he announced that

Lieutenant Colonel Henry Blakes's plane had been shot down over the Sea of Japan. It spun in. There were no survivors . . . Here endeth the tale."

"Magnifique," Eddie said, and I thanked him. It had been a good telling and a particularly good day.

Late in the afternoon the day before, we were both on the rocky side of the island debating whether to light a signal fire that evening, and before judging the conditions to be too windy, we simultaneously noticed a new bit of debris on the rocks. It looked to be a crate. In the midmorning, when the sea got more cooperative, we half waded, half swam, and occasionally crawled out with some simple breaching tools fashioned from scrap. For these scrounging expeditions, we had a floating tool shelf made of a few boards supported by foam-filled life vests that we took out to the metal crate. It was filled with mostly water-logged catalogs, but the top forty or so were still dry enough to burn. We had some plastic trash bags with us and kept them dry all the way back to shore, cursing our luck at not finding anything truly useful.

We made it all the way back to a shady spot in the Mini-Mart, where I slung the bag of catalogs. Eddie rummaged around in our salvage piles, and I pulled out a few catalogs to thumb through as he muttered, "We should have enough shit for you to make a coconut radio, you know that? What's your problem?"

I ignored him. The first catalog was men's shoes and belts. It would burn nicely. It was on page sixteen of the second catalog that I gasped audibly enough to get Eddie's attention. Pages sixteen to thirty-four: women's bathing suits. Handel's chorus pealed in my head. I have no idea what facial expression I made, but he came at me in urgent curiosity.

"What do you got?" he demanded.

I squealed in greedy delight, my first instinct was to grab it to my chest and run, but he was right on me, clutching at the fragile pages. "Get away from us, you fucking creep," I yelled, holding him off.

He made an end run to the garbage bag and, throwing aside one catalog of purses and hats and one catalog of winter coats, found a women's fashion one with at least ten pages of lingerie and nightgowns. We both heard the chorus, which quickly faded to an uncomfortable silence. Neither one of us would lower our eyes or break gaze. The uncomfortable moment hung in the air before we both made our respective moves. He coolly placed his catalog under his arm and faded back into the long grass that led to a quieter part of the beach, as I similarly edged my way to the path to the high spot on the cliff, catalog in both hands.

Later, I watched the sun start to set for a while before I headed back to the shelter, marveling at our lush surroundings. By the time I made it back, Eddie was adding roasted rat to the bubbling taro. He was whistling. I was hoping he'd washed his hands.

"Been a good day, Joe," he said, a look of peace on his face. "A carton of smokes, and this could really be paradise."

I could have really gone for a root beer myself, but I got what he meant.

————————

UNFORTUNATELY, NOTHING LASTS FOREVER, AND that goes especially for cheap catalog pages in a tropical climate, despite the curatorial care we put into their preservation. Eventually, the curvy goddesses that had been helping us with the tension of our situation were little more than ghosts on the tattered disintegrating paper. We were both a little sad and heartbroken the day we admitted to ourselves that there really were no more images on the paper other than the memories we projected upon them.

One midday at the Mini-Mart, while I was constructing another rattrap, Eddie was gingerly inspecting the pages for any semblance of an image and with an obviously heavy heart, announced, "Enough is enough." He took the stack of tattered scraps and walked them back to the fire in front of the shelter and relegated our erstwhile harem to their pyre. I don't think we spoke that night. I recall no stories were told.

The next thing that broke the boredom a bit was another windfall, one that unfortunately led to the Spat, but that came later. A plastic shipping tub appeared on the rocks. It was sturdy plastic that would make a good rainwater basin, but inside was a bonanza of office supplies kept mercifully dry. There were plastic binders that did a great job of reinforcing the soles of our shoes that had been cut to ribbons by the sharp rocks. The markers and highlighters had dried out, but their hollow barrels made decent bobbers for fishing on the calm water. The best of all were the reams of paper, packages of manila folders, and generous supply of pencils. These would have been useless except for kindling, which we didn't need, but luckily, we had Eddie and his remarkable artistic skills.

Eddie was a brilliant illustrator. When we were in school, he had been the darling of every art teacher. The principal of our high school commissioned him to paint a mural in the lunchroom, which had been boldly executed in the style of Soviet-era propaganda posters. Old O'Halloran, our boss at the liquor store, paid him handsomely to paint the brick wall against the parking lot of Tara Liquors, which Eddie transformed into a gorgeous logo. It looked like a parody of a classic beer can logo done in black, white, and yellow, proclaiming Tara Liquors as *Celebrated 'Round the World!* with a logo of a harp superimposed on the city skyline, fancy knotwork and filigree at the corners. The bottom left corner had a small trompe l'oeil of the label lifting from the brick surface, revealing the faces of three characters from an underground stoner comic we used to read. He had talent. He could do fine art, animation characters, portraits, caricatures—you name it. He started getting his artistic muscles back into shape immediately. Within a few hours, he was contentedly scratching away, pausing only to sharpen one of the pencils with scrap piece of metal that had been honed on a rock.

I was peeling the charred skin off some rat carcasses before tossing the meat into the taro slop cooking on the fire when he strode up triumphantly to show me his creation. There I was, wearing the Storyteller mask up on my head the way an umpire pushes his up between plays, holding a bottle clearly labeled *Root Beer*. Eddie was there, cigarette dangling from his mouth, turning a spit over a fire. On the spit, the two women that had talked us into the time-share seminar were tied, roasting away.

The title of the piece was written in bold letters underneath. *JUS-TICE*, it said.

I laughed.

IT MIGHT HAVE BEEN A few days later when I was going to wade out a bit and try to catch some fish when Eddie strode up to the shelter wearing a grin. He took a piece of manila folder and stuck it to a drift-wood post with a pushpin. "Here's something we can both think of to keep our spirits up!" On the tan cardstock, he had done a still life from memory: a pack of his brand of cigarettes and a perspiring bottle of good-quality root beer.

I chuckled. "Okay, but if you come by and the picture is missing and there's a necktie on the doorknob, take a hike for an hour or so."

We both laughed. Then we stopped abruptly, the simultaneous re-alization too shameful to acknowledge. We lowered our eyes and went off to our respective tasks. I took the bait and tackle and headed for the shallow water.

HIS FIRST WORK WAS AN amazing rendering of the long-legged blonde from one of the swimwear advertisements, a favorite of both of ours, and although he captured her features perfectly, his memory had evidently grown dim when it came to the details of her one-piece crossback since he'd omitted the suit altogether. It was remarkable art. In those rough surroundings, the product of his talent was glorious. That first spark of inspiration and the muse was upon him. From then on up until the Spat, he was an artist possessed. He seemed to go through the drudgery of our daily routine more cheerfully, relishing the moments when he could work on his pictorial creations. I, too, benefited from the introduction of high culture to our atavistic island life and felt noticeably less tense and clearer of mind than before.

I'm no humanities scholar by any stretch, but I'm rather an authority on the progression of Eddie's artistic arc, as it was I who witnessed it firsthand. His style was distinctive and representational, showing an attention to detail and a high degree of accuracy. His early work during this period is almost stark when compared to later offerings, which showed a rapid progression of intricacy. His first few pieces were done purely from imagination, but his first collection, *Sci-Fi Actresses Reimagined*, showed such a gift for capturing resemblance and verisimilitude that it took the island's cultural scene by storm. He was to be lauded not only for his ability to reproduce a recognizable face so faithfully, but also his attention to the insignia on the uniforms in the few instances where depicted.

The artist's sophomore work, which was boldly much more personal, was *Attractive Women from Sitcoms from the 60s through the Mid-90s, Imagined Engaging in Nudism*, which while successful, had somewhat less of an audience appeal than the previous series because of some obviously glaring omissions and the fact that some of the portrayals chosen were just rehashed stereotypical bitchy wives and were frankly unfunny, no matter what the artist's personal and incorrect views were.

His next collection, however, was a very daring and brave endeavor that may have been his twisted triumph. *Scenes from Great 80s Horror and Slasher Movies, Remembered and Reimagined* was a bold and shocking exploration of the more perverted aspects of the genre, provoking much thought and reflection, to which the audience responded enthusiastically. His next artistic phase saw a striking collection evolve from a commissioned work: a sensitive rendering of a particularly attractive female Soviet spy from one of a much beloved series of films. This portfolio, provocatively named *Women Who May Kill You but You'd Still Think It Was Worth It*, certainly hit all of the high notes as far as imagination, accuracy, and tone of the subject matter. Eddie was at the top of his game.

NOT LONG AFTER CAME THE Spat. It was our own retelling of the Michelangelo movie starring Moses, the trust broken between an artist and patron . . .

I offered to get the water *and* bring the firewood three days in a row to allow him more time for his art. It had been my request. I had asked for something specific and had traded my labor to offset the energy of its production. Does a patron not deserve some basic respect?

I recall there had been some lively debate after that night's story. Eddie in no way could entertain the thought that the bond between the dolphin and the Florida park ranger could have been based on a mutual need for the other to keep a secret. Simply put, the park ranger knew the cetacean was responsible for a string of indecent assaults upon swimming vacationers, and the dolphin knew where the park ranger had disposed of the body of the teenage boys' mother. Talented though he was, Eddie also had the capacity for extreme naivete.

He leaned his back against a jumble of odds and ends piled near the fire pit, admiring the portrait on which he was currently working. A cute petite woman with a short haircut. He turned the unfinished work toward me and the firelight. "Whaddaya think?"

"Nice," I said, and I meant it. "Who is she?"

"Bartender down the street from my job."

"Yeah, you probably don't have that job anymore," I reminded him.

A night or so before, I'd had a dream about Melanie DiBennedetto. She was a customer at the liquor store when we were in high school. She was only a few years older than us but at the time was the trophy wife of Rocco DiBennedetto. He was a rising star at the fire department, partially due to his uncle Pete, the battalion commander, and partially due to his aggressiveness on the job, which was rumored to be somewhat augmented by steroids and blow. Mrs. DiBennedetto had an adorable face, a will-melting smile, a body to sell one's soul for, and had trouble written all over her in neon letters. She unfortunately also had a voice that squeaked like a rusty gate, but nobody wanted to *talk* with Mrs. DiBennedetto. She would come into the store, always sexy whether dressed up or down, smelling of just a little too much perfume, flirting mischievously. She was always a show. She made sure of it.

"Hey," I said to Eddie. "Next one, give her curly shoulder-length hair and big eyes . . . long lashes. Fuller cheeks than that one and curvier."

"Mrs. DiBennedetto?" Eddie guessed right away. He could have been an FBI sketch artist.

"Yes! Exactly!"

Eddie laughed at my request. "Holy shit, that woman spelled trouble! Probably still does!" He grabbed a fresh sheet of paper and started a preliminary sketch. "She had your number, son! We *all* looked, but you slobbered, Joe! Ha!"

"With good fucking reason."

"Man, she'd come in with a minidress and the high heels . . . No! Better yet, when she'd come in with the tiny cutoff jeans and a bikini top! Jesus! I think I saw you almost hump a pony keg once when she was in a wifebeater and no bra!" He chuckled away as he drew.

"Just do the picture and leave my memories to me . . ."

―――――――

IT WAS, EASILY, HIS FINEST work to date. A masterpiece of pornography ripped from the heavens and applied to the page in #2 graphite. Words wouldn't do it justice.

"Great or what?" he asked during the unveiling.

Words failed me.

WORDS FAILED ME AGAIN ABOUT a week later after returning to the shelter late one morning following a grueling session of scrounging among the fresh jetsam. I was tired and aching. Melanie DiBennedetto was missing. The Spat thundered on the horizon.

Oh, I knew damn well where I'd last set her down, but I searched the shelter nonetheless. I shuffled through the growing pile of perfectly good hand-drawn filth just in case she'd inadvertently been filed away, to no avail. I checked between the bits and structures that passed for furniture and the myriad of materials that stood in for walls to find nothing.

I didn't want to admit it to myself. I didn't want the hideous thing to be true.

That motherfucker.

Since a line had clearly been crossed, I violated an unspoken taboo on the island: I marched off into the grass toward the spit of beach that was his private spot. He didn't venture to my shallow little indentation, not big enough to be called a cave, a bit below the highest spot on the island on the opposite side from the *HELP* sign. And until that moment, I didn't trespass on his private spot, a sandy micro-peninsula with a spit of beach and a nice view of the ocean. But the gauntlet had been thrown. That son of a bitch. I was pissed, but I had enough of my wits about me to announce myself loudly. It was bad enough that he'd no doubt done the transgression; I certainly had no need to witness any of it.

"You son of a bitch!"

You'd think that all those years of friendship, especially the last nineteen months or so of sitting across from this scoundrel watching him chew rat and lizard with his mouth open like a goddamned animal would have counted for something. All the times I helped him move, covered for him with girlfriends and family, gave him my second to last beer, evidently had meant nothing.

"You filthy animal!" I bellowed, crashing noisily through the bushes to make absolutely sure I didn't surprise him in the heinous act.

"You worthless prick!" I stepped into the sandy clearing, and that goddamned weasel was even holding Melanie DiBenedetto behind his back, an obvious and unmistakable sign that he knew fucking well he shouldn't have done it in the first place.

I didn't push him down, no matter what he claims. I have no idea what I *was* going to do to him in my rage, but the clumsy fuck tripped over a tree root, and that was what sent him sprawling on his scrawny ass. For a second, I thought I'd done it with my mind, like the creepy adopted kid from a low-budget horror movie, but I saw the root clearly enough to step over it as I advanced on him. The sight of him sprawled out like that, backing up like a frightened crustacean, filled me with disgust. I stifled the urge to give him the mother of all Indian burns, electing instead to call him a bastard and storm off. It was the last word between us for a long time.

Later that night, when I went to the shelter to eat long after Eddie had finished his dinner, the backstabbing louse was already stretched out on his side of the shelter. The gray wispy ash remains of Melanie DiBennedetto, the sitcom women, the sci-fi women, et Alice, swirled around the feet of the low fire.

––––––––––

OVER THE NEXT SIX OR eight months, we fell into a new routine that served to keep us from having to talk to each other. We still cooked and took care of the shelter in the original spot, but we tended to work and eat in shifts. We still alternated cooking, but we didn't eat together. If I wasn't fishing, emptying rattraps, or scrounging, I spent a lot of my time up in my shallow niche in the ridge.

Eddie worked on his own as well. He even started another system that kept our mutual animosity to a low seethe. He had scrawled on large piece of plywood in the Mini-Mart *You going to use this???* and propped whatever piece of jetsam he had plans for in front of it. I started doing the same. If the item stayed, one was free to use it however they wished. If it had been put back, the future for the item was in dispute, and nobody touched it. This arrangement lasted nearly a year.

––––––––––––

I SHALL NEVER FORGET THE glorious day that brought the renormalization of relations. It was like a Christmas miracle . . .

It had been a gray morning with the sky threatening rain. I had spent a couple of hours cleaning up the area around the *HELP* sign on the cliff, keeping it easily visible and legible. I noticed that the ocean had hocked up some fresh garbage upon the treacherous rocks. There looked to have been something substantial, like the broken hull of a small boat, that I thought might be worth investigating once the weather cleared.

Later that morning, the sun broke through the clouds, and I pushed the floating work-platform out to go scrounge amid the rocks. I checked among the newly deposited garbage for about an hour and a half before I came across a half-floating cube—a Styrofoam box that had been over-sealed with duct tape as if in an attempt to keep a Babylonian demon from escaping. I checked it for biohazard stickers and, finding none, pushed it back to the shallow water with the rest of the crap I'd picked up.

Up on the beach, I sorted the morning's haul into piles—one for the Mini-Mart, and one for the garbage pile that went to making our *HELP* sign bigger and more impressive. I used a repurposed steak knife to slice open the duct tape to get the foam box open, revealing two dense bricks that had been wrapped in plastic with such care as to discourage even the most dogged Babylonian demon yet yielded nicely to the cutlery.

The aroma hit me—a scent reminiscent of a laundry bag from the varsity gym locker of a high school for ferrets and weasels. I got real tears in my eyes, and it wasn't from the waft.

"I JUST BECAME KING OF THE ISLAND!" I yelled in thanksgiving to the sky.

Wrestling the two bundles out of their squeaky cocoon, I danced all the way on the path past the Mini-Mart to the shelter on the other side of the island, yelling for Eddie all the way, the Spat suddenly forgotten.

"Eddie, you son of a bitch! You're not going to believe this!"

He came up the beach at a lanky jog to see the source of my excitement. I handed him the punctured brick. His eyes welled up too. "Please be real," he pleaded to the universe as he clutched the bundle to his chest. "Please, oh please, be real . . ."

Suddenly, his reverie was broken by his next frenzied thought. "Pipe! Paper! Something!" He placed the block of weed down reverently on a crate-cum stool and started ransacking the shelter for a suitable smoking device. I did the same. Had we even entertained the possibility of this kind of windfall, we would have spent some of our ample free time crafting something for the blessed event, but as it was, the thought hadn't entered our minds much since our initial experiments with the flora of the island.

With hands shaking with excitement, I crafted the first workable prototype: a piece of aluminum tube with an irregularly shaped piece of rock wedged a half inch or so in one end that would allow air to pass but hopefully block most ash. I rushed over to the package and pinched out a fragrant green plug and loaded it into the pipe, then lit a long piece of dry grass from the cooking fire.

I probably inhaled too deeply, because the coughing fit soon found me laid out on my back on the sand, hacking and gurgling. For whatever hell it was on my body, our bounty proved to be of the highest quality. My mind was soaring on a Pegasus's wings, up in the cool air among the choirs of angels and the orchestral music of the spheres, my consciousness wrapped in fluffy blanket of pure understanding. When I came back to my corporeal form, I was still coughing, slowly regaining my breath, eventually becoming aware of my surroundings.

Eddie had picked up the tube from where I'd dropped it and used another dry grass match to duplicate. He sat down on a piece of our furniture and took a long slow hit, extinguishing his match in the sand beside him. He leaned his head back with closed eyes, puffed cheeks, and a beatific smile, holding the smoke for an impressive interval before exhaling a thick pale blue cloud.

"Mmm, pumpkin!" he declared.

"Better than a pack of smokes?" I asked.

"Quite possibly . . ." he said thoughtfully. "Better than a root beer?" he asked back.

"Definitely possibly," I replied, still on my back, listening to the glorious chord played by the rushing breeze and rhythmic waves.

That night, even though we would have sacrificed a Christian baby in exchange for a real pizza, the rat, lizard, dumb brown seabird, and taro chowder went down unexpectedly well for a change. For the first time in months, the Storyteller mask got used, the evening seeing a rare double feature, including both the tale of the rolltop desk with the Mathew Brady photograph and an encore of the story of how the annoying child's middle name got to be Rosebud.

"Robert Oscar Sam E-D-W-A-R-D Edward Benjamin Ulysses David!" sang the celebrant and the congregation as one, eyes red and glassy, gaunt limbs permanently speckled with bites and scabs.

We fell asleep in front of the fire that night, only retreating into the shelter when the chill woke us both and the fire was only a glowing smolder.

We fell back into the routine as before the Spat, but now occasionally much more relaxed and lighter of heart. Since we'd worked out a system of survival some time before, we now had spare time to craft drug paraphernalia out of soft green wood, scraps of aluminum tubing, dumb brown seabird bones—whatever seemed worth a try. Sometimes on special occasions, we'd roll a traditional jay with the ideal paper we had at hand that had come from one of those hotel Bibles we found in the glove box of a half-swamped motorboat that had been on the rocks way before we showed up. We referred to these sessions as High Mass, and maybe we should have been less irreverent, but the fact is that it was during High Mass that the Miracle happened . . .

There we were, sitting around the collection of sorted jetsam on the rocky beach. I believe we were celebrating the birthday of Oliver the Humanzee, plus or minus 182 days, but that's not what's important. What's really important is that what Eddie had initially thought to be an eye floater turned out to be a genuine speck on the horizon. When he realized that he was seeing possible salvation, he was struck dumb and only able to communicate with a hoarse bark and a rapid slap on my shoulder. It took me a second or two to see what he was gesturing at, and I let out a hysterical yell like a kid at a carnival. We scrambled up the ridge face to our *HELP* sign.

"Smoke! Smoke!" I yelled, but Eddie was already sprinting back to bring a burning match from the cooking fire instead of having to start one. We had a trench above and below the huge rock-and-nondegradable trash letters filled with tinder and bits of tire and plastic that we hoped would provide good visible smoke. We had decided long ago that if we saw any ships or airplanes during the day, we'd light the top trench so as not to obscure the letters, and if at night, we'd light the one below in effort to illuminate the message. In a matter of minutes, we had both trenches and a fairly big patch of long dry grass burning like an oil rig fire as we ran around screaming and yelling like idiots. The boat on the horizon grew bigger and bigger.

For a bit, I had a waking nightmare of the boat getting bashed on the rocks as ours had, and started yelling and pointing for them to approach the other side of the island, oblivious to the fact that there was no way for anyone to know what the hell I was doing other than Eddie. Of course, it's easy now to realize that whoever was captaining the boat was an actual boat captain and not as dumb as two drug-addled drunks who'd stolen the craft they piloted aimlessly. A bright spotlight winked at us, probably giving us far more Boy Scout credit than we were due. When it became obvious that they were circumnavigating our spit of island, we ran through the path past the Mini-Mart to the shelter on the calmer side.

In a frenzy, we gathered up everything of value, which at this point was a small remainder of cocaine and maybe a quarter pound of our windfall dope, and put it into the Styrofoam box in preparation to swim out to as close as the boat dared come. Before we even got our feet wet, we could see that they were putting a small Zodiac boat into the water.

We put the drugs in our pockets and tidied up the site. Why, I have no idea. Maybe it was because of the Miracle.

And I don't say *Miracle* lightly, because wouldn't you know it, our rescue vessel was the MV *Lamb of the Sea*, the converted fishing trawler that was now operated by the evangelical-environmental group Brotherhood of Purity. We were being rescued by the fucking Salvation Navy!

"*Dios sea contigo*! God be with you! God be with you! *Dios sea contigo*!" a weather-beaten and astonishingly fit-looking woman aged anywhere from sixty to one hundred shouted to us through a bullhorn.

We waved. As soon as boat beached, the old dame was over the inflatable side like a shot, leaving the two young fellows to drag it up the beach until it was safe from being floated away. *"Hola hermanos! Hola!"*

"Holy God! Are we glad to see you!" Eddie said, inadvertently giving our rescuers a rosier opinion of us than we warranted.

"You speak English!" the woman said, clasping her hands in front of her.

"Almost exclusively," I answered for no reason.

"Do. You. Need. Assistance?" one of the younger sailors asked as if he were speaking to members of an uncontacted tribe. Maybe he hadn't heard us.

"You bet your ass we do!" Eddie blurted. I don't think he caught the icy glaze that the three new faces took on. "Our boat wound up on the rocks." He gestured to the other side of the island. "Like a couple of years ago! Can you believe it?"

"We're glad you're safe, brothers, and sorry about your boat," the older woman said.

"Yeah, thing is, it really wasn't our boat," Eddie said.

"Eddie," I cut him off. I could see it was going to take some time to reacclimate him to not make an ass of himself.

"Are there any others besides yourselves?" she asked, her eyes raking our camp.

We shook our heads.

"I'd like to have the doctor check you out. We could take you back to civilization, if you'd like."

"Way ahead of you, sister," Eddie babbled. "Let's get the hell out of here!" he added, making to help handle the small craft back into the water. The two younger sailors poked around the bones of our shelter, which suddenly looked much more dilapidated to me.

"Is there anything you need to take with you?" one of them asked.

"Oh, Christ no! Let it all burn for all I care!" Eddie giggled in joy, oblivious to the horror he was causing in the crew of our only ride home.

"What about your Bible?" the youngest-looking one said, picking up the tattered book reverently.

"Yeah, sure, why not? That's good paper there," Eddie said, perplexing them further.

"We can certainly give you one that's not missing Genesis and Exodus once we get on board," the rescuer said.

"There's quite a few pages out of Revelations too," he replied.

We went to push the boat back into the surf, but the old woman grabbed us by the hands, and the two fellows did the same, leaving us standing in a ring-around-the-rosie circle, and began praying loudly. "Oh Almighty God, thank you for delivering these two shipwrecked

souls to our bosom, and grant them recovery of their bodies and spirits, and bless the next leg of their journey upon your mighty oceans!"
The three kept their heads bowed for a few seconds before adding their
amens. We all turned to handle the boat into the water.

As soon as all five of us were in the bobbing Zodiac and the outboard motor was coughing to life, Eddie turned to me and said in a
loud clear voice: "Whaddaya think, religious nuts?"

Oh Jesus Christ, I thought. I was going to have to keep a lid on him.

I looked gratefully at the old woman. "Apologies, sister. He's been
out here a long time!"

THE DOCTOR THEY HAD ABOARD examined us in fascination. We
were obviously sick, malnourished, and being eaten from within and
without, and that gave him every excuse to load us with tablets, pills,
and shots so the good Lord could heal us. The captain welcomed us
aboard but cooled a bit when he learned we'd been raised Catholic. A
few of the crew shook their heads in pity when they heard about our
former allegiance to the church of Rome. You'd think they would've
warmed up a bit when we told them that we'd left that behind ages ago,
but no dice there either.

We listened to the stories of their maritime environmental and
evangelical crusades, and even kept from laughing at the story of how
they'd lost two of the crew to a tribe of islanders in the Indian Ocean
they had meant to convert. The two missionaries didn't even get a
chance to climb out of their boat full of Bibles before being ventilated
by arrows by the Stone Age tribesmen who didn't go for that sort of
thing, possibly Unitarians. But try as we might, there was no way we
were fitting in with our rescuers. The relationship really took a turn
south when we heard that the MV *Lamb of the Sea* was making its way
to San Diego, and we were told the good news that we would be back
home in the States shortly.

"How soon, do you think?" Eddie asked innocently.

About three days, was the answer.

"Good," he replied. "We'll have to get through all of the coke and grass before we go through customs."

Let me tell you, the reaction was as if we'd told them that we needed to sacrifice a virgin, and on that vessel, we could have. The atmosphere didn't thaw after we were forced to dump all of our chemical and vegetable happiness off the fantail, and I didn't notice anyone praying for us when we walked down the gangplank days later.

AFTER THE US COAST GUARD and State Department checked us out in San Diego and the doctors pronounced us *unlikely to die* and *probably not contagious* from whatever diseases we were carrying, we were put on a plane back home. A few news outlets called us at the motel we'd been put in. Neither of us had thought about the possibility of becoming celebrities.

When we got off the plane in Chicago in mid-December, there were a few cameras and reporters to catch us reuniting with our families after being gone for almost four years. We wore tropical shirts we'd gotten before leaving California for the biting cold.

"Is there anything this incredible experience has taught you?" a slim blond reporter asked on the concourse, holding a foam-covered microphone in front of us.

"As a matter of fact," I said, "Eddie and I were just discussing this on the flight back."

Eddie stopped to address the cameras. "I've always held that the country girl was the one you'd want to boink, but Joe here had another take."

I nodded in agreement before speaking. "My thought is that if you were stuck on the island for that long, the smart thing would be to go after the movie star, and here's why: Say you were with the country girl, and one day, the movie star gave you the green light . . . when that news got around—and it *would*—you'd have broken the country girl's heart and everyone would think you were a bastard. You'd be cut off entirely and only kept around to pedal the bike that powered the radio. Now if the reverse happened, and you were with the movie star and one day tagged the country girl like you wanted to all along, when that fact got out—and it *would*—well, you could talk your way out of that one."

There was silence when I paused. I thought we had them rapt.

Eddie continued, "Look, we all know the movie star is a loose Hollywood type. Hell, she'd probably put the moves on the country girl before anyone else—not to mention she'd probably do the skipper, the professor, and anyone else she needed something from. Yeah, she'd have to forgive you. And if she didn't, the country girl would probably feel obligated to take care of you on account of her being a filthy hut-wrecker."

I could tell we were losing them for some reason. Perhaps we weren't being clear enough. But Eddie plowed on.

"But what occurs to Joe and me now—now that we've gone through what we've gone through and being saved by those kind whack jobs—is that the really smart thing to do would be to put the old rat up Lovey's drainpipe, at least once or twice."

The crowd of reporters stood stunned by our newfound wisdom, although it seemed like a few cameras were being switched off and no more flashbulbs popped.

"Look," I pleaded, eager to help Eddie get the point across. "Okay, so she's old, but I sure bet she looks young in the dark. And if you *do* get rescued, wouldn't you want the wife of a millionaire to be grateful that you scraped the cobwebs from her corners? Hell, Thurston would probably give you a nice portfolio for taking the heat off of him for a while and keeping your trap shut once you got home!"

There was silence apart from the odd loudspeaker announcement.

Strange, we were sure we were onto something there.

———

ABOUT A WEEK BEFORE CHRISTMAS, I got a call from Lenny Issac, the talent agent. The first thing I asked was where he got my phone number. At the time, I was staying at my brother's house, my apartment and possessions having long been disposed of. He told me Eddie had given it to him.

"Look, Joey, pal, you're rich and you don't even know it yet. Wow! What an incredible story! They'll want you two buckaroos, you can bet on that! I'm seeing a book about your story, maybe a documentary, maybe a major motion picture! You two just need someone to handle the details!"

I hadn't thought that anyone would be interested in our tale, but Eddie and I talked it over. Maybe this had all happened for a reason. We wound up signing with Lenny Issac.

The day after Christmas, we sat in a television studio downtown wearing blazers over loud Hawaiian shirts, fresh haircuts, and makeup, waiting for our big moment. Lenny had gotten us an extended slot on the news to talk about our amazing tale of survival. And sit and wait we did. Lenny chain-smoked. I had a few root beers. We were patient men, to be certain. The previous four years had proven that. The scheduled time for our interview came and went. Lenny told us not to worry; waiting is part of the business. *Much like the business of being stranded,* I thought.

After sitting and waiting some more, a production aide came into the guest dressing room to give us the news that our interview had been postponed. As it turns out, the day before, a six-year-old beauty pageant contestant with creepy-ass parents died under strange circumstances out west, and now nobody on the planet cared about what two rat-eating goofs shot with sunburn and insect bites had to say. With that, our time in the spotlight evaporated. Well played, kid.

Lenny assured us all was not lost though. He was exploring all angles: story rights, ghostwriters, movie producers. He assured us everything was well in hand.

Sometime in late January, we sat in his office with a literary agent who'd flown in from New York to see us. Her family and Lenny's had summered in the Catskills together once upon a time.

"I'm seeing something different here," she said, obviously full of ideas. "It's more than a story of survival. It's the story of love between two men once civilization is no longer available to them, finding their passion amidst hostile surroundings."

"Beg pardon?" Eddie said.

"There they are, alone against the elements, with only each other to turn to . . ."

I waited for Lenny to interject, but he seemed to be really listening to the woman.

"Eh, we're not gay," I explained.

"But in the story, you will be." She leaned back in her chair and waved an expensive pen around like a conductor's baton. "Finding your true selves in the harsh crucible, finding each other . . ."

"We're not gay," Eddie said, in case she hadn't heard me.

Lenny seemed to be siding with the agent.

Eddie and I looked at each other, then at Lenny.

"Fellas, let's not be so rigid. She's from a top house. She knows what sells, what the people want. Of course it's going to take some poetic license for us to maximize the potential your dynamite story has!"

"Except we're not gay," Eddie said.

We listened to the two of them brainstorm for about twenty minutes while we shook our heads at one another.

Finally, I'd heard enough. "Lenny—"

He held up a hand to cut me off. "Listen, bubbi, I understand your concerns. Let us talk for a bit while you two catch some lunch, and come back in an hour. If we haven't made some inroads by then, we'll find something else, deal?"

The way the two of them smiled made me suspicious. Eddie shrugged, and we agreed to step out for a bit. The last thing they said before the door shut behind us gave me a chill. "Trust us," they said in unison.

Once the door was closed, Eddie looked at me and said, "But Joe, we're not gay," like I'd forgotten that.

———————

WHEN WE RETURNED NINETY MINUTES later, Lenny and the agent were beaming. Lenny swiveled in his tall leather chair, tapping his pen on a single piece of paper in front of him.

"Boys! Keep an open mind here. Our objective is to sell the best story we can, no matter what trivial facts need to be tweaked and polished."

Oh shit, here it comes, I thought.

"Now, what we're thinking of is this . . ." He lazily circled a number at the top of the sheet. "We sell the rights for the story for this much, top number." He drew a heavy line under the second number. "We set you up with a ghostwriter to do a first-rate job on a draft of your story, and we can get this upon acceptance. And when the studios pick it up, we'll make sure we get this." He drew a box around the bottom number. "Maybe points on top of that, we'll see!" Lenny pushed the paper in my direction.

"We're not gay," Eddie reminded everyone present.

I looked at the numbers and gave a low whistle. I was stunned. I pushed the paper in front of Eddie, who scrutinized the numbers, his eyebrows slowly inching upward.

He looked at me quizzically. "Poetic license? Yeah, poetic license, I guess."

You can't sell out until you sell, I thought. For all I knew, Eddie may have been a little gay.

We signed.

———————

EXCEPT THE MONEY DIDN'T ROLL in. We got a check for the rights to the story, and we sat for hours with the ghostwriter, who mostly asked about how much coke had washed up on the island. After months of work, we had three different treatments of our story turned down, the last one for being "too gay." Our chances of seeing the underlined number in cash seemed to be dwindling.

Eventually, a basic treatment of our story made the rounds of the production houses, and a major studio made a modest offer on our tale. Things were looking up.

Or so we thought. It turns out, sometimes a studio will buy up stories that are similar to projects they already have in the pipeline, just to keep a book or a movie from having to compete against something nearly identical. I suspect some less scrupulous outfits also buy up stories like ours so they can take a little "poetic license" and make something just different enough to ensure they won't have to pony up the full whack to whomever's story it is and not get their asses sued off. I can't say for sure that's what happened here, but I can tell you a couple years later, a major studio put out a major motion picture with major stars and made major bucks on a story that was an awful lot like ours, and we majorly didn't see one extra dime.

They didn't even do the gay angle. Instead, they merely took our basic story and changed Eddie's character from a bungling nitwit to a piece of sporting equipment, if you can believe that nonsense.

And that's where the story ends, pretty much. The experience made it difficult to return to our regular lives. I tried to go back to work, but the second day my alarm clock went off, it got sent hurtling through the window. I couldn't be bothered with the daily grind anymore.

Lenny did do us a solid. Believe it or not, he had a cousin in real estate who sold us the ownership of a duplex in the far suburbs for slightly less than we'd realized from our story. The building's history of a triple homicide didn't bother us much, and we had our separate houses for the solitude and a common yard to share the misery.

We couldn't go back to the grind, but we did go back to routine. This morning I woke up, got dressed, and walked out my patio door, just like I do just about every other day. I let myself in Eddie's patio door, took a root beer from the fridge, and found him as I almost always find him, waiting for me while he enjoys the second smoke of the day.

The Storyteller's mask is probably where we left it, propped up against the rock with the island's laws scratched on it, but the Storyteller migrated with us.

Eddie stood in the center of the living room as I sat quietly in a recliner.

"Hear me! I have come from afar, and I have brought a story to tell!" he announced, holding a shining DVD in front of him as a priest does a communion wafer before placing it reverently in its tray in the machine.

"Oh, Storyteller! Please tell the poor wretches assembled how that shit went down!" the congregation replied.

Eddie sat down in his recliner, picked up the remote, and hit PLAY. Moments later, we were in Mayberry.

www.ingramcontent.com/pod-product-compliance
Lightning Source LLC
Chambersburg PA
CBHW051510150726
47997CB00001B/191